COUNTDOWN

COUNTDOWN

BOOK ONE · THE SKYE VAN BLOEM TRILOGY

CAROL FIORE

Flying Kea
Press

Published by Flying Kea Press
www.flyingkeapress.com

Paperback ISBN: 978-0-9897004-3-6
E-book ISBN: 978-0-9897004-4-3

**Publisher's Cataloging-In-Publication Data
(Prepared by The Donohue Group, Inc.)**

Names: Fiore, Carol.
Title: Countdown / Carol Fiore.

Description: [Tucson, Arizona] : Flying Kea Press, [2018] | Series: The Skye Van Bloem
trilogy ; book 1 | Interest age level: 12 and up. | Summary: "Eighteen-year-old Skye Van
Bloem didn't create the environmental crisis facing our planet, but she's angry about it
... But Skye's about to discover that she's not alone. A race of technologically advanced
aliens called Beholders have offered the animals of Earth a chance to determine the fate
of the biggest threat facing the planet: humanity itself. According to ... a snarky prairie
dog, only Skye can convince them that humans can change and start protecting the
environment instead of destroying it."--Provided by publisher.

Identifiers: ISBN 9780989700436 (paperback) | ISBN 9780989700443 (ebook)
Library of Congress Control Number: 2018938758

Subjects: LCSH: Teenage girls--Juvenile fiction. | Environmental degradation--Juvenile
fiction. | Extraterrestrial beings--Juvenile fiction. | Earth (Planet)--Juvenile fiction. |
CYAC: Teenage girls--Fiction. | Environmental degradation--Fiction. | Extraterrestrial
beings--Fiction. | Earth (Planet)--Fiction. | LCGFT: Action and adventure fiction.

Classification: LCC PZ7.1.F536 Co 2018 (print) | LCC PZ7.1.F536 (ebook) | DDC [Fic]--dc23

Interior design: Kevin Callahan/BNGO Books
Cover design: Rebecca Lown

For Robin "Daisy"

who loved the story
from the first draft

Acknowledgments

This trilogy owes its life to my daughter Robin "Daisy." Her belief in the power of the story and its environmental message encouraged me to keep writing. The story about Quyet was her idea, based on her thesis research in Vietnam.

I also owe thanks to my older daughter, Tia, who helped with the teen language and applauded my decision to write the character Henry.

I wish to thank my friend Janine Crick for her patience and support as I talked incessantly about my characters, and I thank her for allowing me to borrow her name for one of them. The character of Janine is fictional, of course, as are all my characters except Dr. O'Brien and Mel. Aside from these two, any resemblance to real people is coincidental.

The inclusion of any person, group, organization, school, or business is not an endorsement by them or their affiliates for this book and is used in a fictitious manner.

Ultimate Hikes is a real travel company that escorts hikers on the South Island of New Zealand. I thank them for hiking with me on the Milford Track.

I would also like to thank my teen readers for their valuable input on the book.

A shout out to my two spectacular editors, Lindsey Alexander and Salvatore Borriello of the Reading List. Thank you for helping me bring my characters to life.

Lastly, I wish to recognize my late husband, Eric Fiore, an experimental test pilot who gave his life to keep the skies safe. He was brilliant, funny, playful, quirky, and romantic. He looked at nature with a childlike sense of wonder and reverence and never faltered in his support of my career choice to work with animals. I miss him every single day.

1

In a single moment of carelessness, she'd let them approach her. They saw her and smiled, and their smiles were evil.

She'd been warned about the beasts. She knew they were vile creatures. Everyone did. But she'd been daydreaming, distracted. *She had to get out of here!*

She took off, bounding ahead, but they towered over her, and they were gaining on her. One had a sword.

She propelled herself forward, putting everything she had into her legs. They were strong, but not strong enough. The one with the sword stabbed her.

She felt it go through her. *Incredible pain.* As the beast lifted her, she heard her brother in the distance, calling urgently. She thrashed, trying to free herself, but it was no use. *The pain . . .*

She felt life slipping away, and as her eyes began to close, she saw the girl. The one everyone said was special.

But the girl did nothing, standing there with a horrified expression on her face.

2

The toad was dead.

Skye gazed at the poor thing hanging from a stick, and she felt her insides contract painfully. Josh was holding it and laughing with his two loser friends. They had their backs to Skye and didn't see her.

It wasn't the first time Skye had seen them with dead animals. While others were Googling cute puppy and kitten pictures, these three were out murdering innocent animals.

She'd complained to the school counselor, who had done nothing. Didn't animal cruelty lead to people cruelty? Josh was a bully. Skye knew it personally. She'd been taunted and harassed often enough. She knew she'd lose in a fight with him, but even so, she was *so* close to confronting him.

Squeezing her hands into fists, she started to take a step toward the three when she felt her arms being pulled backward.

Janine, her arm linked around Skye's, said one word: "Don't." She said it softly, with all the compassion Skye had always received from her friend.

Hanging on to Skye's other arm and turning her away from Josh and his friends was her other best friend, Henry. He'd been at the receiving end of Josh's fists a couple times.

Skye glared over her shoulder at the three boys as she headed away from Tomsin Valley High School. "Don't you have rehearsal?" she asked Henry.

"I've got an hour. We're going to Schmidts; Janine's treating."

"I can pay," Skye said, glancing at Janine. "You always pay."

"I have money. You and Henry don't. My parents are cool with it so just let me."

"Your parents are the best," Skye said.

"I know." Janine smiled and then became serious. "What were you going to do, Skye?"

"They killed it."

"I know. But there are three of them and they're big."

"But I have to do something," Skye protested.

"It's just a t—"

"Please, Henry," Skye interrupted. "Please don't say it's just a toad."

Henry stopped and released Skye's arm. "I'm sorry. That wasn't fair. I know amphibians are declining. I listen to you."

Janine released Skye's other arm. "Josh is going to end up in prison like his father. Did you see the rabbit last week?"

"Janine," Henry scolded. "Get on board with operation cheer-up-Skye."

"I'm not five," Skye said.

"We all need cheering up sometimes. That's what friends do. Don't you remember last month when it was operation get-Janine-to-chill?"

Skye suppressed a smile. "Katie didn't mean to color all over your lab report, Janine."

"That's what my parents said, but little sisters are so annoying," Janine replied.

Henry put his hands on Skye's shoulders and turned her to face west. "What do you see, Skye?"

"The mountains?"

"No." Henry said slowly, "What do you see?"

"I know what you're doing, Henry," Skye said softly.

"What am I doing?"

"You want me to say that I love the Rocky Mountains, and that this view is the best in all of Colorado. You want me to say that I'm happy when I look at my mountains."

"You know he's right," said Janine. She pointed to a stand of trees. "And there's a bunch of aspens. They're your favorite trees."

Without a word, Skye linked arms with her friends. Her eyes greedily gazed west as she tried to slow her breathing on the short walk to Schmidts Café with her best friends — her only friends.

"The usual?" Janine asked Skye and Henry at the counter. They nodded, and she ordered their drinks.

A few minutes later, sitting at their favorite booth, Skye put her head in her hands. School had sucked today, especially chemistry. And calculus. She was never going to understand it, even with Janine's help.

Janine pulled three chocolate bars from her backpack and tossed one to Skye and then another to Henry. They were 3 Musketeers bars — Janine's favorite. She was fond of saying that the candy was a metaphor for the relationship the three shared.

"We're almost done, Skye," Henry said, running a hand through his curly blond hair. "You never have to see them again."

"I know. It's just that I want to help animals and I watch those three and do nothing."

"You are doing something," said Janine. "What about all the stuff you did to save the prairie dogs?"

Behind the west corner of the high school, partially on the school's grounds, lay an empty ten-acre field — a flat expanse of dirt with hundreds of burrows. The land contained a small prairie dog colony. Each burrow entrance was like a flat donut elevated to give the animals extra height in searching for predators. Skye had started three separate petitions to stop a housing development that would destroy the colony. She'd written two letters to the editor; both had been published in the *Reporter-Journal* newspaper. Spearheading an effort on social media, she'd uploaded a video to YouTube, blasted scores of tweets, and posted on Facebook. Her contact with the US Fish and Wildlife Service had been discouraging, and although local wildlife groups were unconcerned about the animals, she'd hooked up with some well-known environmental groups who had given her excellent advice. Desperate, she'd sneaked out in the middle of the night and removed the for-sale signs, throwing them in a dumpster. If the property was sold and developed, the animals would have to be relocated. If they weren't . . . the alternative was too grim to consider. She was angry that few people seemed to care.

Glancing at his cell phone, Henry said, "Gotta go soon or I'll be late for rehearsal."

"I'm so proud of you, getting the lead. I can't wait to see the performance," Skye said. Henry was playing Jean Valjean, the lead in *Les Misérables*. It was one of Skye's favorite books. She'd heard the director hadn't wanted to cast Henry in the lead because, with his wiry frame, he was the polar opposite of burly Valjean, but Henry's voice and passion had left the casting committee speechless. Like Valjean, Henry's compassion for others was unfailing no matter how badly he was treated.

"Only two more rehearsals till opening night," said Henry.

"You're going to rock the house," said Janine. "Nobody has a voice like yours."

Henry cocked his head and said in a thick southern accent, "Why I do declare. That is awful kind of you, darling."

Skye grinned. "And no one can dance like you either. Have you seen his twirl-turn thing, Janine?" Skye leapt up and spun around but lost her balance and fell, landing on her butt. She quickly looked around the café to see if anyone had noticed. There were only two other people in the place — a child eating ice cream and an elderly woman.

"I'm such a klutz," Skye said with a light laugh.

Henry extended a hand to Skye. Lifting her, he twirled her around and tried to do a dip with her. But Skye was a runner — not a dancer; she was stiff and considerably taller than Henry. This time they both ended up on the floor. Now it was Janine's turn to laugh as Skye and Henry sat on the floor looking somewhat embarrassed.

"You two are so dramatic," Janine said.

Still sitting on the floor, Skye lifted her hand over Henry's head and pointed down at him.

"You're every bit as dramatic, Skye. Don't blame it on Henry," Janine said. "I know it's only Tuesday, but what's the plan for the weekend? Aside from Henry's musical, of course."

"Hiking in Rocky Mountain National Park, but I have to help Oma around the house before I head out," said Skye, scooting back into the booth with Henry. "You know how she is about the windows, and I don't trust her on the ladder."

"Don't wear those hippie sandals on the ladder," Janine joked, twirling her thick, braided ponytail.

Skye looked down at her Birkenstock sandals, which were made from imitation leather. Oma, her grandmother, had special ordered them for Skye's eighteenth birthday just last month. Don't eat animals, don't wear animals. That was Skye's mantra.

"Come on, Skye," Janine said. "Let's walk Henry to practice. We'll take a detour by the prairie dog colony. That always cheers you up."

Henry nodded knowingly. "Maybe that tame one will be there."

Walking back to Tomsin Valley High School, Skye couldn't stop thinking about Josh and his friends and animal cruelty. They'd called her a freak again yesterday — for about the hundredth time. "I hope Josh is gone and there aren't more dead animals. And I'm sick of him calling me a freak." She paused. "Maybe I am one."

Janine pushed her black-rimmed glasses higher on her nose. "You're a little messed up, but you're not a freak."

"Janine," exclaimed Henry.

"It's not her fault," Janine said, turning toward Henry, "but I'm going to tell the truth. That's what friends do. Animals follow her. It's creepy. But hey. Skye's the most entertaining person I know. I'm still not giving up meat for her though, and I don't think *Bambi* is the saddest movie I've ever seen."

"I'm right here," Skye replied. "Anyway, how can you say that? The scene when they shoot —"

"Please, Skye. You see the world through the lens of a Disney camera," interrupted Janine.

"No, I don't." Skye didn't believe in fairy-tale endings. The girl didn't find her prince while surrounded by adorable talking animals, and even if she did, it never ended well. Besides, Skye was no princess. They were beautiful, and Skye knew she wasn't.

"And," Janine added, "you talk to animals. Even my little sister grew out of that."

"Nothing wrong with talking to animals," Henry said, giving Janine an irritated glance before looking back at Skye with a smile. "And you're gorgeous too."

Skye frowned. Now Henry was being ridiculous. *Gorgeous? Yeah, right.* She had mismatched eyes — one the blue-green of the Caribbean, the other a deep forest green. People commented on her eyes frequently, and it made her super self-conscious of them. Then there was her long hair, extending to the middle of her back. It was the same color as a red poppy. Her father used to tease her that garden fairies wove the flowers into long, wavy strands, just for her. She hated her hair color. Last year, without consulting Oma, she'd gone to the best salon in Denver to have her hair colored. The brunette dye washed out in less than a week, hundreds of dollars that she'd saved for years were wasted, and Oma was furious. The hairdresser had insisted it was Skye's hair; it wouldn't hold on to the color. Skye had tried two in-home color kits with even more disastrous results before finally accepting that she'd always have a horrid hair color. It sucked. Most things in life did.

"Stop frowning, Skye," Janine said. "I'm cool with you talking to animals. As long as they don't talk back." She paused. "They don't, do they?"

"I'm not crazy, Janine."

Even though Skye couldn't hear animals, she understood them much better than people; she certainly preferred their company. Whereas people seemed to avoid Skye, animals gravitated toward her. She would never forget the first time a wild rabbit had jumped into her lap, looking up at her with intelligent, dark eyes. There was something unusual about the rabbit; Skye could feel it but didn't have words for it. Oma had been setting up a picnic lunch for Skye's sixteenth birthday. When she saw the rabbit in Skye's lap, she dropped the whole bowl of macaroni salad. Oma had stood over the rabbit for a long time, staring at it intently.

Since then, Skye had taken up with the gray mouse that lived in the walls of their duplex. She had outfitted a shoebox with soft towels for the rodent. The mouse often climbed up her arm and perched on her shoulder when she read or studied, and it seemed fond of watching movies and eating carrot cake — oddly, two of Oma's favorite things.

Skye talked to the mouse frequently, especially when she was lonely. It seemed to sense when Skye was sad and would stare up at her with its tiny black button eyes. It occasionally disappeared for weeks at a time, and then it would reappear. One day last year it vanished permanently, but the rough edge of Skye's sadness dulled when she made friends with a new animal. An amazing animal. Skye's favorite animal.

A prairie dog.

Sitting on the sidewalk next to the colony, Skye took off her backpack. The prairie dog Henry had dubbed "the tame one" scurried toward Skye, sat on its bottom, arms dangling in front of its fat folds, and yipped at her, waggling its tail. Black-tailed prairie dogs had black on the tips of their tails, but this one had an all-black tail.

Henry grinned. "He's sort of cute."

"You *do* know they carry the plague and have fleas, right?" Janine said.

Skye rolled her eyes dramatically.

Henry glanced at his phone again. "I better go or —"

Josh and his friends appeared, stopping some twenty yards away, laughing loudly. Josh pointed a finger at Henry and whispered something to one of his friends, who immediately exploded with forced laughter.

Henry shifted from foot to foot. Trying to ignore them, Skye stared out at the prairie dogs: some standing guard like tiny soldiers, others yipping frantically as they peered from a hole, a few jumping up and back — "Wee-oo." Some seemed oblivious to the activity around them as they munched on grasses.

Josh's voice rose. The word slapped the air, full of hate. "Fag."

Henry, hands in his pockets, looked down at the ground.

Before Skye could react, Janine moved in front of her. "Excuse me?" she retorted, moving her glasses down her nose and staring over the top of the frames.

"What are you looking at, geek?" Josh said.

His gang laughed again and pointed stupidly at Janine.

"Geek? I take that as a compliment." Janine pushed her glasses up and put her hands on her hips. "You'll have to come up with something better than that."

"I can think of something better. It starts with *n*." Josh smiled smugly.

Aghast, Skye jumped to her feet as Henry made a strangled sound. She was not going to let this continue. Janine turned toward her. "I've got this," she said quietly, motioning for Skye to sit back down.

Skye hesitated, but she knew her friend. Reluctantly, she sat down.

"Hey Josh," Janine said, turning back to the three. "I've got a new project for my genetics class. I'm studying how someone without a brain can walk and talk." She paused and tapped her bottom lip thoughtfully. "Oh, how silly of me. Of course you have a brain; it's just really, really small. Like what you've got in your pants. You'd need an electron microscope to find, well, both of them." She smiled sweetly.

9

One of the boys snickered. Glaring at his friend, with face flushed and fists clenched, Josh advanced toward Janine.

"Could you just leave?" Skye asked. She sounded like she was begging, even to herself, and she was angry for sounding like a coward — especially after the racist name Josh had threatened to call her best friend and the ugly, hateful name he'd called Henry.

"What's it to you, freak?" Josh continued his slow, prowling advance.

"Hey Josh," Janine began. "What —"

"Janine," Henry hissed. "Stop taunting him."

"You're next, fag boy." With a cruel look, Josh turned quickly to a still-seated Skye and grabbed her arm.

"Owwwwww!" Josh shrieked, releasing Skye and kicking hard at the prairie dog next to her, the one with the completely black tail. The one who'd just bitten him on the ankle.

There was a sharp yip as the sandy-colored three-pound creature fell over onto its back, its front legs kicking wildly. Furious, Skye helped the animal upright and got the strangest sensation, almost as though he was speaking to her, telling her he was OK.

"That thing bit me," Josh howled, grabbing at his bleeding ankle as he hobbled over to his friends.

Skye rose to her feet, shaking with anger, her mind clearer than it had been in several months. She'd tried ignoring them, but it didn't work. They'd made fun of her friends. They'd stomped her grandmother's flowers, and they'd taunted her with dead animals. Now this.

Skye balled her hands into fists. The helplessness she'd felt grew into something powerful. She walked slowly over to Josh.

"Skye, please," Henry pleaded.

Josh rubbed his ankle, trying not to seem off-balance.

Skye saw her opportunity. She took it.

Her right arm shot out and delivered a solid jab to his nose. Pain shot through Skye's hand and vibrated up her arm. She wanted to drop to the ground as dizziness spread. How could a punch hurt like that? She fought the feeling because this needed to end right now. Trying not to sound breathless, she said, "You're going to leave us alone, and you're never going to hurt an animal again. Understand?"

"You bitch . . . you broke my nose. You're gonna pay." Josh's spiked black hair seemed to deflate as his chubby belly heaved in and out over torn jeans, making his shirt ride up. He pulled frantically at his shirt, trying to cover an ugly scar on his hip. There were other scars. And bruises. Blood ran in rivulets from his nose as the sweat dripped from his forehead. He smelled of tobacco and unwashed clothes.

Skye looked down at her hands, somewhat horrified at what she'd done. She'd . . . lost it. It felt as though her anger, stored up for years, had erupted out of her in a scalding rush.

As Josh's friends advanced toward her, a shout rang out. "What's going on over there?"

There was silence except for Josh's groans of pain.

"Answer me."

Skye recognized the shop teacher — a burly middle-aged Hispanic man, well-liked by students for his kind humor and willingness to help fix their cars.

"I asked you a question, Josh. Is there a problem? What's wrong with your nose?"

"I . . . uh . . . fell."

"Then get home and see to that nose." He took Josh's two friends by the shoulders and motioned with his head to Josh. "Let's go."

As the teacher left with the boys, he gave a sympathetic look over his shoulder.

"Where'd you learn that?" Henry exclaimed after they'd left.

"I think you broke Josh's nose," said Janine, her dark-espresso eyes wide beneath her enormous glasses. "You'll get thrown out of school for this."

"No she won't," said Henry. "Didn't you hear Josh? He'd never tell anyone a girl beat him." He pointed an accusing finger at Janine. "Do you think before you talk?"

"Be glad he didn't have a gun."

Henry threw his hands up in the air. "Great. That'll be next."

Skye was too busy tending to the injured prairie dog to respond. She gathered the creature in her arms. "I've got to get him home and under a heat lamp." She headed down the road in a burst, Henry and Janine huffing after her.

3

Janine and Henry collapsed in the front yard of the small duplex Skye shared with her Oma.

"What was that?" gasped Henry, clutching at his side.

It took Janine several seconds to answer. "Running like you stole something."

"No, not that. We know Skye is unbelievably fast. I mean the karate moves."

"Her temper is going to get her in serious trouble."

"Yeah, but admit it. Josh and his gang deserved to get beat, and Skye totally owned them."

"I heard that," Skye called from the doorway, where she was gently cradling the prairie dog.

Oma waved from her flower bed. She was a somewhat comical sight in her flowered yellow dress and wooden shoes over thick knee-high white socks with her gray-streaked black hair secured in a tight bun. "Goedemiddag, Janine and Henry."

"Hi, Ms. Van Bloem. How are you?" Henry answered, having finally caught his breath.

"Goed. Goed. Thank you for bringing Skye's backpack."

"Oma," Skye called. "Where's the heat lamp?"

Grabbing Henry's arm, Janine said, "Come on. I'll walk you back to rehearsal. I'm sure you're late now. I have to get home and watch my little sister. Later, Skye."

In her bedroom, Skye gently placed the prairie dog in a box lined with Oma's delft-blue-checked dishtowels and clamped a heat lamp, which her grandmother had retrieved from the small garage, to a stand next to the box. Talking softly to the creature, she reassured him that she would return him to his home when he recovered. He looked at her with bright black eyes, motionless on his stomach. *There's something familiar about those eyes*, Skye mused. She had the oddest feeling of déjà vu.

Skye sat on the floor, next to the box, and began dialing the wildlife rehabilitation center; she'd memorized the number long ago. The animal leaped out of the box. Startled, Skye dropped the phone, the clatter it made on the tile floor echoing around her bedroom.

The prairie dog was alert, holding a small orange leaf with double veins and serrated edges that was covered in purplish bumps.

"What's that? Where'd you get that?" Skye took the leaf and set it down on the tiled floor. The prairie dog picked it up and seemed to hold it out to Skye. She took it again.

"Uh, it's a leaf. A pretty one. Thanks." She set it down on the floor.

The prairie dog, sitting on his bottom, raised his front paws to his mouth and then lowered them, repeating the act several times. He retrieved the leaf and placed it on Skye's leg, then he moved away.

Skye picked up the leaf. "Um, I don't eat leaves, but thanks anyway." She set the leaf down, and once again, the prairie dog pushed it toward her.

"O—OK." Skye took the leaf and sniffed it. Odorless. Pretending to eat it, she put it up to her lips and, with a quick flick of her tongue, licked the leaf. It tasted like chocolate and raspberries.

The prairie dog barked a sharp yip, throwing its head backward, and stared intently at Skye.

"You win." Skye nibbled the edge of the leaf. It tasted like the best chocolate raspberry cake she'd ever had. The prairie dog yipped again. Skye took another nibble and finally popped the entire leaf in her mouth. It was delicious.

"About time. I've been carrying that leaf around for months."

Skye shook her head. What was happening? Did the prairie dog . . . speak to her?

"Name's Starion. Thanks for the rescue, princess. Loved the moves back there — impressive."

Skye drew her legs to her chest, wrapping her arms around them. She rocked back and forth. She felt dizzy, hot, like she was going to pass out.

This is what it feels like to go crazy. She got up and stumbled around her room, then she paced back and forth, finally sitting back down on the floor and resuming her rocking.

I'm crazy.

More pacing.

More rocking.

More head shaking.

"Skye, stop it," Starion finally ordered.

Skye stared up at him. "This is a dream. Or I'm losing my mind."

Starion groaned. "C'mon, you've always been able to communicate with animals. The only difference is, now you can understand me word for word."

"This is impossible."

Starion scratched the side of his face with one long claw. "I'm sure you can think of many things that would have seemed impossible fifty years ago, right?"

Nodding, Skye asked, "Can I hear other animals?"

"Open your window and listen."

Skye did as Starion requested. A robin sat perched in a tree outside her window and sang:

*"This is my home;
this is my home;
this is my home.
Mine."*

Skye turned from the window and faced Starion. "I always wanted to be able to understand animals. My whole life I've dreamed about how cool that would be."

"Dream no more." Starion rubbed his head with one paw. "Those boys have issues."

Skye swallowed loudly. "Issues?"

"Definitely." He stared at Skye and gave a slight quirk to the side of his mouth. "You gonna say something?"

"Are you OK?"

"I've got a nasty headache, but yeah, I'm fine. Maybe I'll go give those boys the plague." He made a noise that sounded like a cough. "Joke in the colony."

"Can you do that? Give them the plague?"

Starion snorted. "It's a joke and not a funny one. If any of us had the plague, we'd be dead long before we could hurt any of you humans. Duh."

"Why did you give me the leaf? Why is this happening . . . to me?"

"You're the only one who can help us, who can save this planet."

"'Save this planet?' What are you talking about? I haven't even graduated from high school. I'm going to my parents' university, and then maybe I could help."

"You've been talking to me for almost a year. I know how important college is to you."

Skye's mouth dropped open. "All this time? You understood me?"

Starion spread his short arms in a gesture of surrender.

"Then why didn't you give me the leaf a year ago?"

"I had my reasons. Maybe I was waiting to see what you would become." He bowed. "I'm amazed by you, Skye."

"Amazing? Me? I don't think so."

"Yes, amazing. That's why we need you to save the planet."

"But—"

"No buts," Starion interrupted. "There's been a change of plans. Save the planet first. Go to university later."

"Look, I try; I do. I really, really care. I don't eat animals; I don't wear animals; I recycle; I remember my green bag when I shop. I send emails to Congress when they do things that hurt the environment." Her eyes narrowed. "There's been a lot of that crap lately."

"Good for you, princess, but it's time to step up your game. Be the hero you were born to be."

"I'm no hero."

"Sure you are. Stealing sale signs posted on the colony was a gutsy move."

"You saw me?"

Starion chuckled. "Not to worry. No one saw but us prairie dogs and we think you rock. *So.* You gonna help me save the planet or what?"

Skye frowned. "I told you; I've been trying. Look who was elected to run the country! I didn't even get to vote because I wasn't old enough. There isn't anything I can do."

"You're wrong, princess."

"Stop calling me princess."

Starion raised a clawed front foot. "You know what? You're not the person I thought you were. My bad." He crawled back into the box, pulled a towel up to his chin, and turned away from Skye. "Turn that stupid lamp off. I've got fur."

Brrrrrrrrrrrinnnnnngggg. The alarm on Skye's phone was going off. She quickly silenced it and rolled over.

"What's for breakfast?"

Skye leaped out of bed and stared down at the box on the floor and the prairie dog—Starion. It hadn't been a dream. And he was still talking.

"What does a prairie dog have to do to get some breakfast?"

Skye frowned down at him. "I'm taking you back to the colony today. You'll fit in my backpack."

"Maybe I'll chew up your textbooks while I'm in there."

"You wouldn't."

"Do you have any carrot cake? I've been dying for carrot cake."

"Do all small mammals like carrot cake?" Skye asked.

"Yep. Do you have any?"

"No."

"Maybe I'll ask Janine and Henry."

"How can you ask Janine and Henry? Do you have any more of those leaves?"

"Nope."

"Then how can you ask them for carrot cake?"

Starion crawled over to Skye's backpack and removed a chocolate bar, peeling down the wrapper. "You can translate for me." He took a bite of the chocolate.

"Hey," Skye shouted as she snatched the candy from him. "You can't have that. Chocolate is bad for animals."

"I was just going to have a taste."

"Wait here and I'll bring you something from the fridge."

Starion was investigating a stack of wildlife magazines when Skye returned. "How good of you to return, princess. It's only been like what, a half an hour?"

"I said to stop calling me that." She handed over a plate of fresh vegetables — carrots, lettuce, kale, and peas.

Starion wrinkled his nose. "I detest peas, and kale is vile."

"Here, I brought you a poffertjes." She handed a silver-dollar-sized pancake to Starion, who sniffed it.

"What's the white stuff?"

"Powdered sugar. This is my Oma's family recipe. It's Dutch."

Sitting on his bottom, Starion held the pancake in his claws and nibbled delicately at it, finally popping it into his mouth. "More please."

"You wish. Let's go."

■ ■ ■

Janine and Henry were waiting for Skye at the colony. It was Wednesday, and they always met on Wednesday mornings.

"I just saw Josh," said a grinning Henry. "He's got a huge bandage over his nose. He's telling people he fell playing football."

"How's the prairie dog?" Janine asked.

Skye set her backpack down and unzipped it. Starion clambered out and sat next to it.

Janine stared at him. "He looks fine to me."

"You don't understand," Skye said, running a hand through her red hair. "He talks."

"Sure they do. You've told us all about their 'sophisticated vocalizations,'" Janine said, using air quotes. "I listen to you."

"I'm not making this up," Skye insisted. She'd thought about telling them she could understand other animals too but decided to wait. Way too unbelievable; even she couldn't believe it. She'd had to concentrate on tuning out the chatter that rose up around her like a noisy lunchroom. It was mostly outspoken squirrels and chatty birds. The rabbits seemed to be the only ones with manners.

"Fine, Dr. Dolittle." Henry folded his arms across his chest. "Whatever you say."

Yep. Good thing she'd kept that info on the other animals to herself.

"I know it sounds crazy, but you guys have to believe me. I'll tell him to do something. He understands me."

"How do we know you didn't train him?" This from Janine.

"Then you tell him to do something."

"Hey, prairie dog, open my genetics book to page forty-two," said Janine flippantly.

Henry chuckled. "Prairie dogs can't read."

Starion crawled over to the stack of books next to Janine's backpack. He turned to Skye. "I'm only a small animal. I can't pull it out of the pile."

"He needs you to pull the book out," said Skye.

Janine tossed her head. "Right. Of course he does." She pulled the book out, laying it in front of Starion.

It took Starion a few moments to open the book; claws slowed things down. Using his teeth, he picked up a pencil that had fallen from the backpack and dropped it squarely in the middle of page forty-two.

"Mendel's peas!" exclaimed Janine, falling off the rock she'd been sitting on.

Henry peered over at the book. "How'd he do that?"

The three sat in stunned silence. "Does he have a name?" Henry finally asked.

Before Skye could answer, Starion began writing in the dirt with one of his front claws. "NAME'S STARION. NEED YOUR HELP."

"I'll talk, you translate," Starion said to Skye.

"OK."

"OK, what?" Janine asked.

"He's going to talk and I'll tell you what he's saying," Skye answered.

"There's a conference of animals meeting in New Zealand to decide the fate of the world," Starion began. "I need you to go with me, Skye, and tell them people care about animals and the planet. You're the only one who can do it."

"But people don't care and everyone knows the planet is trashed."

"Then that's a real problem," Starion said.

"What did he say?" Henry asked. "I just heard a bunch of clicking and growling."

Skye repeated Starion's words.

"This is crazy," Henry said, still gazing in awe at the words Starion had written in the dirt. "Why does he want you to go to New Zealand?"

"For a conference of animals," Janine replied. "Pay attention, Henry."

"You and I should leave on Saturday, but I need your friends' help," Starion said. "I've got a plan."

"He wants me to go to New Zealand on Saturday," Skye said. "He wants you two to do something else."

"What?" asked Janine.

"I don't know yet. He says he has a plan."

"What about graduation?" retorted Janine. "You'll lose your scholarship if you don't graduate. You've wanted to go to Colorado State for ages."

"What?" Henry practically shouted. "Graduation? Are you serious? There's a talking prairie dog right there. Shouldn't we call someone?"

"That would be a bad idea," Starion replied.

Skye pointed at Starion. "He says —"

"That it would be a bad idea," Janine interrupted. "Clearly."

"But what are we supposed to do?" Henry asked.

"We listen," Skye said. She knew it was crazy, but something inside her said to trust Starion. He was a talking prairie dog. How many times did you meet one of those? It was utterly impossible, but . . . This was real.

They listened, with Skye translating. Starion told them she needed to convince the animals at the conference that humans could and would change and stop destroying the planet.

Janine looked down at her phone when Starion finished. "I have a test, though how I'm supposed to concentrate after this . . ." She shook her head. "I'm half expecting the music from *The Twilight Zone* to start playing. Let's meet back here tomorrow morning."

"Tomorrow morning?" Henry practically shrieked, pointing at the prairie dog. "What about him?"

The three teens stared down at Starion.

"Starion, can we do this tomorrow?" Skye asked. "Will you be OK?"

"Not OK. I'm working on a deadline here," Starion said. "Let's meet at your house tonight after musical practice."

"What did he say?" asked Henry.

"He wants to meet at my house after your practice," replied Skye.

"I can do that," said Janine. "What time are you done, Henry?"

"Seven thirty."

Starion ran toward a burrow. "Tonight, kids."

The other prairie dogs were chattering away — mostly gossip — but Skye thought she heard one of them say something about bad men in green as she headed for chemistry lab.

4

It was just past seven thirty when the three friends gathered around Oma's battered kitchen table; Oma had left earlier for a friend's house. The back door opened suddenly, as if by magic. In scurried Starion, two orange leaves hanging from his mouth. Climbing up on the kitchen table, he held out a leaf in each paw to Henry and Janine.

"If you eat it, you can understand him," Skye urged.

"I am *not* eating that. He had it in his mouth. Gross," said Janine. "Maybe I ought to get these things to a lab and run some tests. What's in them? Where do they come from? How do they work? What—"

"Janine," Henry shouted. "Eat the thing. I want to hear what Skye's prairie dog is saying." He grabbed a leaf from Starion's claws, chewed rapidly, and swallowed. "I don't feel any different. How long does it take?"

"It's instantaneous," said Starion.

Henry's eyes widened. "I heard him. I heard him! Did you hear him, Skye? He said 'it's instantaneous.' That's what he said, 'instantaneous.'"

"Thank you, Captain Obvious, for that commentary," Starion replied.

Henry began waving his arms. "Wow. He said 'thank you Captain—'"

"Stop repeating what I say, Henry, or I'm going to come over there and give you the plague."

Henry began to laugh, somewhat hysterically. "He says he's going to give me the plague. Can he do that?"

"No," Skye said. "He's joking."

"For Crick's sake." Janine took the other leaf from Starion and popped it in her mouth, swallowing quickly. "I hope you weren't supposed to chew it."

"You missed out on a good dessert," said Skye. "What was yours, Henry?"

"Mine tasted like peach pie," Henry shrieked, his face flushed, jumping up and down.

Janine grabbed Henry and forced him back into his chair. "You're making me crazy, Henry."

"Me too," agreed Starion.

Henry leapt up again. "He said 'me too.' Did you hear him, Janine? He talked!"

Janine stared at Starion and then turned to Henry. "I heard him."

"Super-duper, kiddies. Let's get down to business."

"Let's!" Henry could hardly contain his excitement.

Starion held up a clawed front foot in Henry's direction. "And don't even think about repeating what I say or commenting that you can hear me or that the prairie dog can talk. Put a lid on it." Starion stood up to his full height of about a foot. "There's some serious stuff going down, and I need you to be calm and listen. Can you do that?"

Henry nodded rapidly.

Starion exhaled loudly. "OK then. Here's what's happening in New Zealand." He paused. "What is it, Janine?"

She was laughing, her hands on each side of her overjoyed face. "I won't have to study Spanish anymore. I'll understand it. That is *so* awesome."

"Sorry," Starion replied. "The leaf only works with nonhuman animals. Humanoid speech is too complicated—too many nuances. Guess you'll have to study after all." He smiled. "Siento."

Janine's smile immediately disappeared.

"The prairie dog speaks Spanish," Henry exclaimed.

"Pay attention," Starion continued. "We don't have much time. If we fail, all human life will cease to exist."

"Are aliens going to destroy us from space with a death ray?" Janine scoffed.

"Much worse." Starion paused. "Tell me, Miss Genetics Whiz, how many diseases — viruses primarily — attack only humans and no other animals?"

"There's the flu, and of course it mutates," Janine started. "It doesn't attack animals, and —"

"Wouldn't a virus that kills humans also kill great apes? Genetically we're similar," interrupted Skye.

"Not necessarily," Janine pointed out. "Chimps have an extra pair of chromosomes that people don't have. It's possible they could be resistant to a virus that attacks us."

Starion nodded. "Very good. The Fioretta research scholarship for genetics goes to —"

"Janine." Skye glared at her friend. "Did you get the Fioretta scholarship and then not tell me?"

Janine looked at Henry, who shrugged and said, "She was waiting to tell you. She's using it to go to Stanford University."

Before Skye could protest, Starion said, "That's enough. Janine's a genetics genius. She's incredibly smart for a barely sixteen-year-old."

"She skipped from third to sixth grade," Henry said brightly. "She could have skipped more, but her parents wouldn't —"

"Henry, stop," Starion interrupted. "Let's save the commentary and the drama about who told who what until after we've dealt with this crisis. I realize Earth being under attack is secondary to teenage angst, but —"

"How do you know and I don't?" snapped Skye.

"Skye, please," pleaded Starion. "I saw the letter in her backpack."

"The prairie dog reads too," exclaimed Henry, quickly silenced by a killing look from Starion.

"We don't have time for the full textbook lesson," Starion said, "but suffice it to say that a mutated virus, introduced into the atmosphere and spread through the respiratory system, would be enough to kill all humans. Right now, right this minute, this virus exists. The animals of Earth have cried out for help, and the Beholders have heard their cries. We don't have much time — twenty-one days. And trust me, it's barely enough time considering what we have to do."

"Procrastinate much?" Janine said with a frown. "Why did you wait until there were only twenty-one days left? That's a pretty arbitrary number. You appeared about a year ago so that must mean you've been watching Skye for at least a year. If she's so important to this planet then why didn't she give the speech last year?"

"Because getting the animals together for the conference takes time. She can't give the speech until everyone is assembled. And anyway, a certain person tied my paws."

"What person?" Skye asked.

"Who are the Beholders?" asked Henry. "Ecoterrorists who ate your leaves?"

"Not important who tied my paws. Also not important who Beholders are, just that they have this virus and they will use it. The key to stopping it is the council of animal representatives meeting in New Zealand. We need to be at this meeting, and you, Skye, will have to convince the animals that humans can change. The animals will vote to save humans or end them. We need to stop the countdown, but we have to go now."

"Are Janine and I going?" asked Henry.

Starion shook his head. "I can only take Skye. I need you two to convince her to go with me."

Henry looked at Janine in alarm. "But —"

"No," stormed Janine. "I'm not letting you take my best friend. Why should I believe you? I don't know anything about you. This is crazy, Skye. Please tell me you're not thinking of going with him. Your grandmother would freak out."

"Are you willing to risk your life and those of the people you love, or are you going to trust me?" Starion replied.

"Why didn't the animals speak up for themselves before now?" Janine asked.

"They did. Weren't you listening? Couldn't you hear their screams when their homes were destroyed and they were poisoned and shot?"

The room was silent.

Janine took her glasses off and rubbed her eyes. "Yeah. You're right. So, let me understand this . . . the Beholders are terrorists with an environmental agenda who have your leaves and have decided to save the animals of Earth? I'm guessing they have some sort of antidote or they'll be killed themselves. This is a job for the FBI or the CIA, not us. Have them capture these Beholder freaks and stop the conference."

Starion shook his head. "Your government will not be able to stop them. Every animal on this planet wants the conference to proceed. They are an organized force and they're pissed. They believe humans don't care about the environment."

Henry raised his hand.

"What is it?" Starion asked irritably.

"I care about the planet," said Henry. "Janine too. And everyone knows Skye does."

"I can't give a speech; I'm terrible at public speaking. I got a C in the class," Skye said.

"I know more than some teacher," Starion huffed. "And I say you're a great speaker."

"Henry got an A," Skye said.

"That's because I'm in theater," Henry replied. "He only gives theater people A's and B's. Anyway, you talk about environmental stuff in a way that no one else does. It's hard to explain."

"Henry's right," Janine said. "There's this passion and genuine love for animals that rolls off you. It's amazing."

"Exactly," said Starion. "She's the only one who can do it." He rubbed his paws together. "All-righty then, kids. Skye, are you ready to go?"

"Really?" scoffed Janine. "Right now? You want her to go *right now*?"

"Yes," replied Starion.

"Doesn't she have to ask her grandmother and write a speech?" asked Henry.

"And get some sleep," Janine said. "Seriously? At least let her think about it."

Starion climbed down from the table. "Fine. Tomorrow. Deadline, people." The door swung open, and he scurried off into the darkness.

5

By the time Skye reached the prairie dog colony the next morning, she was breathless from running. She'd tossed and turned all night thinking about Starion's words.

For a split second, she thought she'd taken a wrong turn. A bulldozer was churning up soil in the ten-acre field. Nearby stood a parked van. Its side was brightly painted with animals — mice, bats, squirrels, prairie dogs — dancing around the words "Bob's Extermination — Pesky Pests? No problem."

Skye raced toward the bulldozer, waving her arms, shouting, "Stop! You'll kill them." The dry dust hung in the air, finding its way into Skye's nose and throat as she ran faster, stumbling over clods of dirt and weeds.

Two men wearing neatly pressed lime-green cotton jumpsuits bearing the word "Bob's" across the chest walked rapidly toward her. "You ain't supposed to be in this field, kid," one of them said. He was wearing a bulky belt with various tools hanging from it. He carried a thick baseball bat, streaked with red.

"Please, you didn't kill them, did you? You can't kill them."

"If you don't leave, I'm gonna call the cops," the other worker grumbled. He glanced at his phone as he set his canister of poison on the ground. "Don't make me miss my son's soccer game."

Skye had seconds to act. She was stopping that bulldozer, no matter the cost to herself, because it might save a few prairie dogs. It wasn't just about Starion, but about all the animals she'd worked so hard to save. When had the land been sold? Why hadn't she known? Her eyes darted around for something to use. Then she saw it.

Skye quickly yanked an oversized chisel from the man's belt and ran to the bulldozer, throwing herself on the ground in its path. The bulldozer operator turned off the vehicle and started to climb down from the cab. Losing his footing, the heavy man fell to the ground, cursing. Jumping up, Skye violently jammed the chisel's sharp tip into one of the enormous tires, repeatedly, until a worker grabbed her roughly by the arm.

"Let me go," she shouted through tears.

A few local residents had stopped to watch by the time Janine and Henry reached Skye. A police car roared up to the field, lights flashing and siren blaring, attracting an even bigger crowd.

"What's going on here?" barked a muscular middle-aged female officer getting out of the cruiser.

The second officer, a petite young woman, her black hair wound in a long braid, reached for Skye. "You OK, honey?"

"Honey?" the bulldozer operator shouted. "She threw herself in front of my machine and then tried to pop a tire." He pointed at a tire emitting a soft hissing sound. He began cussing in earnest.

"Watch your language," said the older officer. "Let's see that permit."

"But she's the one in the wrong here."

"Do you want to press charges?"

"I sure do. That's destruction of property."

"While you're at it, you might try explaining those marks on this young lady's arm," said the younger officer, pulling out a notepad.

"Wasn't me," the bulldozer operator protested. He pointed at the two workers.

One of the exterminators glared at Skye. "We put the poison out yesterday morning; most of them were already dead, kid. We took care of the ones that weren't. They're in that dumpster over there."

Tears streaming down her face, Skye screamed, "How would you like to be poisoned?" *They'd been poisoned when she was in class! How could she have not known?*

Henry tried to put his arm around Skye. "Please, Skye," Janine pleaded.

The second exterminator made a sound of disgust. "That's our job. To kill 'em. We've got families to support."

"Your job is murder?" Skye shouted.

"That is it," bellowed the older officer to Skye. "We're talking to your principal since part of this property is technically on school grounds. Let him deal with this. Start walking."

"I've got something to say to him too," declared the bulldozer operator.

"No, you don't," said the younger officer. "We're writing that property damage report right now." She clicked her pen and brought it to the notepad. "Name?"

As Skye was escorted to the school, she gazed out at the destroyed colony. It felt as though a bulldozer had crushed her soul. *All those sweet animals . . . Starion . . .* She'd wanted to tell him that she'd heard other animals; she'd had trouble blocking their voices out. The odd thing was that they couldn't understand her. Now she'd never find out why.

Starion was dead, and it was all her fault.

Skye had been with the counselor for over two hours. The school had called Oma, and now all three sat with the principal, Mr. St. John.

Rising from his chair, Principal St. John shot a stern look out the door at Janine, who was peering in. "Back to class now, Miss Franklin," he ordered her.

Mrs. Wood, the twenty-something counselor, folded her hands in her lap and sighed for about the hundredth time, staring at Skye with a mock-sympathetic face, wiping a wisp of platinum-blond hair from her forehead. She smelled heavily of perfume.

"I'm disappointed, Skye," Mrs. Wood said. "I thought we'd been making progress."

Skye had met with the counselor twice before: once to complain about Josh's bullying of Henry, and the second time about the dead animals. After that, Skye refused to go back. The woman hadn't done anything and seemed to think Skye was the one who needed counseling. Mrs. Wood needed to worry about Josh, not about her. Skye had several descriptive words for the woman but thought it wise to remain quiet. The words were definitely get-expelled-from-school-and-don't-graduate words.

Mr. St. John cleared his throat. "Ms. Van Bloem, you may take her home. She'll be suspended for a week. Since graduation is next Saturday, she'll only have one day — Friday — to take her finals in order to graduate. Be glad the extermination company is willing to forgo pressing charges in exchange for disciplinary action from the school. And you must pay for the tire." He paused. "I'm sorry, Skye. We all know you've been through a lot, and you've always been a good student. Let's try to keep some perspective here. It's too bad about the prairie dogs, but we have progress to consider."

Skye's grandmother, Katrina Van Bloem, rose from her chair with a huff. "This is progress?"

"I think we're finished here."

Before Skye could respond, Oma steered her out of the office and the building. Neither one said a word on the walk home, but as soon as Oma shut the door of their duplex, she turned to Skye. "I know you were trying to protect those animals, but violence is not the answer."

"I'll pay for the tire."

"It isn't about the money, Skye."

"I'm going to my room now."

Oma stopped her with a light touch to her arm. "We could try counseling again."

"Those men are heartless jerks. They're the ones who need help."

"Skye," Oma said, "you don't know anything about those men. Maybe they couldn't find another job."

"Except murder? I hope a bus hits them."

"Skye. Honey." Oma paused. "Many people struggle to support their families."

"Why do you defend people who don't care about animals? I live here and they don't care if they destroy . . ." Skye clenched her hands into fists. "Everything."

Stomping down the hall, Skye locked her bedroom door and threw herself down on her bed. People sucked. They really, really sucked. She thought of the day, *that* day, eight years ago. She'd barely made it through, probably wouldn't have if it wasn't for her grandmother. Because there were terrible people out there.

Now no one besides Janine and Henry would ever believe her about Starion. She could imagine Mrs. Wood's reaction. The counselor would have her locked up.

Her cell phone beeped, a text message from Henry: Sorry, luv u. Janine chimed in and said sorry too and then that she and Henry were coming over after school with all her assignments so she wouldn't fall behind.

Skye's phone beeped again, this time with a short message from Henry: Closing night of musical tomorrow. Suspended or not, YOU'RE COMING.

Skye knew she'd have to find a way to go, even though she couldn't be on school grounds for any reason until next Friday. She was going to miss opening night, which was tonight, but she had to be there tomorrow for the closing of Henry's musical.

Janine was on Skye's porch just minutes after the final bell rang, and she was determined that Skye would not fall behind in her classwork. She'd gone to all Skye's teachers on her lunch break and picked up homework. She spread books and papers on the porch and said, "Come on, Skye. Math is calling you."

Skye stared straight ahead. How could such a beautiful sunny day be so awful? How was she supposed to do homework after everything that had happened?

"Math is calling you," Janine repeated, shoving the math papers in front of Skye.

"If math has ever called me, I'm pretty sure it's gone straight to voicemail," Skye answered. "Languages call me. Ecology calls me. Math does *not* call me."

"It would if you'd try. And you better if you want to pass your final."

"I am trying," Skye muttered. Then, arms were around her and she looked up into Henry's robin's-egg-blue eyes.

"Do you want to talk about it?" he asked, sitting beside her.

"No. I don't want to talk about math."

Henry frowned. "You know what I mean."

"Henry, why are you here?" Skye exclaimed. "Opening night of the musical is tonight."

"I have some time, and you're more important," Henry answered sincerely. "I'm trying to get into my part but all I can think of is that the only talking prairie dog in the universe is gone."

Skye kicked a small stone off the porch as Janine added, "We're here for you, Skye. If you want to talk about the prairie dog."

"I thought I did everything I could to save the colony," Skye said in a whisper, "but maybe —"

"You did. Don't give up, Skye," Janine interrupted. "You're making a difference. You had thousands of hits on that YouTube video you made about the importance of prairie dogs. And it was fun to watch."

"Do you think they suffered?" Skye said, trying to choke back tears.

"Stop torturing yourself, Skye," Janine said softly. "You know what that chemical does. We've talked about it. You're a good writer. When some time has passed, write about it."

"I don't want to walk by that field anymore."

"Of course not," Henry said. "But what about this conference thing?"

Janine shrugged. "Guess we'll never know now." She paused. "How long do you think this leaf works? Holy Drosophila; I'm getting tired of this animal chatter. I can't concentrate."

There was a long uncomfortable pause, and then Janine and Henry had their arms wrapped around Skye. She did everything she could not to cry.

The next day, Skye was up early enough to watch the sunrise. The first sound she heard was chattering robins shouting about their territory. Like Janine, she wondered if she would always hear them. Unlike Janine, she wanted to hear them forever. A text was waiting from Henry: sold out house; went well. He was unbelievably talented, and she'd never missed any of his performances over the years. She needed to make it tonight, somehow. She was glad Janine had been there last night to support their friend. Skye had received a text from Janine too: Henry brought down the house.

Skye filled the day helping Oma with chores, doing homework, and surfing the internet for stories of people who could speak with animals. She found articles about delusions. She searched for plants similar to the leaf she'd eaten but found nothing.

Skye listened to the birds outside her window: robins, scrub jays, house finches, and black-billed magpies, all engaged in talk of foraging, mating, and gossip. When she spoke, they flew away. Why could Starion understand her, but no other animal could?

She ran five miles on her favorite course west of town. Thin — but with muscle definition — and five nine, she was three inches taller than Henry and five inches taller than Janine. Skye's gym teacher had noticed her athletic talent at the beginning of high school and had encouraged her to go out for the cross-country team. Skye had refused. The uniform was expensive, not to mention other fees, and she refused to ask Oma to scrimp and save.

The coach was furious — such a waste of talent, she'd repeated — but Skye was decisive; she refused to reconsider. She wasn't a joiner anyway, preferring her solitude in the foothills of the Rocky Mountains. There she watched elk and deer, the varied bird life, and in the plains beneath the mountains, her favorite mammals — black-tailed prairie dogs.

Skye loved running, but she preferred to do it alone. She felt alive when she ran solo on the Colorado back roads, and it gave her an outlet for the anger she sometimes felt building inside her. In winter, she often noticed a red-tailed hawk gliding quietly beside her. In the summer, an American kestrel, with its boldly patterned head, followed her in a circling, buoyant flight pattern. There were other birds over the years and during different seasons. They always seemed to accompany her on runs, following her to and from school, joining her on errands. Sometimes at night she would see a small screech owl, sitting in a cottonwood tree outside her bedroom window, watching her with large yellow eyes.

She never thought it was that peculiar. She felt a connection with animals that she shared with no one else aside from Oma, Henry, and Janine. Before her parents died, she seemed to recall, she'd liked and trusted most people. But that felt like a long time ago.

Later that afternoon, Janine came over with a suitcase full of makeup. She opened it with a flourish. "I have a friend in theater who is friends with a makeup artist who loaned me this."

"Henry's friend Mel?" Skye asked.

"Precisely," said Janine. "Only she's doing makeup for a wedding and can't come, which is a shame because she is truly an artist."

Skye frowned. "What good is all this stuff without Mel? Do you even know how to use it?"

"I do," responded a voice from the hall outside Skye's bedroom. Oma slipped into the room carrying a black wig that was tinged with gray. She held up a flowered dress. "Let's turn you into me. Henry needs you tonight."

"Don't cry," Janine hissed in Skye's ear, "your makeup will run."

Skye dabbed at her eyes and tried to think of something happy, but Henry's performance as Valjean was so moving, so beautifully acted, his voice so powerful and pure, she couldn't help it. Her face was a mess by the time the actors came on stage for their bows. Henry was last, and the crowd erupted into cheers, everyone rising to their feet amid thunderous applause. The sold-out auditorium practically shook. Skye could feel the joy radiating off Henry, and the audience cheered louder. She was so proud to be his friend.

As people began to head for the exits, Janine shoved a program in Skye's hand. "Bury your face in this and hold your head still. I think your wig is slipping."

"Oh, Katrina. Wait up, dear."

"Oh no," Skye whispered to Janine. "It's one of Oma's friends."

"Slump over a little and keep your head down," Janine said. Turning to the elderly lady pushing toward them, she called out, "Ms. Van Bloem isn't feeling well."

"Feel better," the friend called. "Don't forget tea next week."

Skye waved a hand behind her as she hurried to the auditorium exit.

"Check out the hottie at ten o'clock," Janine whispered in Skye's ear.

A young man sat sprawled over an aisle seat near the exit. He had a short midnight-black ponytail and nearly perfect features. He winked at Skye.

Blushing, she quickly looked down. She'd only gotten a glimpse, but when she looked back up, he was gone.

"Who was that?" Janine said. "He acted like he knew you. Or maybe he knows your grandma."

"I've never seen him in my life." She would have remembered someone that good looking, and he was . . . incredible. Strange. There was something oddly familiar about him.

Principal St. John headed in their direction. "Quick," Janine said. "Follow me." They slipped out the side door and crouched behind a dark-blue van. Skye peered around the vehicle and saw the principal, hands on his hips, surveying the parking lot. Finally, after what seemed like an eternity, he walked back inside. Janine and Skye looked at each other with relief.

"You'd better not go back in to congratulate Henry," Janine said. "Text him."

"Thanks, Janine. You're the best."

"You say that a lot." She glanced back toward the school. "Hurry, before St. John sees you."

Skye stayed near the trees, in the shadows, on the short walk home. Five houses from hers, she heard the metallic clinking of a garbage can lid before she caught a whiff of a foul smell.

"Ah . . . fries," a voice exclaimed. Masked eyes stared at Skye. The raccoon was perched atop an open trash bin, holding the lid like it was a tray.

"Gross," Skye muttered as her phone rang. Henry.

"You looked great tonight. Thanks for coming." There was a short laugh. "Janine told me all about the makeup."

6

When Skye returned home, Oma handed her a small box wrapped in blue-and-white-checked tissue paper. "This belonged to your mother. I was saving it for your graduation, but I think now is the right time to give it to you."

Opening the box, Skye lifted out a delft porcelain locket on a silver chain. Opening the locket, she stared at the two pictures of her parents.

"Your father gave this locket to your mother," Oma said. "I put pictures of them inside. They would be so proud of you, Skye." She handed Skye a purple gift bag stuffed with white tissue paper. "This is a gift from your parents' friends at the university. Happy early graduation." She paused. "And this is from me." She handed Skye an envelope with vouchers to the IMAX theater and a crisp $100 bill.

"Oma, this is too much money." Skye tried to force the money back into her grandmother's hand.

"Don't you dare. I saved that money for you."

"I should pay for the tire."

Oma shook her head. "Nee."

Skye opened the purple gift bag and removed a check. She felt her jaw drop. So. Much. Money. With her scholarship, this money should cover college if she was careful.

After thanking Oma, Skye went to her room and curled up on her bed, clutching the locket, wondering what her life would be like if her parents were still alive. Eight years ago, they'd left to do research. Skye still fantasized they would return. Today, more than most days, she felt like she'd let them down. She'd let the prairie dogs down too. Those sweet, gentle animals . . .

"Are those tears for me, princess?"

Bolting upright, Skye stared into the intense black eyes of Starion. "You're alive!"

Starion put his front foot on Skye's hand and patted it gently. "I know you tried. I watched."

"I'm really sorry." Staring down at her hands, Skye said, "I don't understand what it is you want me to do in New Zealand. Push for world peace? Make people stop killing prairie dogs?"

"Yep, something like that." He pointed with one long claw. "Is that necklace new?"

Skye opened the locket. "My mom. She was so beautiful." She gazed at her blond, forest-green-eyed mother before pointing to the picture of her father. "That's my dad. We had so much fun together." She ran her finger over the picture of her smiling father, also blond but with soft green eyes, the color of tulip stems with a tinge of blue.

"I'm sorry you lost them."

"Thanks. Did you know the colony was going to be destroyed?"

"Maybe."

"You should have told me. That wasn't fair, to make me go through that."

"Fair?" exclaimed Starion. "Life isn't fair. If life were fair, then animals wouldn't be poisoned and bulldozed and a thousand other horrible things. People wouldn't kill each other. The air and the soil and the oceans wouldn't be polluted. There wouldn't be jerks in power, passing hateful laws."

"But what can we do?"

"Skye, I can save you, but I'm not sure I can save your friends. Time is running out." He paused. "And there's someone else who knows about this."

There was an abrupt knock on the door.

"Come in," Starion called out.

The door opened slowly, and in walked . . . Oma.

Skye stared in confusion at her grandmother. She glanced at Starion, then back at Oma. Her chin dropped. "Oma?"

Oma glared at Starion. "You couldn't have waited one more week?"

"Things are bad, Katrina," Starion replied with a clipped tone.

Starion knew her name? "How . . . how can you know each other?" Skye asked in a choked voice.

Oma took Skye's hands in her own. "I've known about the Beholders' conference since you were a child. Your father was supposed to give a speech. And hence . . ." She nodded her head toward Starion. "Him."

Skye pulled her hands away and scooted back on the bed. "But how could you know about this? I don't understand. All these years . . . you've lied to me."

"Technically she didn't lie," Starion said smoothly. "She omitted certain things."

"What things? And why do you think I should be the one to give this speech?"

"Because you're the only one who can save this planet," replied Starion.

"Humans aren't allowed in the conference hall; not since Pieter is gone," Oma said, facing Starion. "You'd be putting Skye's life in danger. I will not allow it."

"I can protect her."

"I'm still here, you know," Skye practically shouted, her shock turning to anger. "Stop ignoring me."

"Just a moment, Skye." Leaning forward, Oma waved a finger in Starion's face. "I grow weary of that cocky attitude. You haven't changed at all."

"It's you I'm weary of," Starion snapped. "I've followed all your ridiculous rules, for all these years. I'm not going to let anything happen to her." Starion rubbed a claw down his cheek. "The situation is serious. That's why she has to come with me. Right. Now."

"What's going on?" Skye demanded.

Starion's gaze shifted to Skye. "I believe your honesty and passion can win the animals over. Your father Pieter knew this day was coming. He and your mother were going to speak for the humans at the conference."

Skye swallowed loudly. "But I'm not my mother or my father."

"You're more like them than you know."

"Starion," Katrina said, "have you asked *your* father for permission to bring Skye?"

"I'll deal with my father."

"I see," said Oma. "I've learned he's sent Tane to check on you."

"I know. How did you find out?"

Oma dropped her gaze.

Starion shook his head sadly. "You're playing a dangerous game. There's only one place you could have obtained that information. You do not want to be involved with *them*."

"I'm not going to dignify that with a reply." Oma spit the words out.

Turning again toward Skye, Starion said, "Skye, the future of everyone on this planet depends on you. Will you go with me?"

"No! Who is 'them'? Why would a prairie dog's father know about this? You've both been lying to me and I'm not going anywhere with you. Who are you really?"

Starion let out a long, weary breath. "I'm a prairie dog; admittedly, a brilliant one." He spread his arms, wiggling his long whiskers. "Are you ready to save the world?"

"I'm not going anywhere with either of you. Do you hear me?" shouted Skye, shaking. "Me, save the world? Are you kidding me? I wasn't even able to save a small colony of prairie dogs. They suffered and died, and I can't stop thinking about them. No one listens to me. No one! I've been suspended and if I don't graduate, I will lose my scholarship. The only thing I've ever dreamed of is going to my parents' school. And now you're telling me to ditch graduation, give up my scholarship, and do something I can't do. Go find a famous scientist to give your speech. Animals want to destroy evil humans? Fine. Let them." Jumping off the bed, she grabbed her running shoes and headed for the door.

"Skye, wait. Please," Oma begged.

Wheeling around, Skye shouted, "Why should I? So you can tell more lies?"

"Please, Skye. Sit and I will tell you the truth."

"Fine." Skye sat on the bed and laced up her running shoes. "You can start by telling me how you know so much about these Beholders and about *him*."

"I know about the Beholders," Oma said quietly, "because I am one."

Skye gasped; Starion groaned with disapproval.

Pointing at Starion, Oma said, "Out. Now. This is between Skye and me."

Skye, shaking uncontrollably, watched a protesting Starion leave. Still unable to form a coherent sentence, she allowed Oma to guide her into the living room to the couch.

"Beholders are not terrorists. We're explorers from another planet. Occasionally, we intervene in other worlds. I'm not involved with this conference, but I've known about it because of Starion's role and because your father was supposed to speak."

Skye's voice was barely a squeak. "So you're not my real grandmother."

Oma tried to take Skye's hands, but Skye backed away. "Sweetie, you don't have to be related by blood to be someone's grandmother."

"Did my parents know?"

Oma nodded.

Skye's head throbbed and her stomach lurched as she curled up on the sofa, trying to think.

"Skye, what do you want to know? I will try to answer your questions."

Skye's voice was a whisper. "You're an alien. Why did you pretend to be my grandmother? Why would my parents let you do that?"

Oma was quiet for several seconds. "Pieter was afraid for your safety. He felt I could protect you if something ever happened to him."

"You mean the people who murdered my parents are after me?"

Oma shook her head. "No. That isn't what I mean. Pieter wanted me to make sure you were taken care of. I don't know who killed your parents. I have tried to find out, but I'm not good with the money system or the legal system used on your planet. I hired many, many investigators to find the murderers, but they were never found. I'm so sorry, Skye. That is what happened to all the money — why we had to move."

"I'm glad you tried to find the killers," Skye answered. "But why did my parents think you could protect me? Because you're from another planet? Do you have super powers or something?"

"Beholders can change shape — into animals; our laws forbid transforming into humanoids."

Skye bolted upright. "WHAT?"

"Should I show you?"

Skye nodded and watched with wide eyes as Oma — the woman she had called grandmother her entire life — transformed into a small owl. Huge yellow eyes blinked at Skye from behind a feathered face. Then, the owl became Oma.

A sudden coldness spread over Skye. This woman in front of her had been spying on her for years — following, watching, disguised as various birds. Rising, she stumbled to the door.

"Don't leave," Oma pleaded. "Please, Skye."

Skye never looked back as she let the door shut behind her.

7

"Dr. Franklin, may I stay with you?"

"Skye, come in," exclaimed Janine's mother. "You know the guest room is always ready for you. But honey, what is wrong? Did you run all the way over here in the pitch dark?"

Mr. Franklin, peering over his wife's shoulder, shouted, "Janine. Skye is here."

Janine was soon bustling around her parents. "Are you OK?"

Skye nodded and whispered, "I need to stay with you."

"Does your grandmother know where you are, Skye?" Janine's father asked.

Skye shook her head.

"Then we are going to call her so she doesn't worry. Agreed?" said Janine's mom.

Skye nodded.

Janine's father put his arm around her mother. "We're going to leave you two to talk. Skye, let us know if we can help."

Janine walked Skye up to the second-floor guest room and sat on the king-sized bed with her. "Talk to me, Skye."

"Oma's an alien."

"I know," said Janine. "She's from Holland."

Skye shook her head. "She's a Beholder."

"She's one of the ecoterrorists?"

"No. She's an alien from another planet." Skye told Janine everything that had happened. It was rare for Skye to see Janine speechless, sitting there, her mouth hanging open, shaking her head.

"Do you believe me?" Skye finally asked.

Janine took out her cell phone. "Henry, get over to my house now."

Twenty minutes later, Janine ran downstairs when she heard the doorbell ring. In seconds, Henry was hugging Skye. "What happened?"

"Henry, I'm so sorry. Janine shouldn't have told you to come. I know you were at a cast party and —"

Henry put his fingers to Skye's lips. "You're more important. Spill. What's going on?"

He was quiet as Janine and Skye related the events.

"You don't believe me, do you?" Skye asked, looking at both her friends. "You think I'm crazy."

Henry extended his open palm and Janine put her hand on top. Skye reluctantly added hers to the pile. "Friends always believe friends," he said.

Janine nodded. "We absolutely believe you, Skye. But seriously, how awesome is this? Your grandmother is from another planet. I always knew there was life on other planets — every Trekkie does. Of all the people on Earth, I have the honor of being here at this historic moment." She bounced on the bed next to Henry, exclaiming, "Aliens. *Wow.* My best friend's grandma is an alien."

Even Henry had to admit it was awesome.

"She lied to me all these years," Skye said. "I don't think I can ever forgive her."

"Wasn't she keeping a promise to your father?" Janine said. "Seriously, no one could ask for a better grandmother."

Henry nodded in agreement.

"What's the name of the Beholders' planet?" Janine asked.

"I don't know. Who cares? They're Beholders. The planet Beholder, I suppose," Skye said.

"Starion's one of them," Janine insisted. "You know I'm right. Did you ask your Oma about him?"

Skye shook her head.

Henry, still in full makeup, looked thoughtful as he twirled a strand of blond hair — straightened for his role — on his finger. "If Starion was a Beholder, he wouldn't be a prairie dog, would he? Why not take the shape of the president or someone important? Then he could make a bunch of laws and fix this whole environmental mess and you wouldn't have to give a speech."

"Cause politicians do *so* much to help the environment," Skye said sarcastically. "Anyway, Oma said Beholders can only take the shape of animals, that it's forbidden to change into a person."

"Are you going to give the speech?" Henry asked.

Skye moved off the bed and began to pace. Janine and Henry were both silent, watching her. Finally turning to them, Skye said, "No. I told them to go find a famous scientist."

Skye spent a restless night of pacing, going back to bed, pacing some more. Oma had dropped off a suitcase with some of her things, including a white blanket covered in sparrow drawings that her mother had given her as a child. Skye had refused to speak with the woman.

She thought about her parents. She tried to do homework, which of course Oma had also dropped off. She went back to sleep. She got up. She sat down on the floor, hugging the sparrow blanket. In her other hand, she clutched the delft porcelain locket — the one with pictures of her parents.

I will not cry . . . I will not cry . . .

Carolina, Skye's mother, was American, and she had been a licensed wildlife rehabilitator with a PhD in animal behavior and ornithology. She often let Skye help her with injured animals because Skye had a gift for calming the animals. Skye's father, Pieter, a world-famous

Dutch botanist, had called her his own Dr. Dolittle. They'd lived in the Netherlands when Skye was young, on a farm near Haarlem, by the coast in North Holland. Skye missed the mute swans that gathered in groups by the canals. She had secret names for several of them and often snuggled up next to their soft white feathers.

Skye adored helping her father in his flower laboratory, looking under microscopes and helping him to plant, but her real love, like her mother's, was for animals. When Skye was six the family moved to the Northern Colorado Front Range, into a beautiful Victorian home on 125 acres with several horses, so her parents could pursue research at Colorado State University. CSU was her mother's alma mater. Skye missed Holland, but she fell in love with the Rocky Mountains and the abundance of wildlife there. Her parents took her hiking and camping in the mountains, and she was a regular in the university labs. The graduate students nicknamed her "Sky Flower" since her Dutch last name of Van Bloem meant flower. Her parents were popular professors at the university, and there was always a waiting list for their classes.

Skye's father was widely known for breeding a special tulip he called the Skye Tulip. It was the color of a red poppy, like Skye's hair, with two stripes: one a dark green and one a soft blue-green.

Right after Skye's tenth birthday, Pieter's mother, Katrina Van Bloem, had come from Holland to care for Skye in Colorado while her parents went to Costa Rica to do research. Skye had trusted the woman, loved her, always called her Oma.

Skye's parents never returned. For a long time, she pretended they would come home.

Shortly after Skye's sixteenth birthday, with their funds depleted for a reason Skye only now understood, Katrina sold the Victorian home with its acreage and moved with Skye into a small duplex near the high school. Skye had stood looking out over the property for a long time the day they left, her face set in grim lines, her fingers curled into fists. She vowed that one day she would buy it back.

Oma soon took to talking to her flowers, which she fussed over daily in her tiny garden. Sure, she'd taken care of Skye for all these years. Admittedly, she'd been the best grandmother possible, but what did it matter if their relationship had been unique and special? It was all a lie, a betrayal.

Skye was never going back.

8
....

Skye fell into a routine at Janine's house, even reading to Janine's little sister Katie and telling her stories. The girl loved it when Skye talked about animals and would listen eagerly to the tales.

Janine continued to help Skye with math and chemistry as they both prepared for finals on Friday. While everyone in the house was at their jobs or school, Skye worked on the computer. By Tuesday, she felt well enough to go running.

Skye sped down a remote road near the foothills, enjoying the breeze, the aspens shimmering in the light. And then she stopped and wheeled around, screaming at the small falcon that she'd spotted following her, "Go away, Oma. I know you're pretending to be that kestrel. Stop spying on me."

Anger causing her to stumble, Skye raced back to Janine's house and locked the door behind her. Why couldn't that woman leave her alone?

After taking a shower, Skye sat on the bed, gazing sadly at the picture on the cover of a wildlife magazine Henry had dropped off for her. A mother polar bear sat clutching her cub on a piece of ice barely big enough to hold them.

The cub hadn't made it.

Skye exhaled loudly. The world was such a mess. Climate change was driving more than polar bears into extinction and some people didn't even believe it existed. But what could she do? Starion was wrong about her — she was nobody special. She couldn't give a speech. Who would listen to her?

She curled up on the bed and shut her eyes, still holding the magazine. She was so tired, emotionally and physically. If only she could make a difference.

A real difference . . .

Skye hurled the magazine to the floor. What she really wanted to do was give a speech to all the humans. Stop destroying the planet. Stop making climate change worse. Fix it!

Reluctantly, she walked over to the desk and sat down in front of the computer. She typed climate change into the internet browser. It was time to dig into the specifics of global warming.

On Wednesday, Skye called the Tucson office of a leading conservation group and asked to speak to Ryan — one of the directors who'd given her advice about the action she'd taken to help prairie dogs. After some pleasantries, Skye asked, "Ryan, what are people doing to save animals?"

On Thursday, instead of studying for finals, which were tomorrow, Skye spent the entire day reading articles on the computer — all of them about environmental issues.

Every single day, she thought about the dead prairie dogs, and she mourned for them.

On Friday, after taking her finals, she returned to Janine's house and spent the rest of the day writing. That evening, she asked Janine to call Henry over. After they'd finished a pizza, Skye retrieved a set of papers from the printer. "I wrote a speech."

Henry and Janine gave each other a knowing glance.

Skye looked from one to the other. "You've been talking about this, haven't you?"

Henry's words were careful. "What if that prairie dog is telling the truth? What if they really are going to kill us all? Why would a scientist be better at convincing a group of animals than you, Skye?"

"Why didn't you say something?" Skye exclaimed. She looked at Janine. "All week neither of you said anything."

"We couldn't tell you what to do, Skye," Janine said softly.

"But you knew I was thinking about it?"

"Don't be mad," Janine admitted, "but I checked your browser history." She paused. "Why can't you see what Henry and I see?"

"Yeah, what's that?"

"That the prairie dog got it right," Henry said without hesitation. "If anyone can convince a bunch of animals not to kill us, my money's on you."

Nodding, Janine said, "Tell your grandmother to find the prairie dog and meet us at your house tomorrow night after my graduation party. Henry and I are going with you to New Zealand." She held her hand out. "Let's see the speech."

Skye handed the papers to Janine. "I looked up a bunch of statistics on the internet. I even made an outline." She chewed at her bottom lip. "But I barely got a C in public speaking. I was terrible."

Henry shook his head and exhaled loudly.

Skye fidgeted as Janine read the papers, nodding at times, sighing at other parts. She finally handed them back. "Nice. Well organized. You've listed the facts about progress that's being made to save species and their habitats, along with references. Very scientific." She stuck her thumb in the air.

Henry grabbed the papers and began reading. Frowning, he shook his head several times. Holding the papers out to Skye, he said, "It reads like a term paper. This isn't you, Skye. It lacks passion. A collection of figures isn't going to sway anyone. I think it would be better if you spoke to them the way you speak to us about environmental issues. You care about this more than anyone I know."

"You're wrong, Henry," Janine said. "Skye needs actual real statistics." She looked at Skye. "If you wrote this for a class you'd get an A."

"But she isn't writing it for a class," Henry argued. "It's dull. Skye should be Skye. She's trying too hard."

Skye groaned in frustration. "Should I rewrite it?"

Henry put his arm around her. "Be yourself when you give the speech. Look at your audience; watch their reaction; change it if you need to."

"What if I can't?"

"Sweetie, of course you can," answered Henry. "Aren't you always telling me I can make it on Broadway? You've got this one. Honestly."

"And Skye," Janine said, looking her directly in the eyes. "Stop being a jerk to your grandmother."

9
....

Except for Janine's irreverent valedictorian speech and Henry's powerful vocal solo of the national anthem, graduation, held outside in ninety-degree heat, was boring and long. Skye threw her cap in the air with the other seniors, walked off the football field, and ran right into Oma. Skye knew she'd be there. Oma was always there.

Oma turned to leave with a quick apology. Skye stopped her.

"Oma . . . I . . . uh . . ." Tears threatened as Skye grabbed Oma in a tight hug, and then they were both crying. "Tell Starion I need to talk to him."

Janine had been asking Oma questions ever since the three newly-graduated friends had arrived at Skye's house. Oma refused to answer direct questions about Starion, instead saying that he would answer them when he arrived. She told them about not just her planet, but another one too.

The Beholders had a dependent relationship with a neighboring planet called Vanger. The Beholders imported most of their food from Vanger, which in turn received ships in order to explore space, searching for agricultural samples so it could grow new types of crops. It was one such mission that had reported the ecological mess occurring on Earth. The aliens' Earth contacts had been Skye's parents.

The Vangers wanted to take cuttings, soil, seeds, and other samples and leave, but the Beholders insisted on fixing the mess. Skye sympathized with the animals, but killing all the humans? Though she still doubted she was the best-qualified person for the task, she'd decided to give a speech and fight for the environmentalists, scientists, and wildlife heroes who worked every day to make things better. Everyone else? Skye had never been that fond of people, but she figured she wouldn't tell the animals that. Or the Beholders. Or, she supposed, the Vangers either.

Oma remarked that the two planets had been in contact for a mere nine hundred years, but it was widely thought that their peoples had descended from a common ancestor, though Vangers could not change shape. Each planet had its own language, but most inhabitants were bilingual. The two planets interacted like a dysfunctional family: squabbling, stealing, backstabbing, threatening, gossiping, arguing about money and resources.

"Ms. Van Bloem, you look tired," Henry said. "Go sit in the living room. Janine and I will help Skye with the dishes."

After Oma had gone into the living room, Janine whispered to Henry and Skye. "This is so awesome. It's better than an episode of *Star Trek*."

A few minutes later, Oma called from the living room. "Skye, someone is here to see you."

Skye walked into the living room and froze. A young man leaned casually against the wall, smiling at her. His fair skin had the same smooth, flawless texture as hers. A lack of facial hair added to the overall softness of his features: high cheekbones, full lips, and immense black eyes crowned by ebony eyebrows. His midnight-black hair was straight, pulled back into a ponytail that reached almost to his shoulder blades. Wisps of hair cascaded around his face. Smallish sideburns framed perfectly sculpted ears. A small gold hoop pierced the lobe of each ear. He looked like he was posing for a photo shoot.

He was unbelievably gorgeous.

"Hi," the young man said, looking at her with amusement.

Skye opened her mouth, but no words came out.

The man held out his hand. He was wearing faded, ripped jeans and a long-sleeved black silk shirt. He was the same height as Skye. Stunning dark eyes peered out from behind strands of hair as he smiled seductively.

Skye temporarily lost the ability to speak. *Wow*. He was . . . *Wow* . . . Her brain felt as though someone had stuck it in a blender, then sucked out all her thoughts with a straw, leaving only one.

Wow.

"I hope I didn't startle you," he said. Perfect gleaming white teeth blazed from a slightly off-center smile.

"Hey," exclaimed Janine, pointing at the visitor. "That's the guy we saw in the theater after Henry's musical. Who is he?"

"This is Starion," Oma answered.

Skye was stunned.

But only for a minute.

He walked slowly toward her. Smiling, he reached out for her hand. In one swift movement, she kicked his feet out from under him, landing him on his back in a pile of pillows. She placed her foot in the middle of his chest and glared down at him.

Janine burst into laughter while Henry attempted to hide a wide grin behind his hand.

"What? What did I do?" Starion complained.

"Hey Starion," Janine said, still laughing, "not a smart move." She turned to Henry. "Told you he was a Beholder. Nailed it."

Henry high-fived Janine.

"You should have told me you were a Beholder." Skye glared down at Starion.

"Hiding the truth isn't a lie."

Skye pushed her foot down harder into Starion's chest as her eyes narrowed. "Yeah. It is. No more lies." She paused. "Or I'm not giving this speech."

Starion grinned. "Giving the speech, huh? Decided to be a hero after all?"

"I'm not a hero," Skye muttered as she lifted her foot and backed away, allowing Starion to stand.

"Let's see you change into a prairie dog," said Henry.

One minute, Starion was human, and the next, he was a prairie dog. He sat on his bottom, claws dangling in front of his chest, and barked. Returning to his human form, wearing the same clothes as before, he spread his arms out wide. "Convinced?"

"Awesome," exclaimed Henry.

Janine nodded in agreement. "Impressive." She paused. "Here's the deal. Henry and I don't trust you. If you're taking Skye, we're going with you. Right, Henry?"

Henry nodded. "I have to tell my mom though. So she doesn't worry."

"Sorry, kids, that's a no-go," replied Starion. He tapped his upper right shoulder. "I have a module, about the size of a quarter, embedded under my skin, that allows me to transport almost anywhere, but since Skye doesn't have one, I must carry her. Can't carry all three of you. Sorry."

"Can you get Vanger transport modules for them?" Oma asked.

"Yes, but I don't have them on me." Glancing at Skye, he pushed back a wisp of dark hair. "Skye is the only one I need." He winked.

"Starion," snapped Oma. "You're not winning points with me right now."

"Let's see how it works," Janine demanded.

Starion pressed a hand to his shoulder, spoke strange words, and disappeared.

Henry swiveled his head around and exclaimed, "Hey, where did he—"

Starion reappeared on the other side of the room.

"Amazing," exclaimed Janine, talking rapidly. "It's a combination transporter-communication device. I have questions. Lots of them. What is a Vanger transport module and how can I get one? This is going to change science. And by the way, why does your planet think they can interfere on our planet? Ever hear of a noninterference directive?"

Skye smiled. "I knew you'd say that."

"If you're Beholders," Henry said, looking at Oma and Starion, "just tell them to stop this conference, that you met humans and we're nice and we care about stuff."

"I'm afraid it's not that easy," Oma said. "No one is going to listen to an old lady."

"What about you?" Skye pointed at Starion.

Oma blurted out a laugh.

"What?" Skye looked from Oma to Starion.

"My father is in charge of the conference," Starion replied. "But I just do his bidding. He doesn't listen to me."

"Can't you make him?" Henry asked.

"No," Starion and Oma said in unison.

"So . . . back to the plan with Skye's speech then," Janine said. "What do the Vangers think of all this?"

Starion shrugged. "They just want to collect their seeds and leave. They don't want to get involved."

Janine looked over the top of her glasses at Starion. "Maybe you ought to listen to them."

"Vangers are farmers and artists. They are often a source of ridicule for the people of my planet, which consists of many businesspeople and entrepreneurs. Beholders tend not to listen to advice from Vangers."

"Sounds like you're from the wrong planet," Skye mused.

Starion looked thoughtful then turned to Henry. "Nice performance in *Les Mis*, by the way. That's some voice you've got."

"You saw me playing Valjean?"

"Yep. Impressive." Starion paused, rubbing his hands together. "All-righty then. Skye, are you ready? Only eleven days till the conference. Time to go."

"Right now?" Skye asked, panic in her voice.

"Yep. Right. Now."

Oma stomped over to Starion. "No. I absolutely forbid it. Look at her. She's exhausted. Look at the dark circles under her eyes. She needs a good night's rest. She can't give a speech if she gets ill." She pointed menacingly at Starion. "Leave."

"But—"

"No buts. Out now."

When Starion hesitated, Oma shouted, "NOW!"

Henry put an arm around Skye as a cursing Starion left. "Your grand-mother is a badass." He eyed Skye closely. "You really don't look well. Janine and I will come back in the morning. Get some sleep."

When Skye finally stumbled into the kitchen the next morning, Henry was already there, having a cup of tea with Oma.

"Is Janine here?" Skye asked.

"She's on her way. I just got a text," said Henry.

"Starion?"

"I sent him out to the porch," Oma replied, staring down at her tea.

Henry attempted to hide a grin. "Skye, may I talk to you? In your room?"

"Sure." Once they were in her room, she shut the door. "Henry, what did—"

A scratching at the window interrupted them. "Help. Please, help."

Henry's eyes widened. "What was that?"

Skye lifted the blinds on her window and pulled back in surprise. A fox squirrel was frantically scratching at the window.

"I can hear him," exclaimed Henry.

"Help me. Please help me. Come out through the back door." The squirrel motioned frantically with its small paws.

Skye and Henry ran out of the bedroom and through the back door.

The squirrel came around the side of the house and sat in front of Henry and Skye. "She's here," the squirrel called out.

Two men appeared. One was bald with a crooked nose; the other had shoulder-length russet-streaked brown hair. Silver guns flashed in the sunlight.

Henry screamed.

Starion came running with Janine following. He shouted strange words, and almost instantly, a red-tailed hawk glided down and grabbed the squirrel in its talons.

Shielding Skye with his body, Starion addressed the two men in a language Skye had never heard. They replied with the same foreign sounds. The words soon rose to an angry pitch; hands gestured, faces reddened, nostrils flared. The hawk perched calmly in the branches of a cottonwood tree to the side of the house, the squirrel squirming and crying, firmly held by the raptor's talons.

With a dramatic flourish, the two men pointed their guns at Janine and Henry. Then they disappeared.

The hawk flew down and dropped the squirrel into Starion's hands. With a *key—rrrrrrr* sound, the bird took off around the side of the house. A moment later, Oma came running.

Starion squeezed the squirrel tightly and spoke to it in the same foreign tongue. The animal thrashed and tried to escape, but Starion maintained the pressure.

"Tall man. Eyes odd," the squirrel choked.

"What are you doing to that squirrel?" Skye demanded. "Let him go."

"It seems someone is taking bribes," replied Starion, glaring down at the squirrel in his hands.

"No humans at the conference," the squirrel squeaked. "Let 'em all die."

Skye gasped and stepped back.

Oma motioned at the squirrel. "Kill it," she ordered Starion. "We can't risk it."

As Starion started to squeeze the life from the squirrel, Skye screamed, "Stop!"

Oma shook her head rapidly. "Skye, honey. Those men found you because of this creature. He can't live."

Skye tried to pry Starion's fingers from the squirrel. He was so surprised he opened his hands. Skye took the squirrel and gently set it down on the ground. The animal quickly ran off, pausing and looking back at her. Then it disappeared around a corner.

Without a word, Skye turned toward the house. Going into her room, she closed the door quietly. The animals wanted the humans to die. What was she going to do? She loved animals, sympathized with their plight. She couldn't blame them for wanting to get rid of humans. Yes, there were bad people, but . . . what about Janine and Henry? There were people who cared about the environment and tried to make a difference. But then she thought of the men who'd destroyed the prairie dog colony. And Josh. And greedy oil companies. And corrupt politicians. She put her head in her hands and sobbed.

Her animal friends wanted her dead.

When Skye finally joined everyone in the living room, Henry was the first to hug her. "It was one squirrel."

"Squirrels are nuts anyway," Janine added. "Seriously. And brains? None in those tiny heads, I promise."

Skye put her hands in the pockets of her jeans shorts. "We can go whenever you want." She paused. "Why were those Beholder men here?"

"They were not Beholders," Starion answered. "They were Vangers."

"What?" Janine shouted. "You said Vangers didn't care about the conference."

"Those men are working independently from the central authority. Janine is correct — Vangers don't care about the conference. That squirrel tipped them off to your location, Skye. They threatened to come after Janine and Henry if they couldn't get you." Starion frowned. "I have no idea who they're working for, because clearly they're hired thugs."

"Why are they after *me*?" Skye said, rubbing her hand nervously across her forehead.

"They don't want you to speak at the conference," said Henry.

Janine looked thoughtful. "Maybe. Anyway, we've got to come so we can protect you."

Starion scoffed. "How? You're no match against Vanger thugs. You don't have weapons, and if you did you wouldn't know how to use them."

Henry put his hand in the air and smiled. "I do."

"Oh, please, Henry," Janine retorted. "The gun you used in *Les Mis* was fake."

Skye put her arms around her friends. "If Starion can't take all of us, I can't go. If I leave, they'll come back here and hurt you. I'm not putting your lives in danger."

"We could fly there," Henry suggested.

"Oh and how much fun would that be?" said Janine. "Thousands of dollars, fifteen hours on a plane, the TSA with all their drama, rude flight attendants, tiny seats with no leg room. I *love* to fly."

"How does your transport thing work?" asked Henry.

"Really? We're going to waste time explaining that?" Starion said irritably. He glanced at the three teenagers glaring back at him. "Fine. Here's the short version. There's a transport control ship, or TCS for short, hidden in your solar system. It's manned by soldiers from both planets. All Beholders have an embedded module that can get them immediately up to the TCS with a code. The Vangers don't have their modules embedded unless they are military, but they can get up there too. Then, one of the soldiers on the ship can send them anywhere on the planet, or to another ship in space. Transport-module identification numbers are encrypted and you need clearance to get access to them. The system operates on a space-folding principle."

"Space folding?" Janine exclaimed. "How cool is that. How does it work?"

"It's classified," Starion snapped.

"What if they make a mistake and send someone into the middle of the ocean? Maybe I don't want to do it. I can't swim," Henry replied in a horrified voice.

Starion gave Henry an irritated glance. "You're not going anyway."

"Stop it, Henry," Janine said. "Just because you and Skye are incompetent with machines, that doesn't mean the rest of us are. The science behind it must be fascinating. How do I get a clearance?"

Oma chuckled. "A clearance is a difficult thing to obtain on our planet, but you are bright enough that you could probably understand the transport science, Janine. Goodness knows, I would not."

Janine beamed.

"How do they get all the animals to the conference?" asked Skye.

"There is a specialized room, located at the site of the conference in New Zealand, which operates like the TCS," Starion said. "It has a huge control field that can transport hundreds of tagged animals at once. It's rather complicated and took years to construct."

"There's no privacy if you think about it," Skye said. "If someone knows your module number, they could transport you anywhere, find you anywhere."

Janine looked thoughtful. "Good point, Skye. That could be scary. Maybe that's why the Vangers don't have their modules embedded. Interesting." She looked at Starion. "Another point for Vanger. That makes two."

Ignoring her, Starion looked at Skye. "Will you come with me? I can't take your friends."

"Not if Janine and Henry are in danger."

"Skye, I'm aware of the danger to them." Starion inclined his head at Oma. "Katrina has already spoken with Henry's mom and Janine's parents and they've agreed to let the three of you go on a vacation."

"Sweet." Henry smiled.

Skye looked confused. "They're coming with us?"

"No. Henry and Janine will stay here and Katrina will protect them."

"What? A vacation here? Definitely not sweet," Henry blurted.

Skye looked over at her grandmother. "How are you going to protect them?"

Oma instantly transformed into a mountain lion. A terrifying snarl echoed through the room. Henry gave a squeak of fright, and Janine dropped her glass.

Transforming back, Oma asked, "Convinced?"

"I feel safe now," Henry said, his voice shaking.

"Me too," gasped Janine.

"Katrina has another talent," Starion said. "She has the gift of shapesight. It is a rare ability on our planet. She can detect a Beholder in animal form. She will know if an animal is an animal or a Beholder pretender."

"Can Vangers change shape?" asked Janine.

Oma shook her head.

Janine threw her hands up. "What good does that talent serve when the bad guys are Vangers?"

"Don't worry, you'll be safe here," replied Starion. "Skye, are you ready?"

Skye turned to Oma. "You promise you won't let them get hurt?"

"I will guard them with my life."

"Go," Janine said. "We'll be fine."

Skye slung her backpack over her shoulder and picked up her small duffel. "Wish me luck everyone."

Janine coughed loudly. "You're wearing shorts to New Zealand? In the middle of their winter?"

Skye blushed. "Oh. I knew that." She ran back into her bedroom. In a few minutes, she returned wearing her thickest jeans, hiking boots, and a heavy forest-green hoodie bearing the Colorado State University emblem. "Wish me luck."

"You don't need luck, sweetie," Henry said, kissing her on the cheek. "You'll be amazing."

Janine hugged her. "Come back, OK?"

"Bye, Oma," Skye said to her grandmother. "I'll try not to disappoint everyone."

"Oh, Skye, you could never do that." Oma turned to Starion. "You remember what I told you."

Starion bowed with a sarcastic flourish. "Yes, professor."

"Professor? What?" Janine asked.

Gazing sternly at Starion, Oma said, "He was one of my students."

Before Skye could ask, Starion said, "I'll tell you about it later. Katrina. Valjean. Janine. We'll be back after Skye's speech."

"How long will that be?" Henry asked.

Starion shrugged. "It depends on how long it takes to get there and start the conference. We can convene early, but if the vote isn't concluded within ten days from tomorrow, it's the same as a no vote for the humans."

"That would suck," Henry murmured.

"Yup, it would suck. Ten days, people. Tick tock."

Janine frowned. "Then get going. We're going to be worried."

"And bored," agreed Henry. "On vacation. In your house."

"Skye," Starion said. "May I have permission to pick you up?"

Backpack over her shoulder, she nodded and clutched her duffle to her chest. Starion lifted her, his eyes flashing, and asked in a husky voice, "Comfy, princess?"

Skye looked into those gorgeous dark eyes set in that too-perfect face. She was so not falling for him. Not now. Not ever. "Keep it up and you'll end up on the floor again."

"Well," Starion practically purred, "we can't have that, can we?"

"*Starion*," scolded Oma.

"Press down on my transport module." Starion paused. "Or anywhere else you'd like."

"*Starion*," Oma repeated.

Skye placed a hesitant hand on his shoulder, over the transport module. She could barely feel the outline of the small device. As Starion spoke strange words, Henry's giggles began to fade into the distance.

The room spun.

10

....

"**R**ichard," said Starion, addressing the man in front of him. "It's good to see you."

"Put me down," ordered Skye, still in Starion's arms.

"Skye, this is Professor Richard Leven," said Starion, setting her down in a spacious living room with plush black couches and tall bookshelves lining two walls.

"It's nice to meet you, Skye," said Leven, extending his hand.

"Nice to meet you too," replied Skye, shaking the hand of the thin fiftyish man with gray hair and a bushy mustache.

"Starion told me you'd probably like to get some sleep and relax before the conference begins. Much rests on your words, young lady."

No pressure there, Skye thought. The doubts came rushing back. Could she do this?

Leven patted her on the shoulder. "Don't look so terrified. Starion is convinced you can sway the delegates, and he's usually right."

"Usually?" Skye asked breathlessly. "Usually?"

"Yes, of course I'm right." Starion turned to Richard and embraced him warmly. "Thank you for helping us. Have you heard from Tane?"

"Not yet."

"How do you know each other?" Skye asked the two.

"He was my student for a short time," answered Leven.

"Are you a Beholder?"

Leven shook his head. "No, I'm a human professor at the University of Otago in Dunedin. Starion was in one of my classes there several years ago."

"Have you studied kea?" Skye asked.

"Yes, indeed. You'll see them down here, cheeky parrots."

"Really?" Skye squealed. "They were my mother's favorite bird. I've seen a couple at the Denver Zoo but never in the wild."

"All that noise for a bird?" Starion said. "I thought prairie dogs were your favorite?" He pretended to pout.

"They're OK, I guess." Skye grinned. "Am I in Dunedin?"

"No, we're about three and a half hours from Dunedin. You're in Queenstown, on the South Island of New Zealand, in one of the apartments for out-of-town guests of the university. The university maintains facilities here because it's closer to the fiords — easier for study." Leven motioned for Skye to follow him to one of the bedrooms. "This is the best room in the house, Skye. We reserve it for VIPs. I think you'll enjoy the view. Starion always has." He motioned for Starion to open the drapes covering an enormous window.

With a flourish, Starion pulled the drapes open. Skye gasped as she stared at rugged mountains — snow-tipped, majestic, towering over an ink-blue lake. They were different from the Rocky Mountains she called home, but there was something familiar about them.

"Do you recognize them?" Starion asked with a grin.

Skye frowned. "No. How could I? I've never been to New Zealand."

"Think. You've seen these mountains dozens of times."

Staring at them, Skye loudly exclaimed, "It's the Remarkables — the mountain range in *The Lord of the Rings*. They filmed part of the movies here. They're my favorite books, and I've watched all the movies with Oma, and —" She stopped. "I guess I won't have time to see the town or anything, right? I have to go save the world." Her voice was full of despair.

"Skye," Starion said gently. "We have time."

"Brilliant," Leven said. "Starion, you know your way around town. Skye, grab a coat and scarf in the closet by the door. It's winter here."

Queenstown reminded Skye of resort towns in the Rockies. People carrying skis and snowboards jostled for places on the many buses running up to the lifts, and the restaurants and cafés overflowed with tourists. They strolled by the shores of the lake, stopped for hot cider, and listened to street musicians.

"I'm starving," Starion said. "What type of food do you feel like?"

"Chinese?" Skye pointed to a small restaurant.

"Chinese it is," answered Starion, opening the front door for Skye.

Seated at a small table near the window, Skye said, "Just so you know, this is not a date or anything."

Starion had trouble suppressing a grin as he opened the menu. "Of course not." His grin quickly turned into a frown and then into anger as he shut the menu with a snap.

"What's wrong?"

When he didn't answer, Skye opened the thick plastic menu and frowned. "They serve shark fin soup here."

"Do you want to leave?"

"Yes."

Starion shook his head. "They're also serving European eel and Acadian redfish — all overfished and endangered."

On the way out the door, Starion told the manager why they were leaving, and Skye described the cruel way fishermen harvested fins from sharks. A family waiting to be seated overheard them.

"After that horror story," said the mother, "I think we'll leave too."

"Let's go," the man declared.

"Mom, I told you," the young teenage girl whined. "I want waffles, not some nasty seafood stuff." She turned to the manager and with a loud snap of her gum, said, "What you're doing is gross and mean, jerk-wad."

"Young lady, watch your language." The woman smiled apologetically at Skye and Starion.

After they all herded themselves through the door, Starion asked, "Where are you from? You don't sound like Kiwis."

"Iowa," the man replied. "My wife wants to see the fiords."

"C'mon, Daddy," the girl whined. "You promised to buy me a new backpack because of that bird." She shoved a ripped backpack in his face. The zipper flapped in the wind. There was an enormous hole in one side.

"A bird did that?" Skye asked.

The girl's mother looked irritated. "I told her not to leave it on the picnic table at the ski resort, but she didn't listen. When we came back to get it, there were three big birds destroying it."

"Were they kea?" Skye asked in awe.

The man nodded. "Yes. I believe that's what the guide called them. They were green with big beaks."

Skye turned pleading eyes to Starion.

"We'll see them. I promise."

As the woman bustled her family down the road, the daughter's words sailed back toward them. "He is so hot."

Turning to Skye with a grin, Starion said, "Did you notice the sticker on the girl's backpack?"

Skye exhaled loudly. "From the Jane Goodall Institute. What's your point?"

"You're not the only one who cares, Skye."

She paused. "OK, fine. Three people are environmentally conscious. That still leaves millions who don't care."

They walked in silence for several minutes before Skye spoke. "Thank you for that — for telling the manager it was wrong. People think I'm weird because I'm a vegetarian. I usually don't get after people about what they eat, well, unless it's veal or foie gras, but shark fin soup?" She stopped and looked at Starion. "Are you a vegetarian?"

"When you can understand animals and alter your shape to resemble them, it changes your ideas about what's acceptable food. Beholders don't eat meat."

"Beholders don't raise animals for meat? No feedlots or slaughterhouses?"

"Nope."

"What about Vangers?"

"No. Only crops."

Skye smiled at him. "You got points for that."

"And what can I exchange those points for?" He winked.

Skye drew back. "Nothing."

"Ah . . . but I can hope," he purred. "How about that place?" He pointed to a second-story Italian restaurant with a brightly painted sign of a comely woman holding a bowl of pasta. "Richard and I have been there a couple times. You can pick from over a dozen different sauces served over homemade pasta, all vegetarian. If we were in Dunedin, I'd take you to my favorite pub. It's called the Cloaked Sovereign. Richard and I spent quite a bit of time there."

"This is amazing pasta," Skye said, finishing a large bowl of rigatoni drenched in a garlic-olive oil sauce with mushrooms and artichokes.

"I can't believe you ate that entire bowl." Starion scooted his chair to Skye's side of the table. "Can I have the last bite?"

"I suppose you think you're pretty charming."

Starion leaned closer. "I was hoping you did."

"Go back to your side of the table."

Starion laughed and moved his chair back across from her.

"Now," Skye began, "I want some answers and I want the truth."

"Anything for you, princess."

"I mean it." Skye folded her arms across her chest. "Is it rude to ask how old you are?"

"I'm twenty Earth years old."

"Why are you in charge of this conference?"

"My father's in charge of the UEE. I'm only the facilitator."

"The what?"

"The UEE stands for United Earth Ecosystems. That's the name of the conference of animal delegates."

Skye frowned. "You told Oma you'd deal with your father. He's an important scientist, right? I guess he doesn't want me to speak at the conference, does he? Is he the one after me?"

"My father doesn't know about you, and he won't be there." Starion looked thoughtful before continuing. "Don't worry about him. I've been punished before and lived through it. Richard will tell you that I'm often in trouble. You'll be meeting Tane soon. He'll tell you the same thing."

"Is Tane a Beholder like you?"

"Yes. He's my best friend—a military general."

"Really? That's cool, I guess. Was my grandmother really your teacher?"

"Yes. She thought I was a brat. Can you imagine?" He pretended to be shocked.

Skye tried to suppress a grin, but her face quickly became serious. "Why were those men after me? And what did you say to them?"

"As I told you, they're from Vanger. They refused to say who they were working for—not the Vanger government. I told them that kidnapping you would start a war between our planets."

"Who am I?" Skye asked. "Helen of Troy or something?"

"Who?"

Skye waved a dismissive hand. "They don't want me to speak at the conference, do they?"

"Maybe not; there aren't supposed to be humans present—your parents were a special exception. But I feel like something else is going on. It's just a hunch, because truthfully, I don't know." He leaned closer to Skye. "I'm breaking the rules by bringing you, but don't worry. I've spoken to Tane. He'll protect us. Uh, I mean you. He'll protect you."

Skye took a long drink of water. Something felt weird about all this. Maybe the Vangers secretly wanted all the humans dead. Maybe the reason for that had nothing to do with saving animals or collecting plants. Maybe she was standing in the way of something.

"Do the Vangers want us all to die?"

Starion frowned. "I'm not sure why they would. They didn't care before."

"Before? How many times has your planet interfered like this?"

"A few times. Once about fifteen years before I was born. The advanced life forms were destroying the lower life forms, so they were terminated."

Skye felt her mouth fall open. "You just killed them all?"

"I'm afraid so."

Skye ran a hand through her hair nervously. "Just like that. You killed an entire species."

"So others could live."

"Maybe the Beholders want us dead, just like those other people."

"No. We're supposed to remain impartial. That's how it's done. Those other 'people,' as you refer to them, were not like you and I, and they were an extremely violent race, destroying their planet, themselves, and all the other life forms there."

"We're violent and we're doing all that," Skye said, her voice barely a whisper.

They spent another hour talking. Starion told her stories about places he'd traveled, praising the beauty of Vanger. Skye got the impression Starion didn't like his home planet because he changed the subject whenever she asked questions about it.

His face beamed when he spoke of New Zealand — his favorite country on Earth. He even had a place in Dunedin, which he often visited, though he admitted Dr. Leven had never seen it.

Starion had an easygoing manner, and Skye felt herself drawn to him. Being around him was comfortable; there was nothing forced or pretentious. As much as she wanted to deny it, they had a connection. They even finished each other's sentences. And he made her laugh.

"Are you ready to go?" Starion finally asked.

Skye looked down at her plate and nodded hesitantly. For a few minutes, she'd forgotten the task at hand. She'd forgotten her fear. And then she remembered.

"My speech." Skye rose quickly from the table, grabbing her coat. "I forgot my papers. We have to go back to Colorado. I suck at public speaking. I can't wing it. I need my notes."

"Let's drop off our coats at Leven's and I'll tell him where we're headed." Starion threw some bills on the table and followed Skye out the door of the restaurant.

"What's wrong?" Oma asked when Starion and Skye appeared in her living room.

"Skye forgot her speech notes," Starion said.

Oma frowned. "Doesn't the TCS have a record of all this darting back and forth? Keep it up and your father is going to locate you."

"I'll get Tane to delete the logs," Starion said. "Skye, make sure you've got everything."

Startled, Henry rolled off the couch onto the floor. "What time is it?"

"Sorry, Henry," Skye said. "I know it's early here."

Janine staggered out of Skye's bedroom in an oversized T-shirt, smoothing down her highly textured hair, now freed of its braid. "That was fast. I guess the vote went well."

"No vote yet," Skye said. "I forgot my speech. I came back to get it."

Skye disappeared into her bedroom, returning with a handful of papers. "We can go now." She stuffed them into her backpack and slung it over her shoulder. "I guess we're going to do this conference thing now."

"Not right away," Starion replied. "I have a few things I need to do first. Stay here and get some sleep, and I'll be back in a couple of hours."

Janine made a sound of disgust. "You are the king of procrastination. First you say time is running out and then you —"

"I've got it covered," Starion snapped, "but I have something I need to do first."

Oma groaned. "Attention to detail, Starion. Start making a list. Your loosey-goosey attitude is what gets you in trouble."

"Loosey-goosey?" Starion repeated. "Whatever the hell that means."

Henry giggled.

"Where are you going?" Skye asked.

"I have to tag some reptiles outside Alice Springs, Australia, for transport to the conference." Starion glared at Oma. "Apparently I should have made a list."

"Can't I go with you?" Skye asked.

"No." Oma's voice was firm.

"Why?" Skye demanded.

"Because I can protect you better here."

Starion groaned. "I can protect her, Katrina. How many times do we have to discuss this?"

"Australia sounds awesome," Henry said.

"Henry's right," Skye exclaimed. "I'm coming. They have amazing animals there. Isn't Alice Springs in the Outback? I want to see kangaroos."

"Sorry, princess. The professor here" — Starion gave a wave of his hand — "doesn't think I'm capable of protecting you from scary kangaroos."

"Can I go then?" asked Janine.

"If I have to give a speech then I get to be the one to go," Skye declared. "Unless Starion can lift us both."

"Only kidding," Janine said. "I have no interest in going to the Outback. Do you know how many poisonous snakes there are?"

"Can I go then?" Henry asked. "I want to see a kookaburra."

"No," Skye and Starion answered in unison.

Turning to Oma, Skye said, "Nothing is going to happen. I'll see kangaroos and Starion will do this tag thing and then we'll go back to New Zealand and I'll give my speech."

"Poor Skye," Starion said, shaking his head with fake sadness. "Cheated out of kangaroos."

"Oma, *please*," Skye pleaded.

Oma threw her hands up in defeat. "Don't wander off. You *must* stay with Starion." She turned toward Starion. "And you. Do not let her out of your sight and call me when you return to Richard's."

Starion winked at Skye.

"Thank you, Oma." Skye threw her arms around her grandmother.

"We need to hurry," Starion said. "It's almost dusk in Australia. The Outback is dark at night."

"Take some water," Oma said, "and my credit card and the money in the black wallet, in case."

"I'm ready," Skye called, rushing out from the kitchen, her backpack slung over her shoulder. "Bye, everybody." She leaped onto Starion's back. "Let's go."

Skye hopped down and twirled in the warm dry air. She kicked reddish dirt with the toe of her boot. "We're in the Outback, aren't we? This is so cool."

"It is pretty cool," Starion agreed. "I can't transport in animal form, but I need to change back into a prairie dog. I'm taking a bit of a chance out here in the open, but we'll try to find a more secluded spot."

"Would it be bad if the animals saw you like this?"

"Not exactly," Starion explained. "Since they can't tell the difference between humans and Beholders, to them I am just another human. Most of the animals don't trust *any* humans, so I would not be successful in putting the conference together. It has taken me some time to gain their trust as a prairie dog. Imagine if they saw me transform. They would be frightened and confused. The conference needs a facilitator and that facilitator needs to be an animal they trust." He spread his arms out, "Me."

"Why did you pick a prairie dog?"

Starion looked down, then directly into Skye's eyes. "Because it's your favorite animal."

"I'm not sure what to say to that."

"You asked for the truth. That's the truth." He handed her a small cloth bag. "There are small tags in there. First, I ask the animal's permission to attach it to their bodies so they can be transported to the conference at the appropriate time. If they say no, then I find another animal from that ecosystem."

"Isn't it hard to do with prairie dog paws?"

Starion smiled mischievously. "I'm multitalented."

"Are you—"

Skye's words were interrupted by a deafening pounding as massive red kangaroos surrounded them. One kangaroo, balancing on its tail, lifted its back legs and knocked Starion to the ground.

Skye screamed, dropping the cloth bag. As the kangaroos moved closer, Skye turned her back to an unmoving Starion, attempting to protect him.

"Don't hurt my friend," she pleaded in a shaking voice. She never thought she'd be frightened of kangaroos, but at that moment they seemed scarier than any bear she might have encountered hiking in the Rocky Mountains. And there were over a dozen of them.

Coughing sounds and grunts rose up. Several of the animals thumped their huge feet.

Skye threw everything she had into her words—her passion, her love of animals, her sincerity. "He would never hurt you. He wants to help you."

"Is that so?" A giant reddish-brown male moved closer. He looked almost six feet tall and around two hundred pounds. "He looks like a hunter to me."

"You can understand me?"

Murmurs went around the group of kangaroos. "Why can we understand you?" a youngster asked.

"She's the one," the giant male answered.

More murmurs and sharp barks.

"Kill her," several shouted.

"*Please*," begged a terrified Skye. "I haven't done anything and neither has my friend. He's not a hunter."

"You're the one who wants to talk at the conference," the male declared. "You'll try to influence the vote."

"How do you know that?" gasped Skye.

"We all know."

"But he —" Skye's words stopped in her throat as she turned to point at Starion.

She stared, then blinked rapidly, thinking the growing darkness of the night was deceiving her. Starion was gone.

"Where is he?" she stammered.

"Disappeared," a smaller blue-gray kangaroo said. "Saved himself and left you to die."

The kangaroos moved closer. One shouted, "You humans kill us and make us into gloves and shoes and food for your pets. Why should we let you live?"

Skye closed her eyes. This was it. She was going to die, killed by animals she'd loved her whole life. Starion had obviously transported back to his ship, or wherever, to save himself, leaving her to die.

She braced herself and wondered if it would be over quickly.

11
. . . .

Blazingly bright spotlights illuminated the area, shining into the eyes of the kangaroos. The animals froze. Shielding her eyes, Skye saw men sitting and standing in four battered pickup trucks, holding rifles. She hadn't heard them approach.

"RUN!" she screamed to the group of kangaroos. "HUNTERS!"

The big male took off, with most of the group following. While Skye stood there helplessly, the men fired. Two kangaroos twitched and fell; red blood spewed onto the red soil.

"Weeee-aaaaah," whooped one man. "I got me one of them flyers."

A female kangaroo, recovering from the spotlight's stun, tore off at top speed. Skye watched in horror as a joey flew up and out of her pouch, landing with a thud and rolling on the ground.

Skye sprinted to the animal. "Please don't be dead," she murmured as she picked it up. It was heavier than she thought — around twenty pounds. The animal wasn't moving.

She shifted her backpack to the front of her chest, threw out the water she was carrying in it, and gently placed the baby inside, fastening the straps. She ran back toward the vehicles. One truck had already sped off in pursuit of the kangaroos.

Two of the beat-up trucks raced around the downed and injured animals. "Get it in the feet," a man hollered, firing erratically.

"I'm going after that boomer," a skinny man in a third truck shouted. "That roo was huge." The truck screeched out of sight.

"What are you doing?" Skye screamed as she approached the men, forgetting her own safety.

"Looky here, mates," a man hanging off the back of one of the trucks sneered. Skye could tell he was drunk. "We've got us a little sheila out for some action."

"We're going to round up the rest of them roos," the driver called out to her. "Don't get in our way."

Both trucks turned to follow the other two. As the driver pulled away, his drunken partner tumbled off the back, the rifle flying from his hand.

Skye raced for the rifle, picked it up, and aimed it at the hunter. She'd never held a gun in her entire life and had no clue how to fire one. But she could pretend she did. She pointed it at the man's head.

The man sat on the ground, his fear sobering him up. "There aren't any laws 'gainst killing roos."

"Of course there are," Skye insisted, sighting down the barrel of the rifle. "The Australian government wouldn't let you slaughter their national symbol."

The man shook his head desperately. "You're not from around here. The government don't care. Thinks they're pests."

Skye's mouth fell open as she lowered the rifle. Could it be true? Was it possible that a country's national symbol could be murdered like this? For sport? The man scrambled to his feet and ran off. Skye watched as one of the trucks came back and someone hauled the man up and onto the vehicle.

She watched the truck roar out of sight and realized she was alone. In the Outback.

In the growing darkness.

The joey in her backpack began to kick and grunt. "It's all right. I'll get you —"

She froze at a howl directly behind her. She turned slowly. Five dingoes were closing in on her. She could barely make out their ginger-colored coats in the advancing darkness.

"We know who you are," said the lead dingo in a menacing voice. "We have no quarrel with you. Give us the roo and we'll let you go."

The baby in Skye's backpack began to cry plaintively.

Skye aimed the rifle at the middle dingo. "I'll shoot you," she threatened, once again sighting down the barrel.

"But you'll only get one of us before we rip your throat out. Give us that roo and you walk away."

"No." Skye's voice was shaking. "I won't give him to you."

"Then die," one of the dingoes growled.

"There are two dead kangaroos back there." Skye motioned with a flick of her head. "Why can't you eat them?"

The dingoes continued forward.

Skye started to squeeze the trigger and then stopped. Everything she'd ever learned about dingoes and about animal behavior flew through her head. She thought about the gunshot wounds she'd seen on animals at the wildlife shelter in Colorado. She remembered the books she'd read, the wildlife shows she'd seen, and the images of hunters killing the animals she loved.

She threw the rifle to the side.

Skye Van Bloem, who'd never thought herself brave, moved her feet slightly apart and stood in the middle of the Outback, with darkness closing in, dust and sweat streaking her cheeks. "I can't kill you. But I won't let you have this baby."

The dingoes continued their slow advance. The leader growled, his eyes wild. His mouth opened slightly. Sharp teeth gleamed.

Skye doubted she could outrun them, but she would try. Pivoting to the side, she bent her knees slightly and moved her right foot forward, preparing to sprint.

"Last chance," the leader rumbled menacingly. "Drop it."

Skye shook her head. Everything was quiet. Too quiet. She tightened every muscle and wrapped her left arm over the backpack.

"If that don't mess it all up," the lead dingo said. "Kinda hard to kill her now, mates." He sat on his haunches.

"Why?" asked a youngster. "Why can't we kill her?"

"She's a brave one," said the lead dingo. "I gotta respect that. And I don't want any trouble from that miniature pretend-dog running the conference."

"She's the one," an older male blurted out. "Let's kill her. Weren't those foreigners going to give us a reward if we killed her?"

"We're not working for any men," growled the lead dingo. "Guess we better let her go." He motioned in the direction of the dead kangaroos. "I smell blood, mates. Supper's waiting."

As they trotted off, the leader turned back toward Skye. "You better find yourself some shelter, before something gits ya."

Skye exhaled with relief. "Where am I? Can you show me how to get to a town?"

The dingo gave a barking laugh. "Do I look like a bloody guide?"

The darkness was almost complete, and it surrounded Skye like a suffocating tarp. The baby in her backpack continued to cry, but now Skye recognized the noises as hunger sounds. She stumbled around the brush trying to get away from the smell of the dead kangaroos and the sounds of the dingoes ripping flesh.

She finally came to a mound of large rocks. If not for the stars, she wouldn't have been able to see enough to walk a single step. She sat down under a rocky outcrop and removed her backpack. It was getting cold, and she was thankful she was wearing jeans. She untied her hoodie from around her waist and pulled it on over her T-shirt.

She didn't have any water to offer the joey, and she knew it would be foolish to stumble around in the darkness looking for the water bottles she'd tossed out of her backpack. She tried not to think about her own thirst as she wrapped her arms around the animal. It was warm and furry and drove away some of the cold.

In the morning, she would have to start walking toward a town, but which direction? Starion had transported her directly here. She knew the town of Alice Springs was close, but how close? And what about the joey? She had another life besides her own to worry about now. Maybe she'd be able to see the tire tracks from the trucks and follow them to town.

Those hunters killed kangaroos for "fun." They clearly weren't interested in the meat. If she ever made it to the conference, what was she going to say? *You're right; humans are bad. Release the virus cause there's no hope for us.*

The cold was nothing compared to the cold that seeped into her heart. Why did people have to be so cruel?

Skye woke to something hard being poked at her. As her eyes flew open, she looked into the face of an old, dark-skinned man with a broad nose and several missing teeth. He nudged her with a long staff. His hair was dirty, frizzy, held back with a colorful piece of cloth. He was shirtless and wore torn baggy shorts that extended to his knees.

He pointed to the baby kangaroo in Skye's arms. "Kuja."

"Excuse me," Skye said, sitting up and clutching the baby. "Who are you?"

But she already knew. He was an Aborigine. What she didn't know was whether he wanted to eat the joey.

He touched the baby, who didn't seem at all frightened. "Kuja."

"Is that Aboriginal for kangaroo?" Skye asked.

The man smiled and again repeated the word. He reached for the baby, and before Skye could stop him, he had it nestled securely in his arms. "Kuja." He removed some sort of root from his pocket and chewed it up, then spit it into his hand. The baby immediately swallowed it.

"Thank you," Skye said, standing up. "He was hungry." She pointed to the baby. "Kuja." Then she pointed to herself. "Skye." She excelled at foreign languages, especially French, Spanish, and Dutch. How hard could his language be?

The man pointed to Skye. "Skee." Then he pointed to himself. "Coorain."

Skye smiled. "Coorain. It's nice to meet you."

"Coorain . . . gamarada."

Skye shook her head. "Gamarada. Not sure what that means."

Coorain extended his hand to indicate Skye. "Skee. Gamarada." He touched the kangaroo still nestled in his arms. "Kuja. Gamarada."

Ah. She knew what *gamarada* meant: friend. He pointed and motioned for Skye to follow. "Gunyah." He pointed across the scrubby land. "Gunyah."

"I hope that means town," Skye said as she began walking across the Outback.

Skye followed Coorain and watched him make several stops: freeing a snake trapped under a fallen rock, pulling a nasty-looking splinter from the wing of a pink-and-gray galah parrot, stopping her from accidentally trampling a family of blue-tongued skinks. Coorain was like a wandering wildlife rehabilitator; the animals seemed to show no fear of him.

It was amazing.

They finally arrived at a dwelling that officials in Colorado would have condemned. It was a shack that appeared to have no electricity or running water. As they approached, Skye saw a small outbuilding that was obviously the toilet. Coorain pointed to the outbuilding and nodded happily as though it were a ritzy privy at the Hilton.

Skye did her business and hurried out. Coorain was waiting with a metal bucket filled with muddy water. Skye dipped her hands in and then shook them out.

After Skye followed him inside the shack, Coorain pointed to a chair at a wobbly wood table. He set the joey down on a blanket and placed a tin plate in front of Skye. The plate contained a few dried vegetables, a piece of bread, and a honeycomb. Coorain grinned and indicated with a motion of his hands that she should eat it.

Skye stared down at the plate.

"You can eat it."

Skye jumped up from the chair and looked around. The voice had not come from Coorain. "Who is that?"

"Down here."

Skye looked down and saw a bearded dragon on the floor in front of her. The reptile was waving a front foot. "G'day."

Coorain pointed at the beardie and said, "Ngarrang."

"That means bearded dragon, right?" Skye asked, squatting down next to the reptile.

"Sure does."

"What does gunyah mean?"

"That's Aboriginal for a place of shelter," answered the beardie.

"Do you know how to say town or airport?" Skye asked him. "I need to ask Coorain if he'll take me there."

"He knows a few English words. He'll take you, but first you should have some manners. That's the last of his food."

"Why would he give me that?"

The beardie inclined his head at Skye. "He's a good man."

"I can see that. How long have you lived here with him? Are there any other people?"

"No other people. I've been with him for many seasons. We watch the sunset together and he does his best to look out for the land and the animals." He motioned over at Coorain, who was chewing up a tough-looking root for the joey. It was obvious the joey, like the other animals, trusted him. Skye had learned long ago that animals have a sense about people.

"Aborigines eat meat," the bearded dragon continued, "but he's a vegetarian. Sometimes he goes hungry."

Coorain patted her kindly on the shoulder. His bare arms seemed to be made of weathered leather. He smelled as though he hadn't showered in years, he was in serious need of dental care, and he had a face most would call ugly.

Skye met his kind eyes. Standing in front of her was a good, kind, decent human being.

They existed.

Skye had a glorious day with Coorain, the bearded dragon, and the joey. Whenever worries about Starion or the conference seeped into her thoughts, she worked hard to banish them. A day like this was never going to happen again. She had so much to learn.

She drank billy tea flavored with eucalyptus leaves that Coorain prepared in an old metal can with a wire handle over an open hearth. Skye watched, fascinated, as he lit the fire by striking two rocks together; she'd always wanted to do that. He handed her a miniature loaf of bread with reverence; he'd baked it in a small clay oven he'd built himself.

According to the bearded dragon, Coorain helped a local merchant — fluent in the Aboriginal language — in the town of Alice Springs. In exchange for his work, Coorain received food and a supply of bottled water during the dry season, which was beginning now. He hadn't made a trip to town for some time, and his supplies were almost gone, including his water.

Skye soon learned several Aboriginal words. Coorain taught her to search for roots and how to prepare them. He told her stories, and though she didn't understand many of the words, she delighted in the sound of his voice. The two went on a hike, the joey secure in Skye's backpack, the bearded dragon riding on Coorain's shoulder. Smiling down at the joey, Skye spoke gently to it. She was certain Coorain would care for it when she left in the morning. The beardie told Skye that Coorain planned a long walkabout. He could be gone for months.

Coorain pointed out many of the native animals and continued to rescue several of them who were in trouble. He had an amazing sense of direction. Skye didn't think it was possible for him to be lost, even in the vastness of the Outback. He'd found Starion's sack of tags, which Skye tied to a loop in her jeans, and the broken water bottles. Though

Starion may have deserted her, she didn't want him to get in trouble with his father. She would have tagged the animals if she could.

The thought of leaving caused a lump in Skye's throat, but she knew this couldn't last forever. Even the smelly outhouse and the lack of a shower seemed minor inconveniences in a magical day.

As dusk approached, Skye saw several kangaroos creeping close to Coorain's home, but whenever she tried to speak to them, they hopped off. The joey made no move to leave her and stayed snuggled inside the backpack for most of the day, only coming out to take some of the chewed food Coorain offered.

Sleeping under the stars on a bed of heavy blankets, Skye snuggled the joey while the bearded dragon rested near her head. She dreamed of Starion. He was injured and searching for her, but she didn't want to leave the Outback. She knew there were more good people like Coorain, and she had to find them.

She woke with a start. The sun was coming up over the sweeping expanse of the Outback. A kangaroo was staring down at her.

Quickly sitting up, she automatically cradled the joey to her as she looked for Coorain. He was squatting over a bubbling pot of billy tea. He smiled and indicated a group of kangaroos in the distance. "Kuja."

There was only one reason a single kangaroo would venture away from the others, so close to a fire. The joey squirmed and fussed, and Skye released it. The animal immediately leapt into its mother's pouch, then peered out at Skye, a contented look on its face.

"I'm glad you came back for him," Skye said. "He belongs with his mom." The mother kangaroo hopped off to join the others.

The large male who had threatened Skye moved closer. "We're thankful for what you have done. We will spread the word to the other animals that you are not to be harmed on your journey, but walk with care. There are strange men who seek to hurt you and not every animal will listen to our words."

"Thank you," Skye said, rising to her feet. "I'll tell people about the terrible slaughter of kangaroos. I'll try to help you."

The giant male gazed at her with doubt and then after a slight nod to Coorain, he hopped off with the rest of the group.

Skye looked down at her backpack — empty, as it should be.

After breakfast, Coorain attached a dozen weathered-metal jugs to a cord and slung it over his back, then he picked up a long walking stick. He handed Skye a smaller jug containing all that remained of the water. She put it in her backpack.

"I'm going to miss you," Skye said, bending down to the bearded dragon. "Take good care of Coorain."

The bearded dragon nodded his flat head and waved a clawed foot. "I wish you well at the conference."

Skye estimated the journey to Alice Springs was about six miles. After hiking through scrubby flat terrain for most of the morning, they arrived at a store outside the city limits. A red tin sign hanging over a dusty wooden building read "Esh's Outpost and Market."

A small bell jingled as they walked in.

"Ay Coorain," exclaimed a short man behind the counter. "Come ova' here." He switched to the Aboriginal language, taking Coorain over to several stacks of boxes and pointing to a piece of paper. Even speaking Aboriginal, Esh's voice was loud, full of energy, and somewhat nasal sounding.

"I'm Esh." The fortyish man extended a hand to Skye. "Welcome to my store. Coorain tells me he found you alone in the bush, schlepping around a joey. What were you doing out there all alone? Young girl like you? No parents? Oy."

Skye shook his hand. "It's a long story."

"Coorain says you need to get to the airport."

Skye nodded. "Is it far?"

"You're almost there. Walk another mile down that road and turn left at the end. You can't miss it." He reached up to a shelf, taking down a box. He pulled out a wrapped piece of jerky and handed it to Skye along with an ice-cold bottle of lemonade from a refrigerated case.

Skye stared down at the jerky and handed it back to Esh. "Thank you, but I'm a vegetarian."

Esh nodded toward Coorain. "So's he. He loves these things. Read the label."

Skye smiled as she looked at the wrapper. It was 100 percent vegan — soy and spices. She took a bite. "This is good. Thank you." She took a big gulp of the lemonade. Nothing had ever tasted better. "I hear a New York accent."

"I'm from Brooklyn — born and raised." Esh removed another package of jerky from the box. "Coorain," he called, throwing the jerky.

Walking over to Skye, Coorain placed the food in her hand and stepped back. Skye shook her head and tried to hand it back, but Coorain moved back and smiled.

"Why won't he take it?" Skye asked Esh.

Esh sighed. "Because he thinks you need it more."

"Can you give him another one?"

"Of course, but he'll give that to you too."

"He has to eat something."

"He will. After you've gone, he'll make some deliveries and do some cleaning and then he'll feel he's earned it. The man refuses to take a handout. I'll get his water jugs filled and have them delivered to his home tomorrow." Esh paused. "He says you're going to save the world."

"I . . . uh . . ."

"Oy. So much drama these days. Saving the world and such. You get to that airport and go wherever you're supposed to go. Do you need anything else?"

Skye took a piece of paper and a pen from the counter and began to make a list. She handed it to Esh. "When you deliver all his water containers, will you also deliver the things on this list?" She took out all the money Oma had insisted she carry in her backpack. She handed it to Esh, asking, "Will this be enough?"

Reading the list, Esh nodded. "Sure is. And if there's any extra left I'll put it in his account and bring more supplies next time." He motioned over at Coorain, who was busy sweeping the floor. "Better not tell him though. He'd see it as a handout."

Skye nodded. "Thank you and don't forget the flour and potatoes. And please include some of that jerky. It's really good." She paused. "He's going on a walkabout. Maybe you should send it when he gets back."

"I was thinking the same thing. You are a generous young —"

The tingling of the bell over the door cut off Esh's words. As two young men walked in, Esh froze. Skye turned around and felt hatred boiling inside her.

"Crikey," yelped one of the men. "That's the red-headed tart we saw the other night. Hanging out with an ignorant boong and a big-nosed Jew."

Esh's face reddened. Coorain stood completely still, a broom in one hand. Skye looked from one to the other.

Esh turned to the men. "You're not welcome here."

"That so. It's a free country, last I heard."

Skye glared at the two hunters. "You will *not* call Coorain a hateful name, and your anti-Semitism is disgusting. Nobody talks to my friends that way. And you're going to pay for killing those kangaroos."

"Ooooh." The men laughed.

Something dangerous flickered in Skye's eyes. She moved into a fighting stance, one she'd learned from a body-combat exercise class: feet apart, hands in fists to protect her face, knees bent. The two men in front of her were half-drunk, out-of-shape losers. Taking them down wouldn't even break a nail. "Esh told you two losers to get out of his store. I know people and I will call them. If you ever bother Esh or Coorain, you'll go down and never get back up."

There was a moment of silence before one of the men grabbed the other and steered him toward the door, slamming it behind them amid a string of curses.

Esh threw his hands up in the air. "Young lady, you have chutzpah."

Saying good-bye to Coorain was difficult. Skye was quite sure she'd never see him again, and a great sadness seeped through her.

Spreading his arms wide, Coorain said farewell in his native tongue. Esh translated. Reaching up to indicate the sky, Coorain said, "Skye, our protector, believe in yourself, for only then can you believe in others. Go in bravery and remember what is most important." He spread his hands down toward the ground. "I shall sing to the animals and the plants of your quest, and they shall watch over you."

Had the bearded dragon told Coorain about her mission? Esh didn't seem concerned with Coorain's words; he couldn't have known about the conference. Maybe Coorain didn't know either. Maybe his words were an Aboriginal farewell and nothing more. She wanted to go with Coorain on his walkabout. There was something undefinable about the Outback—primitive, natural, so alive in its quietness. It was real in a world full of plastic and consumerism and fakeness. She'd heard people say the Outback was lonely and dead, but here she didn't feel alone, and there was life everywhere. She felt as though she was part of something special—this world of wonder and diversity. It was what she loved about the vast expanse of the Rocky Mountains back home in Colorado. It was that sense of belonging to nature, of being part of it instead of separate from it, that she craved. She'd often told Janine and Henry that she could never leave the splendor and quiet of her beloved Rockies.

She could live here.

But without those horrid men who slaughtered kangaroos. Skye had added the marsupials to the growing list of animals she had vowed to protect. The slaughter was going to stop.

12

Skye kicked at the red dirt on the side of the road as she walked slowly to the airport. Arriving, her first stop was a pay phone — thankfully, they still existed. She placed a collect call to Oma because she'd lost her cell; maybe it was at Professor Leven's.

"My dear Skye. I've been worried sick. Richard called when you and Starion didn't return. Where are you?" Oma exclaimed — worry, hurt, and fear all weaving through her words.

"I'm at the Alice Springs airport, and I don't know where Starion is," Skye said. She told Oma everything that had happened, concluding with her accusation that Starion had abandoned her.

"Skye, he would never leave you voluntarily. Something has happened."

"Is it his father?"

"I don't know, but stay there," Oma insisted. "I have no idea what's happened to Starion, but this adventure is over. Do you hear me? Over. You're coming home. I'll send Tane for you with instructions to bring you home immediately."

"What does Tane look like?"

"You'll know him when you see him, I promise, and he'll identify himself. Do you remember what those men looked like, the ones Starion stopped?" There was fear in Oma's voice.

"Yes."

"If you see them, run."

Skye hung up the phone and considered her next move. If she was the only hope for saving the world, she couldn't go home. But how could she find the conference site without Starion? And where was he? Maybe his friend Tane would know. For now, her best hope was the professor.

She picked up the phone receiver. It took almost ten minutes, several irritated operators, and the university switchboard to find him. "Dr. Leven?"

"Skye, where are you?"

She explained and then asked, "Where's Starion?"

He didn't know.

"Do you know where the conference is being held?" Skye asked.

"It is somewhere off the Milford Track, a couple hours from Queenstown. But Skye, you cannot find it on your own. It's winter in New Zealand and the Milford Track isn't even hiked at this time of year. It's too dangerous. Your grandmother wants you home, so that's where you need to go."

Skye hung up the phone and leaned against the wall. She checked the departure board for flights to New Zealand. There was one leaving for Dunedin in two hours. She could get a connection from there to Queenstown and be at Leven's apartment by late evening. As she moved toward a ticket counter, Oma's Visa card in her hand, a small sparrow flew over and perched on a railing near her. "Men are after you. By the door."

Skye wheeled around. The two men she'd seen with the squirrel were scanning the terminal. She quickly ducked behind a counter and sat on the floor. "I'm so screwed," she mumbled.

The sparrow sat on her leg. "Stay here. We'll make a distraction." The bird flew off.

Skye peered around the counter at a gathering crowd. Several kangaroos had entered the small terminal and surrounded the two men.

The sparrow flew back to Skye. "Run!"

Skye was confused and tired, but she ran. She was sure they were the same men, the ones Oma and Starion had said were Vangers — a bald guy with a crooked nose and the other with russet streaks in his brown hair. Why were they following her? How many animals were working for them? How could they have found her, way out here? If they could find her, why hadn't Starion found her? Unless . . .

What would his father do to him? She tried to disperse the fear that began to ripple through her, rationalizing that Starion could take care of himself. Anyway, what could she do? She didn't even know where to start looking for him.

Racing down the dusty road, she spotted two things almost simultaneously: a large public bus and the rotting wooden bus stop it was pulling into. She put on a burst of speed.

The doors were closing as she stuck one arm inside. Panting, she climbed aboard and handed the driver Oma's Visa card. The middle-aged woman frowned and pointed to a sign that read "Cash only."

"I'm sorry; I don't have any money with me, but this card is valid. I promise," Skye said.

The driver shook her head and pointed to the doors. "Out you go. No cash, no ride."

"Please," Skye begged, looking outside. "You don't understand. Two men are following me. I have to get on this bus."

The driver rested one arm on the wheel of the bus and wiggled her finger at the doors. "You're breaking my bloody heart. Now git."

Before Skye could answer, a woman about her age shoved money at the driver and hauled Skye to the back of the bus. The doors closed and the bus took off.

Skye stared out the back window of the bus but didn't see anyone following. She turned to the woman in the seat next to her and extended her hand. "Thank you so much for that. My name is Skye."

The woman backed up slightly in her seat and put her hands flat beside her. She was wearing a University of Sydney T-shirt and cut-off jeans shorts. She wore a wide brown belt studded with stones. Two long pouches, decorated with colorful beads, dangled from each side of the belt. "You'll excuse me if I don't." She touched her nose and wrinkled her face before removing a Harry Potter–branded cosmetics bag from her backpack and tossing it at Skye. "Use whatever you need."

"Oh . . . I'm so embarrassed," Skye stammered. "I know I must smell really bad. I've been . . . uh . . . hiking." She opened the bag to find numerous tubes of mascara and eye liner. She used several scented disposable wipes on her hands and face. She was in desperate need of a shower and several bars of soap.

She handed the case back. "Harry Potter is the best."

"Too bloody right," the woman agreed. She eyed Skye. "Better." She extended her hand. "I'm Rob."

"Rob?"

The woman made a dismissive gesture with her hand. "It's better than my full name."

"Which is?"

"Roberta. Have you ever heard such a lame name? What were my parents thinking?"

Skye took a good look at her. Rob was about the same height, about the same age, wearing artfully applied makeup. She was curvy with platinum blond hair and blue eyes that matched — exactly the look most women would envy. Exactly the look Skye wished she had.

"And of course I live in this bloody lame town with my lame parents and . . ."

Skye sighed. It was going to be a long bus ride. She finally interrupted Rob. "Where are we going?"

Rob gave her a condescending look. "To the central bus stop. Where else? Then you transfer to another bus. Me? I'm going to Darwin."

"Where's that?" Skye asked.

"Northern Territory. Top End. My parents think they're sending me there to work in their other hotel, but really, there's this bloke I like. He's in a boating event, so I'm going to see him." Rob rambled on about the boy's looks until Skye interrupted her again.

"Do you think they take credit cards at the main bus terminal?"

Rob shrugged. "Where're you going?"

"New Zealand."

There was a bark of laughter from the seat across the aisle. "American girl thinks she can take a bus to see the Kiwis." The woman's loud voice sailed through the bus and soon several people were laughing.

Skye slumped down in her seat.

"Isn't there a boat or a ferry to New Zealand?" Skye asked Rob. "If I could get to the coast I could book a ticket."

"No passenger ferries," a voice shouted. Now the whole bus was eavesdropping.

"Why don't you swim?" another called. "It'd be a piece of piss."

Laughter rocked the bus as Skye's face turned scarlet.

"She ought to hitch a ride with the Maoris," someone called.

Rob explained that a group of Maori people had flown over to have a festival with some of the Aborigines and would be returning to New Zealand in old-fashioned wooden boats.

"The guy I like is one of the Aborigines in the program with the Maori. We'll ask him if you could get a ride." She leaned closer to Skye. "My parents'd be bloody mad if they found out. I'm already in trouble." Rob clapped her hands excitedly. "You should come to Darwin with me, Skye. *Pleeeeeasssse.*"

It was the best idea Skye could think of. Those men would be watching airports, but she was betting they would never think to look at a port. She had to get to New Zealand. There was only about a week left until the conference deadline.

"I'll go," Skye said.

"Ace," exclaimed Rob. "When we get off at the station, follow me and we'll get tickets. And some food. I haven't had brekkie."

Skye glanced out the window. Was she putting Rob's life in danger by traveling with her?

You learn a lot about a person when you sit next to them on a bus for so long. Especially when it's a dark night and a long, dreary, hot, dusty day. On rare occasions, you're pleasantly surprised. This was one of those instances.

Rob turned out to be funny, kind, and virtually a math genius. Skye couldn't remember quite how the topic of math had come up — perhaps when she was talking about how much she missed Janine and Henry. She'd related how Janine had helped her pass math. Rob had asked Skye what problems had confused her.

Pulling out a pad of paper from her backpack, Rob explained several concepts with ease. Skye was speechless. Then Rob went on to discuss integrals and differentials.

"Calculus I get," Rob said, "Blokes I don't get. They say they like me, then . . ." Her voice trailed off. "Blokes don't want to date a math geek."

Skye tried to convince her otherwise, to no avail. She couldn't help but think how disgusted Janine would be about Rob dumbing herself down.

The problem with the trip wasn't Rob. Every time the bus stopped for bathroom breaks and they disembarked to stretch their legs, Skye noticed animals watching her, but when she spoke, they either said nothing or moved away. Were they spying for those Vanger men? Or did they hate her because she was going to speak at the conference? Skye, who had always been comfortable around animals, was nervous.

A sense of unease built in her. A group of button quail followed her to the restroom at one stop, rock wallabies watched her from behind acacia trees at another, and skinks slithered across the gray-brown cracked soil at her feet when she and Rob stopped to change buses.

It wasn't Skye's imagination; other passengers remarked about the animals following her. Even a few nonnative animals stopped their grazing in the tall grasses and open woodland: water buffalo, donkeys, camels. All of them watched her.

None of them spoke.

Rob insisted on buying food for them since several of the remote stopping places didn't take credit cards. She ate so many packages of candy, mostly Hot Tamales, that Skye lost count.

"How long have you been a vejjo?" Rob asked her.

"A what?"

"A vegetarian."

"All my life," Skye said. "My parents were vegetarians too."

"Maybe I'll give it a burl someday," Rob remarked.

They talked and told stories. Skye tried not to think about the animals watching her. She was more afraid of them hating her than she was of the two men following her.

Rob told Skye about her life in Alice Springs; her parents, who owned the biggest hotel in town and another in Darwin; and her semester-long suspension from the University of Sydney. Rob had caught her boyfriend sleeping with her roommate and retaliated. She wouldn't tell Skye exactly what she'd done, but it involved several cans of spray paint.

"The bloke I like now is better than that wuss in Sydney," Rob insisted. "How about you? Seeing anyone?"

Skye didn't answer immediately. "I thought maybe there was something with this one guy, but he ran off and left me." She hesitated. "I promised to do something so I need to do it, but then I don't want to see him again."

"Yes you do."

"No, I don't."

Rob rolled her eyes.

By the time the bus stopped for a late dinner, Rob felt sick from all the candy and insisted Skye go into the roadside café without her. Handing her a wad of bills, Rob said, "Get me something for later."

"It won't be candy," Skye replied.

"Yeah. I've had enough lollies; maybe get me a sanger. Get yourself something too. And don't yabber about the money. I've lots."

"I'm going to pay you back, Rob. I promise." Why didn't any of these places take credit cards?

Rob waved a hand irritably. "Leave off, will ya. It's a prezzy. Repay the favor to someone else."

It was getting dark as Skye climbed off the bus. She wasn't looking forward to sleeping on the bouncy, uncomfortable bus. Again. Hadn't they heard of coaches in this country? This bus was nothing more than a converted school bus.

Another bus had pulled up ahead of them, and a large crowd of people began crowding toward the café.

Skye frowned. She wasn't that hungry, and Rob certainly wasn't. With a shrug, she turned back to the bus rather than stand in a long line. There probably wasn't anything vegetarian anyway. Then she saw a skinny dark-haired girl and her dog getting off the other bus. It was the dog she noticed first — a scruffy little black-and-tan terrier. He limped across the dusty ground, following the girl closely. They disappeared around the back of the café.

Skye followed.

Peering around the corner, she saw the girl glance around before digging into the garbage bin. The dog, around fifteen pounds or so, whimpered near her feet.

"Hi," Skye said.

The girl wheeled around and stared at Skye with frightened eyes. She had bruises on her cheeks and neck. A dirty cloth was tied around her left forearm, and Skye could see dried blood. The girl looked about seven or eight.

"Go away," the girl whispered.

Skye moved closer and extended her hand. "My name's Skye. What's yours?"

The girl shook her head. "Can't tell."

The dog whimpered and moved in front of the girl.

"Are you hurt?" Skye asked, bending down in front of the dog. "I think you have something in your paw. If you let me look, I'll try to help."

The dog sat and lifted the injured paw. The girl gave Skye an incredulous stare. "He's never done that before. He don't like strangers. Me neither."

Skye inspected the dog's paw. "I don't like strangers much either, but you're a stranger and already I can tell that I like you." Holding up a burr that had become embedded between the dog's toes, she said, "That must have hurt."

The dog reached up and licked her face.

"Bandit likes you," the girl said. "He doesn't like anyone but me." She started to cry. "He was going to shoot Bandit because I was bad, so I had to run away. Please don't tell him where I—"

"Hey, you two. What're you doing back here?" A middle-aged man with sweat marks under his arms and a dirty apron stood glaring at them.

Skye quickly put her arm around the girl. "My friend was upset because her dog was hurt. That's all."

"Either get inside and order or go back to your bloody bus."

Skye nodded and moved the girl toward the front of the store. "Let's get some sandwiches."

The girl stopped abruptly and tried to squirm away from Skye. "Can't. No money."

"When was the last time you ate?"

The girl hung her head.

Skye bent down and whispered to the dog. "Stay by that tree near the bus. I promise I'll take care of her."

The dog trotted obediently to the tree and sat down. "Bandit," the girl cried out, "don't leave me."

Taking the girl's hand, Skye said, "Bandit won't leave you. He's going to wait right by the tree for you."

Skye bought sandwiches, apple juice, and water. She took napkins and a disposable bowl from the condiment cart as she headed out the door.

Bandit was waiting under the tree for them. Skye handed the girl a peanut butter sandwich and a bottle of juice, and she poured water in the bowl for Bandit. The girl immediately fed her sandwich to the dog.

Removing two peanut butter sandwiches, two bottles of water, and two bottles of juice from the bag, she handed the rest to the girl. "For later."

The girl took out a Vegemite sandwich and quickly devoured it. She smiled at Skye. "Thanks. Bandit doesn't like Vegemite." She fed Bandit another peanut butter sandwich.

"Skye," called Rob, walking over and holding her stomach, her backpack hanging from one shoulder. "Stop mucking about. The bus is leaving." She looked from the girl to Skye and back at the girl. "Who're you running from?"

"Nobody."

"Uh-huh," Rob said. "Your bus is going south. Where're you headed?"

"Alice Springs."

"Family?"

The girl hesitated, then nodded.

Rob pulled a notebook out of her backpack and wrote furiously. She ripped the paper out and handed it to the girl. "See that name and address? That's my brother. He's a good bloke. Give him this note and he'll help you. His place is near the Reptile Centre, one block north on the left. There's a huge tree in the front and a green mailbox shaped like a croc."

"But Bandit . . ." she pointed down at her dog.

"No worries. He loves dogs." Rob leaned closer to the girl. "My brother will help you. I promise he won't send you back." She motioned to Skye. "Hurry up."

"Do what my friend said. OK?" Skye called back as she walked toward the bus.

Bandit scurried after Skye and sat in front of her. Leaning down, Skye said to the dog, "Take care of her and make sure she goes to see Rob's brother." She whispered in the dog's ear.

Looking through the window as the bus pulled away, Skye watched the girl and her little dog get back on the bus headed to Alice Springs.

"She'll be OK," Rob finally said.

"Someone beat her."

"I know, but my brother will help her." Rob paused. "If she goes."

"She will."

"You think?"

Skye nodded. She'd repeated Rob's directions to Bandit. He would take the girl there. "She's running from something. It's so sad."

"Sure, it's bloody sad, but you can't save everyone."

13

CLUNK. BANG.

"What was that?" Skye exclaimed.

Rob groaned loudly. "If this bloody bus breaks down, I'm going to throw a wobbly. I wanted to fly, but my parents made me take a bus." She raised her voice to an annoying pitch and scrunched up her face. "You can take the bus, Roberta, and think about what you've done." She shook her head angrily. "A day and a half on the bus and now it'll be more if it breaks down. Bloody hell."

The bus rolled to a stop in the middle of the deserted highway.

Rob wasn't the only one shouting. Angry passengers, about forty or so, began yelling. The driver stood at the front of the bus. "Leave it off all of ya," she shouted. "I called for another bus. Be here in the morning. Nothing I can bloody do about it."

She opened the doors to the bus and pointed. "Git off and sleep in the bush if ya don't like it in here."

Rob grabbed her backpack, blanket, and duffel and motioned for Skye to follow her. "Any of you blokes want to help me build a fire, follow us." As she marched off the bus with Skye following, she said to the driver in a too-sweet tone, "Maybe you ought to see what's wrong with the bus. Seeing as you're the bloody driver."

About half of the passengers joined Skye and Rob around the bonfire—the only source of light and heat in the chilly darkness of the Outback. The rest were still on the bus or had broken off into smaller groups.

Rob pointed at two seedy-looking men standing well away from the group, their heads close together as they smoked. "Look at those two dipsticks. They get near you or me and I'm taking 'em out." She patted her belt.

"I feel safe now." Skye grinned at Rob.

"Too right. I don't let pissed-up whackers hurt my friend."

My friend, Skye thought. She felt a smile float across her face. With the exception of Janine and Henry, Skye didn't have friends. Until now.

There was one child in the group of passengers—a six-year-old clinging to his mother and whining. The mom was promising him all sorts of presents and candy when they got to Darwin, but it only increased the whining.

"Holy dooley," Rob exclaimed. "I'm *never* having kids."

Skye leaned toward the boy and said, "I'll tell you a story if you stop fussing."

"What kind of story?" the boy demanded.

"Listen," Rob replied. "She's a greenie and I've never met anyone who knows more about animals than her."

"They follow her too," said another passenger.

Skye looked at the boy. "Have you ever heard of an animal called a prairie dog?"

The boy shook his head.

"I'll tell you about one," Skye began. "His name is . . . Sta . . . Stan."

Skye had never thought she was much of a storyteller, but even the adults were listening—leaning forward, nodding or frowning at various parts of her tale about a snarky little prairie dog who saves his colony from destruction through cunning and intelligence. Managing to sneak in information about habitat destruction, Skye weaved a story that ended happily.

If only real life were like that.

Several passengers stood up when she finished, clapping and cheering.

The mother of the whining boy thanked Skye, saying, "You're a born teacher." She took the now-smiling boy back to the bus to sleep.

"How about another?" a passenger called to Skye.

Two older teenage boys and a girl sneered and poked at each other, their laughter clearly directed at Skye.

Skye tried not to notice them as she ran a hand through her red hair. "Why do you allow your national symbol to be slaughtered?"

There were confused looks around the fire until Rob said, "The roos. Skye saw some boofheads shooting them."

Many people shrugged. The three teenagers laughed. No one seemed surprised. The comments ranged from hunting being legal to how tasty roo steaks were to the justification that animals had no feelings.

"You don't really believe that," Skye exclaimed. "How can you say those things?" She told them in graphic detail what had happened. One of the two teen boys — a blond with a pierced lip — seemed to be listening as Skye spoke. "Do you want tourists to boycott Australia? Is this something you want your country to be famous for? Red kangaroos exist nowhere else on the planet. Your country is special in so many ways, but the slaughter of these animals for sport is wrong."

"There's nothing we can do," several people protested.

"There's *always* something you can do," Skye replied angrily. "You can start petitions and boycott kangaroo products. You can lobby your elected officials and raise public awareness. You can start a campaign to shame hunters into stopping. Write letters to your local paper and publish essays online. Use social media to get international attention. Contact the tourism board for help."

The teenage girl burped loudly and then laughed. One of the boys joined in the laughter.

"Go back to the bloody bus if you're going to be daggy," barked Rob. "My mate's talking."

The blond-headed teen muttered an apology, but his two friends pulled him to his feet, taunting him, and dragged him toward the bus. A couple others followed behind them.

"Red kangaroos are just trying to survive — like all of us," Skye continued. "The Outback is their home and it's a harsh place. Why can't people allow them to live in peace and care for their joeys?"

When her words were met by silence, she continued. "They're such amazing animals. They could hop a marathon in a little over an hour. They have an elaborate social structure, so you know they're fairly intelligent. We don't have red kangaroos where I live in Colorado. You're the only ones who have them and it's your duty to protect them. Just like it's my duty to protect prairie dogs. We can't give up."

Before she knew it, the four remaining people were planning fundraisers and petition signings.

Skye hoped it wasn't just talk as she yawned, finally resting her head on her backpack. Rob flopped down on the blanket beside her.

"I only convinced four people," Skye whispered sadly to Rob.

"Four's better than none," Rob replied. She motioned toward the blond boy huddled by the side of the bus. "Maybe it's five. He needs to ditch the loser friends."

Skye shut her tired eyes. Had she done it? Made a small difference?

"Don't. Move." Rob's voice was laced with fear and warning.

Skye blinked into the bright morning sun; the bonfire to her left was nothing but embers.

"Don't move," Rob repeated.

Ignoring Rob, Skye rolled onto her stomach, head propped in her hands. She saw three things: Rob, standing with her hands on her belt; one of those seedy men to Skye's right, motionless, with Oma's Visa card held in one hand; and . . .

"Hey, sweetie," Skye said to the olive-colored snake coiled on the right side of her backpack. In her sleepy state, she forgot her wariness of the animals who'd been watching her.

The snake's scales of varying shades of brown and gray glittered in the sun as it rose up in front of the man holding the credit card.

"Drop it, now," Skye ordered the man.

He dropped the credit card, but stood paralyzed with fear as the snake rose higher.

"Thanks," Skye said to the snake.

The snake lowered itself to the ground. The man ran to the bus.

Sweat ran down Rob's brow as she struggled to speak. "Sweetie?" she croaked.

The snake rose up in front of Skye and swayed slightly from side to side.

"Good day to you too," Skye said to the snake.

The snake slithered off and Rob relaxed her hands, bringing one to her forehead. "Bloody hell. What was that about? Are you Harry Potter, talking to snakes?"

Skye shrugged and replaced Oma's credit card in her backpack. "I'm glad he was there or that jerk would have stolen my grandmother's credit card."

"Who gives a bloody hell about the credit card? Do you know what that was?"

"I'm not great at reptile identification. I know rattlesnakes, and corn snakes, and bull—"

"Skye," Rob shouted, "that was an inland taipan. The most venomous snake in the world. If you get tagged by it, you're dead in less than an hour!"

Skye stood up and slung her backpack over her shoulder. "I guess it's a good thing he didn't bite me." She tried to suppress a smile. She had at least one friend in the Outback. The snake was protecting her.

"Someone go kill it." It was the thief's friend.

Skye stomped over to him. "No, you won't. Snakes aren't monsters out to kill you. I know people who are more dangerous." She pointed at his friend, who was cowering by the side of the bus. "If you or your loser friend try to rip anybody else off, you'll regret it." She turned to the group of passengers and loudly said, "His friend tried to steal my grandmother's credit card. Watch your belongings."

There were angry murmurs as people moved away from the thief. Several women clutched their handbags tightly.

A cloud of dust rose up in the distance, followed by a rumbling sound. A brand-new bus drove into view and stopped in front of the tired and dusty passengers.

Skye sighed with relief. It was a coach, an honest-to-goodness coach, not some converted old school bus. It even had a flush toilet and sink — advertised in bold letters on the side of the bus.

Rob and Skye piled into the bus and sat in oversized, comfortable, soft seats.

"You're bloody ace, Skye," Rob exclaimed. "Did you know that?"

"So are you," Skye replied, giving Rob a high-five.

At the central bus station in Darwin, the two friends fell out of the bus, their arms around each other. "Come to the hotel with me, Skye," Rob pleaded.

"I can't stay," Skye reluctantly insisted. "I need to find a way to New Zealand. I've been gone too long already." The vote was in six days. There was still time, but if something else happened . . .

Rob gave her an appraising look. "You need a shower. *Deffo*."

Skye looked down at her filthy clothes. Rob was right. What was an extra hour or two?

The staff at the hotel all recognized Rob and rushed to get her anything she needed. Instead of acting like a spoiled brat, Rob was kind to everyone and addressed people by their first names. She insisted on carrying her own bags. When she requested food sent up to the suite, she said please and thank you and announced loudly, "My friend is a vejjo, so no meat."

Skye was thrilled with the lavish room, the huge fluffy towels, and the incredible view overlooking the water. Coming out of the shower, she saw a new outfit laid out for her: khaki capris, a peacock-blue T-shirt, even underwear.

"Rob, I can't accept this," gushed Skye.

"It's a prezzy. Besides, your clothes ought to be burned."

"You've been great to me."

"You're my friend now. When I first saw you, I thought you could use a mate. Repay the favor to someone else someday; then the world won't be so bloody awful. True, right?"

"You're right," Skye agreed, dressing in the fresh new clothes.

"You better call or write." Rob shoved a piece of paper into Skye's hand. "That's the name of my parents' hotel, with the website address. And that's my personal email and cell number."

They ate a late lunch together after Rob had showered and changed into another pair of too-short jeans shorts, a bright-purple, low-cut tank, and that same rather odd belt with the dangling pouches. Her blond hair was pulled to the side with a matching purple ribbon. The look was intended to appear thrown together, but Skye knew it was anything but. Rob pulled it off well, though Skye thought the belt was odd.

Rob's cell phone rang while they were eating. "What's up?"

There was a long pause as Rob listened intently. "Really?"

Another long pause.

"You're ace. Thanks, brah."

Hanging up, she said, "That runaway and her dog are with my brother. He's taking care of them."

"That makes my day," said a beaming Skye.

Rob frowned. "My brother said the dog was pawing at his door with my note in his mouth. I guess the girl was trying to get it to leave."

Skye's smile increased.

Rob leaned across the table. "Can you talk to animals?"

"Of course not."

Rob stared intently at Skye for a moment before insisting she come with her to find the guy she liked. "He'll know if you can get on a ferry or something." Rob refused to take no for an answer.

Then they would have to part ways, Skye told herself. She could not put her new friend in danger. Who knew what scary weapons those Vanger men had? If they were willing to hurt Janine and Henry, they would hurt Rob. If they'd come when the bus had broken down, there would have been nowhere to run.

Skye slung her worn, dirty backpack over her shoulder and smoothed down the clothes Rob had given her. Perhaps Rob would visit her in Colorado when all this was over.

Provided those men didn't find them.

The immense port smelled of oil and fish. It took a while to find Rob's crush. Rob seemed to know next to nothing about him; she'd only spoken to him once outside class — at a party.

"Maka," Rob called excitedly, waving. "I came to see you off."

As Skye expected, Maka seemed surprised to see Rob. At least he remembered her name. "Uh . . . Rob. What are you doing here?"

After some awkward conversation, Maka left for a meeting with his teammates. He didn't think Skye could get a ride on a freighter, and she couldn't go with the Maori back to New Zealand. He'd only been kind to her, she suspected, because she'd mentioned Coorain. Maka was a distant relative.

"Isn't he ace?" Rob said to Skye after Maka left.

Skye nodded, pretending to be enthusiastic. Maka could have been from Colorado — rather average looking, much lighter skinned than Coorain, and not nearly as interesting.

"Look." Rob pointed to a crocodile floating in Darwin Harbor. "He's a big saltie."

Skye stared at the reptile. Normally she'd have rushed closer for a better look, but the past two days had made her wary. A flock of birds was one thing, an enormous croc was quite another. He was watching her, swimming in slow circles.

Rob shook her head. "You have a freaky effect on animals."

Skye hugged Rob, and they said their tearful good-byes. It was time to move on and find that ride to New Zealand. Skye was tempted to go to the airport. If she couldn't get a boat ride, she would have no choice. She considered calling Oma, but she knew the woman would demand she come home.

After finding the information center for the port, Skye read a sign in the window indicating the attendant had left for a half-hour break. On a bench overlooking the water, she waited. The area seemed deserted; maybe it was a holiday or something.

"Oh, my gosh, you're beautiful," she gushed without thinking as a rainbow lorikeet, about the same size as an American robin, settled on the bench next to her. The parrot was striking: bright-blue head, green wings, distinctive red markings on the neck and chest, and yellow under the wings. His long tail was slightly pointed at the end, the vibrant colors catching the light.

"I suppose you aren't going to talk to me either," she mumbled.

"Skye," the bird sputtered, flapping its wings in excitement. "I'm watching over you."

"Why?" Skye stammered. "Who sent you?"

"Coorain."

"Did he eat a leaf? Is that how he could talk to you?" Skye asked.

"He sings," the lorikeet replied. "Coorain has always sung. The animals who hear him tell others of his song." The bird cocked its head. "We've all been watching over you on your trip. So you'd be safe. Haven't you seen us?"

Skye raised shaking hands to her mouth. "Everyone? All those animals? You want me to be OK? You don't hate me?"

"Coorain sings to us that you're good. He tells us to watch over you. We know you'll speak for the humans, but Coorain is a good human."

Tears formed in Skye's eyes. The animals . . . her friends . . . gamarada.

"Is Coorain on his walkabout? Is he OK?"

The lorikeet began to preen.

Skye coughed. "Is he OK?"

The lorikeet continued preening.

"Mr. Lorikeet?"

The lorikeet flew up to Skye's shoulder. "I'm not a bloke."

"Oh, sorry."

The parrot hopped down onto Skye's lap. "No worries. I'm watching for the bad men."

The bird began to preen in earnest.

After several more minutes of preening, the bird tucked her small head under one wing and shut her eyes.

Skye smiled. The lorikeet was a poor lookout.

Skye was afraid to move with the sleeping lorikeet in her lap, so she let her mind wander while she waited for the information booth to open. She thought of Starion. She felt herself sigh and almost immediately became angry with herself. She was not falling for him.

Not, not, *not*. For so many reasons. She didn't need an across-galaxies relationship with an alien who deserted her at the first sign of trouble. She had plans, like college and stuff. So what if he had an adorable smile? Arrgh. She wanted to scream at herself. *Stop thinking about him.*

She thought about Janine and Henry instead. She couldn't wait to tell them about Rob. The thought of her and Janine together made her smile.

Rob—Skye could see her now. *Wait!* Skye could actually see Rob now. She was standing behind the information booth, peering out with an odd expression on her face.

Standing up, Skye wakened the startled lorikeet who began flapping and screeching, "Bad men! Bad men!"

14
....

Rob stepped out from behind the booth. The two Vanger men who'd been following Skye each had a hold on Rob's arms. One pointed a weapon into her side.

"I think I found those two whackers who were following you." Rob's voice was strong.

The lorikeet flew off. Skye froze. Running was not an option — they had her friend.

"Come." The man with the russet-streaked hair spoke in heavily accented English. "Or friend die."

"Please," Skye said without hesitation. "I'll go with you, but let her go."

The bald man with the crooked nose replied, "On ground. Hands on head."

Skye obeyed. "Now let her go." She looked up to see the men release their hold on Rob, who did not run. Instead, she knelt down by Skye. "Oh, Skye," she wailed loudly. Then she hissed in Skye's ear, "We've got this. I'll take baldie. You've got the other."

Rob stood up and winked at the bald man with the crooked nose. Then she blew him a kiss. He drew back in surprise, and that's when

Rob began wailing punches on him, dislodging the gun from his hand. Skye quickly kicked the other man in the shins — hard. Taken by surprise, both men were soon on the ground.

"Run, Skye," Rob yelled. They took off, ducking behind a building and peering out. The big croc that had been watching earlier had the two men cornered.

The lorikeet reappeared and sat on Skye's shoulder. "Bad men," she scolded.

"Old saltie's gonna eat them," Rob exclaimed.

"Bad men," the lorikeet repeated.

Rob gasped as a massive man appeared out of nowhere and aimed a weapon at the two men. Taking a small device from his pocket, he spoke into it. All three disappeared.

"What the bloody hell was that?" exclaimed Rob.

The croc called over, "Are you hurt, Skye?"

"No," she called. "Thank you."

"Who are you talking to?" Rob asked as the croc made his way back to the harbor.

"Never mind," Skye stammered. "Where did you learn to fight like that?"

"I have three older brothers. I'm an Aussie. You have to learn to defend yourself. And what the bloody hell did I just see?"

Skye hugged her tightly. "I'm glad you're OK. I'm so sorry for getting you into this. You have to leave. What if they come back?"

Skye slumped to the ground and Rob sat beside her.

"Who are they?" Rob asked. "Is that some secret government tech?"

"I don't know. Those two who had you have been following me, but I've never seen that other guy."

"Bad men," the lorikeet repeated.

"And now you're attracting parrots," Rob said. "Something's going on here."

They heard Maka's voice. "Rob, are you OK? Where are you?"

Rob rose to her feet and waved. "Over here."

Running over to them, Maka exclaimed, "Someone saw you fighting. What's happened?" He frowned at the lorikeet sitting on Skye's shoulder.

Rob put an arm around Maka. "Skye and I were having some bloody fun with a couple of pissers."

"Rob saved me," Skye said.

"That so?" Maka replied.

"Too right," Rob declared with enthusiasm. "We don't muck about. Taught them a lesson, eh Skye?"

Skye nodded with conviction. The least she could do was help Rob look good in front of her crush.

Maka was clearly impressed. "Where'd those blokes get off to?"

"I have them," came a deep voice.

The lorikeet squawked loudly as the three spun around and stared at six and a half feet of muscle. The man who'd taken the two Vangers wore a one-piece flight suit, sleeves rolled up, in a vibrant lapis blue. The suit held assorted patches on the chest and sleeves, and he wore heavy ankle-high black boots. With jet-black hair cut close to his head, a prominent forehead, and a square jaw, he looked around thirty. Piercing dark eyes focused in on Skye. He pulled something from his pocket. Silver glittered in the sun.

"Run," Maka shouted. "He's got a gun."

They ran.

The man shouted, but Skye couldn't hear over the rush of the wind, the frantic thumping of her heart, the pounding of her boots on the pavement. She decided to take a chance and separate from Rob and Maka.

Without a word, Skye veered sharply away from them, running in the opposite direction. "Bye, Rob," she whispered, glancing over her shoulder to check that the man was following her and not her friends.

Skye was off, putting on a burst of speed and heading for a busy street away from the shore. The lorikeet flew in front of her with rapid wing beats. "Behind you, Skye. Run faster."

Ducking behind a building, Skye ran through an open door and up the stairs. Rounding a corner, she dove into a dusty room with broken windows. She peered out onto the street below, the lorikeet on her shoulder. The man was not in the street. She listened. There was no sound except for her frightened breaths.

The lorikeet shrieked.

As Skye wheeled around, the dark-headed hulk of a man grabbed her by the wrist.

"Let me go!"

The man grinned slowly, an amused look spreading across his face. "Calm down, Skye." He released her wrist. "Starion sent me. My name is Tane." He tried to suppress a chuckle. "Been having quite the adventure, have you?"

Skye's shoulders sagged with relief. "Oh . . . Tane . . . Oma told me about you."

"Professor Katrina; yes. She called me demanding I return you to your home. I spoke with Richard Leven, and of course Starion is concerned."

"Where's Starion? Is he all right? He abandoned me in the middle of the Outback. We came to Australia to put tags on this—"

"Skye," Tane interrupted. "Starion would never voluntarily leave you. His father demanded he be fitted with a device that automatically transports him to the closest ship if he is injured and loses consciousness. That is precisely what happened."

"Is he OK?"

"Yes." Tane looked skyward and shook his head. "He is furious with me for keeping him on my ship. He threatened the doctor unless he removed the medical monitor. If his father finds out . . ." He ran a hand through his short hair. "I had to disable his transport device so he could not leave. He was badly injured; he is lucky it was not worse."

"A red kangaroo kicked him."

"Is that an animal?"

Skye nodded.

"The roos like you now, Skye," the lorikeet exclaimed.

Extending his hand, Tane spoke to the bird. "Step up, little friend." When the parrot was resting happily on Tane's finger, the man said, "Thank you for watching over her. You may go now."

The bird sailed through the window with a high-pitched shriek.

"Can you change into an animal too?"

"Yes," Tane replied, "I must take the shape of an animal while I assist Starion at the conference."

"What animal?"

"It shall be a surprise."

"I hate surprises."

Tane chuckled. "You may find that Starion is full of surprises."

Skye had to smile in return. "You don't speak like Starion. I've never heard an accent like yours."

"I cannot speak English as well as he."

"Who were those two men who've been following me?" Skye asked. "Starion and Oma said they were Vangers, but they didn't know what they wanted from me."

"A moment." Tane took out a small device and spoke rapidly. There was a short reply in the same foreign language he used.

"The two men are now in a holding cell on my ship," Tane said. "A retina scan revealed they are petty criminals, wanted on Vanger for stealing. They were hired by someone but refuse to talk. I do not have an answer to your question."

Skye began to pace in front of Tane. "I still don't understand why Starion thinks I should speak at this conference. Everyone keeps saying humans aren't allowed."

"He is afraid the animals will vote against you. He wants to save you and your friends."

Skye stopped pacing and looked Tane directly in the eyes. "Can he?"

"No."

"What?" Skye began to protest. "Then we're all going to die and all this is for nothing?"

Tane held a hand up. "I did not say that. If the animals vote against the humans, there is nothing Starion can do. However. He thinks you can convince the animals that people can change, thus preventing a kill vote."

"A *kill* vote?" Skye sat down on an empty crate and rested her head in her hands. "He should get someone important like a famous scientist. My parents could have done it; they were brilliant, both of them."

Tane pulled up a crate and sat beside her. "You are obviously someone important, Skye. Those men were hired for a reason, and I will find out what that reason is. In the meantime, we should return to Richard Leven's apartment, even though Katrina demanded I return you to Colorado. Then I will call my ship and have them release the lock on Starion's transport module. He is most anxious to see you."

Tane held up an aqua-colored oval disc about the size of a quarter. "This is a Vanger transport module." He handed the device to Skye. "Do not lose it. Attach it securely next to your skin."

Skye took the device and stood. "Turn around, please."

Tane obeyed and Skye shoved it inside her bra. "Weird," she murmured. "It sticks to my skin like there's Velcro or something on it."

"Are you ready to depart?"

"Hold on," Skye demanded. "I want answers before I agree to go anywhere with you." She sat back down on the crate.

"Very well. Please be quick. I fear for my men who are watching Starion."

Skye couldn't help but smile at that. "I want to know my friends in Colorado are safe. Can you give them transport devices too?"

"I saw them."

"Janine and Henry?"

"Yes. Katrina was quite frantic for your safety, so I went to reassure her that I was searching for you. I gave them transport modules. It is up to Katrina and Starion whether they come. You must speak to them about it."

"Fair enough," Skye said.

"Your friends threated to phone something called Homeland Security and report me as a terrorist if I let anything happen to you."

A grin spread across her face. She missed Janine and Henry and intended to convince Starion that they should come. The danger from those Vanger men seemed to be over.

"I have one more question," Skye began. "What is Starion—"

The sound of a rifle being cocked echoed through the room.

"Put your hands on your head or I'll blow your bloody brains out." Maka, his finger poised on the trigger, pointed a rifle directly at Tane. Rob stood next to him, a bowie knife in each hand.

Quickly rising to her feet and rushing over to Maka, Skye waved her hands frantically. "He's a friend. Maka, put the gun down."

"The bloody hell I will," Maka hissed.

Tane stood.

Without a word, Rob threw both knives and they embedded in the wall directly behind Tane's head, one on either side. Tane looked amused as he crossed his arms over his chest.

Rob walked slowly toward Tane. "Start talking, big man."

When Tane stared at her blankly, she scowled. "The disappearing act."

"That is classified information," Tane replied flatly.

"Uh huh." She turned to Skye. "You can't go with him."

"No, no. It's fine," Skye protested. "Really, it's safe. He's—"

"A terrorist with secret tech," finished Rob.

Maka nodded and continued to point the rifle at Tane.

"Rob," said Skye softly, "He isn't. I promise. Look at his uniform. He's working for a government organization."

"What government?"

"That is also classified," Tane said.

Slowly, Rob pulled the knives out of the wall behind Tane's head and put them in the beaded pouches hanging off her belt, all the time staring intently at him. Walking back to Skye, she asked, "Who is he?"

"This is Tane. My, uh, friend's best friend," Skye said.

Rob gave Tane another appraising look.

"Trust me, Rob. I know what I'm doing," Skye said.

Maka was still aiming the gun at Tane as Rob walked over to him and put her arm over his shoulders. "Leave it off, Maka." He slowly lowered the weapon.

Tane turned to Skye, "Are you ready to see Starion?"

"Is that your friend?" asked Rob. "Starion? Is he the one who left you in the bush?"

Skye nodded.

Rob shook her head, a frown firmly planted on her face.

"Where's he from?" Maka asked.

Tane and Skye looked at each other. "Colorado."

"Are you still going to New Zealand?" Rob asked.

"Yes. There's this—"

"This thing. Uh huh. Are you flying?"

Tane and Skye looked at each other again and nodded before Skye said, "I guess we'd better be going. Uh . . . to the airport."

"Need a lift?" Maka asked. "I can call one of my mates."

"No," Tane said. "I have transportation."

There was an uncomfortable silence before Rob groaned loudly. "Oh bloody hell, Skye. I'm going to miss you."

The two friends embraced. "Thanks for coming to my rescue, Rob."

"No worries." With impressive speed, Rob drew one of the knives from her side and held it under Tane's chin. "You hurt Skye and I'll find you."

"Too right," Maka agreed.

Rob put her knife away and blew Tane a kiss. He opened his mouth, then he closed it without speaking and shook his head. Leaving with Maka, Rob turned back to Skye and said, "Don't do anything I wouldn't."

After the two were gone Tane said, "Are you ready, Skye?"

"Yes. Let's get Starion. What do I do with this transport thing?"

Tane instructed her to push down on it and repeat some odd words.

Then they were standing in Leven's facility in Queenstown. No jet lag, no lost baggage, no rude flight attendants, no security hassles.

This was the way to travel.

"Skye," exclaimed Richard Leven, "I'm delighted you've come back safely. Your grandmother has been calling constantly. There's the phone on the end table. Please call her right away." He shook Tane's hand. "Good to see you again after all these years, General Tane."

"Richard, you look well."

Skye's phone call to Oma was short. Her grandmother couldn't stop crying, and Skye repeated apology after apology.

"Will you get Starion now?" Skye demanded, tapping one foot impatiently after she hung up the phone.

Tane pulled out a communication device and called his ship. Skye couldn't understand his words, but she heard Starion's name.

In only a few seconds, Starion was standing in front of her. "Skye, are you all right? I didn't mean to leave you, and then—"

"You're the one who was hurt. I'm fine."

"I want to hear all about it," Starion insisted. "Every detail. But first . . ."

He strode over to Tane and punched him in the gut. Tane barely flinched. "Was that supposed to hurt, Star?"

Leven's mustache quivered as he tried to suppress a chuckle.

Starion shouted, "You're not helping, Richard. Do you know what he did? Keeping me a prisoner up on that ship of his?"

"He told me what he did, and I agree that it was the right thing." Skye's eyes challenged Starion to disagree.

"You're not serious."

"You were hurt. I thought that kangaroo killed you."

"Better that roo than Katrina. She's going to kill me," Starion said with a strangled sound. "What if you'd been injured?"

"But I wasn't. I had Coorain and Rob and Maka and dozens of animals looking out for me."

Starion ran a nervous hand down the side of his face.

"She is quite a lady," Tane remarked.

"Yes, she is," agreed Leven.

"I know that," Starion muttered.

Skye stood in the middle of the room, hands on her hips, and said, "Don't we need to be at a conference?" She pulled out the small bag of Starion's tags from her backpack and handed it to him. "Sorry. I didn't know which animals to tag."

"I do," said Tane, taking the bag from Starion. "I will get it done."

"And when you get back," Skye said, looking directly at Starion, "Janine and Henry will be here to go to the conference with me."

"You can do this alone. You were going to tag the animals yourself. You don't need Janine and Henry."

Skye looked down, then into Starion's eyes. "Ever since my parents died I've tried to do everything alone. Just because you can do something alone doesn't mean you have to."

15
·······

Skye had been worried that reuniting with Starion would be awkward. She felt different, changed. She missed Coorain and Rob. She thought about Esh and the girl with the scruffy terrier. She wondered what would happen to that boy on the bus, the one with the loser friends. It was ironic: Skye had always disdained the company of people in favor of animals, and now she found herself thinking about her new friends. Her human friends.

And then there was Starion. She could not imagine ever being bored around him. He was interesting and unpredictably quirky. He was, as Tane had alluded to earlier, full of surprises.

Their relationship fell into an easy, effortless rhythm immediately, as though they'd always known each other. They were once again finishing each other's thoughts and laughing with ease. Starion insisted they needed a day or two to relax. They still had six days.

It was late when they finished dinner with Dr. Leven. All three retired to the living room and talked into the evening, with Skye telling them everything that had happened to her in Australia. Tane had not returned, but Starion seemed unconcerned, insisting that his friend — whom he had begrudgingly forgiven — had other duties.

"I don't understand what happened with the leaf," Skye said, her brows drawing together. "I could understand the animals, but they couldn't understand me — not until the kangaroos. I thought the leaf only worked one way. None of this makes any sense."

"It makes perfect sense. You could understand me as a prairie dog so it was easy to accept that you could understand other animals," said Starion. "But talking to them required a deep belief in yourself and your connection to them. Perhaps when the kangaroos confronted you, then, you believed."

Skye frowned. "You're making that up."

"Am I?"

"Can I get either of you anything before I head to bed?" Leven asked, rising from the couch.

"I'm fine, Richard," said Starion. Skye shook her head.

"Those were good times in The Cloaked Sovereign, were they not?" Leven's smile held a twinge of sadness. "Goodnight."

Starion's eyes followed Richard. When the bedroom door shut with a quiet click, Starion put his chin in his hands and stared at the door.

"What's wrong?" Skye asked, moving over to the couch to sit next to Starion.

"Not my story to tell."

"I can tell you're good friends," Skye began. "I can also tell that, whatever it was, you were there for him."

Starion rubbed at the back of his neck. "Truthfully, I didn't have much regard for humans until I met Richard. And of course, there's you. And your friends."

"Henry and Janine are awesome." Skye used to think that aside from Oma, they were the only good people out there. Now? There were a few more.

"I'm still learning, Skye. From you. You don't turn away from injustice with an indifferent shrug." He exhaled with a long, troubled sigh. "But I did."

"I don't believe that."

"You're the only one who can convince the delegates to give humans a chance to change." He held up four fingers. "In only four days, you changed the opinion of dingoes and kangaroos and dozens of other animals in Australia. I stand in awe of you, Skye."

"I don't know what I did."

Starion gently placed his hand across her heart. "I know."

The next morning, Skye was dressed when Starion knocked on the door.

"You have visitors," he said, without any emotion.

Skye heard voices coming from the living room.

"Do you think we were sparkly when we transported?" came Janine's excited voice.

"Why am I dizzy?" Henry's voice.

"You'll get used to it." Oma's voice.

"Oma! Henry! Janine!" Skye shouted, running to hug them all.

Only after all the embracing was over and Skye had introduced everyone to Dr. Leven did she notice Starion sitting alone at the kitchen table, a cup of coffee in front of him.

"Oma," she whispered to her grandmother, motioning toward Starion. "Did you yell at him?"

Katrina shook her head. "No. I should have guessed his father ordered him to be monitored. Starion is treated like a dog, but Tane told me the device was removed. His father will have less control now. But, can you imagine what would have happened to the conference if Starion had been killed? The vote would have been taken, and without you there..."

Skye swallowed loudly.

"The humans on this planet might die," Oma continued in a strained voice. "Starion wasn't supposed to interfere or have a human speaker, but he obviously cares about someone on this planet." She stared toward the kitchen, where Starion was slumped over his coffee. "I never thought I'd see him care about anyone but himself."

Before Skye could answer, Henry and Janine each put an arm around her and steered her toward the kitchen.

"I'm starving," complained Henry.

"I need hot chocolate," added Janine. She began rummaging in the pantry before turning back to Skye. "Where's the Greek god?"

She gave Janine a blank look. "Who?"

"Starion's best friend," Henry explained. "Tane. That guy who speaks all formal and stiff with that crazy, cool accent."

Still sitting at the table, Starion replied, "That's because he doesn't know your language as well as I do. Contractions and slang are difficult in English. And to answer your question — he's not back yet."

"Tane's too old for you, Janine," said Skye jokingly. "But he does have a body like the Greek god Ares. Or maybe Zeus."

Henry grinned. "He totally does. And I'm older than Janine. Just saying."

Skye gave Henry a quick kiss on the cheek. "You're such a cutie, Henry. You'll find someone. I promise."

Henry frowned. "I don't want to be a cutie. I want to look like a Greek god."

"I know what a Greek god is, but I doubt Tane will." Starion quirked his head at Janine and said in a roguish voice, "What do I look like, Miss Genetics Whiz?"

"A fool."

Henry giggled.

"Who put my friend's life in danger," Janine added.

"But —" Skye began.

"Don't, Skye," Janine interrupted. "He must have known what could happen."

"And what do you think, Valjean?" Starion turned toward Henry.

"I think you're trying to save the world." Henry frowned at Janine, who gave a disgusted huff.

"Rather like a superhero, wouldn't you say?" Starion asked sweetly. "Shall I retrieve my cape?"

A smile tugged at Skye's lips as she threw an arm around Henry. "Which superhero do you think he is, Henry?"

Janine was the first to answer. "Darkwing Duck."

Starion opened his mouth, then shut it without a word.

"Who's that?" Henry asked.

Oma chuckled in the doorway. "It's an old Disney cartoon. I'm surprised Janine knows what it is."

"Do you know what it is?" Henry asked Starion.

Starion's eyes flashed angrily. "Yeah, and I don't appreciate being compared to a caped duck who yells about getting dangerous."

Skye handed Starion a biscotti from a tray on the counter. "I was going to say Superman because he's an alien, but still tries to save Earth. He flies too."

"I can fly," Starion said, taking the cookie. "So can the Greek god."

"Oh, *please*," Janine said, measuring hot cocoa into a cup.

"When are we leaving for this conference?" Janine asked after everyone had eaten breakfast.

"Whenever you're ready," Starion replied.

"Are we going to transport again?" Henry asked.

Starion and Leven exchanged looks.

"Skye, would you like to go the old-fashioned way: in a car, then a boat, and a tramp through the woods?" asked Leven. "If it gets to be too much, you can always let Starion transport you. This way you can see a wee bit of my country."

"I would love to see the countryside." She frowned. "Wouldn't that be selfish of me when we have to, you know, save everyone?"

"No," Starion replied firmly. "A couple hours will make no difference."

"Always with the procrastinating," Janine mumbled. "It's going to bite you one day."

"Can we drive by the Remarkables?" Skye asked with hesitation.

"Anything for you, princess," Starion said.

"I think I'm going to be sick," Janine grumbled.

■ ■ ■

"Our driver should be here shortly," Dr. Leven assured the group as they piled out the front door of the building. Everyone wore a coat, gloves, a scarf, and a backpack. Katrina had opted to stay behind, but not before she gave Starion a lecture about keeping "her" Skye safe.

"It's cold," Henry whined.

"I warned you," scolded Starion.

"Where's Tane?" asked Janine.

"He'll join us on the trail," Starion replied.

Skye stared up at the six-story building — gray, plain, fire escapes snaking down the sides. She noticed a windsock on the roof and knew there was probably a helipad there. A similar building stood across the street, but it had an abandoned look. Pointing to it, she asked the professor, "Is that part of the university too?"

"It used to be. It's empty at present. The helicopter landing area on the roof isn't used anymore."

A black Land Rover Defender with huge tires and bright-red lettering proclaiming "See the LOTR film sites" came roaring around the corner, screeching to a halt in front of the group. A young man with unruly blond hair and a dimpled smile stuck his head out the window. "Climb in, mates."

Leven put his hand in the open window and shook the younger man's hand vigorously. "Dylan, good of you to come. I think you know where we're headed."

Once aboard, Leven introduced everyone to his "star pupil." Dylan, a native of Australia, worked part-time for a tour company in Queenstown driving 4WD amphibious vehicles to visit *The Lord of the Rings* filming locations.

"That's one of my favorite books," bubbled Skye.

"I'll point out a few sites," said Dylan, "but I think the professor here wants to drop you off at the head of the Milford Track. Nasty time of year, the winter season. I'll be back to get you when you're done. Isn't that right, professor?"

"Yes, but I'm not staying. Wait for me, Dylan, while I take the kids to meet their guide."

"Will do, professor." Dylan looked in the rearview mirror at everyone in the back. "It'll take a couple of hours to get to Lake Te Anau Downs where you'll take a one-hour cruise to the trailhead, so settle on back." He glanced over at Leven, sitting shotgun. "You know the catamaran isn't operating this time of year. Right?"

"A local fisherman is taking us," Leven replied.

Skye spent the next hour talking excitedly about all aspects of *The Lord of the Rings* as Dylan pointed out several filming sites. Starion's face was one big smile as he listened to her, but Henry and Janine finally exclaimed in unison, "Enough, Skye." Instead, she told them more stories about Rob.

"I want to meet her," Henry said.

"She sounds crazy," Janine commented.

Starion smiled. "But a good crazy."

Dylan spoke about the New Zealand countryside. He addressed Dr. Leven with awe and respect, making Skye wonder if there was something more to the relationship than just teacher and student.

A small fishing boat was waiting when they reached the boat launch at Lake Te Anau. Leven shook Dylan's hand and whispered something in his ear. Dylan beamed. "Be careful," he called after them.

As the boat sped across the dark blue-black waters, Skye stared out at the rugged mountains jutting up in the distance.

Henry leaned over the railing. "The water looks cold."

"Let's go downstairs with the professor and Starion," Janine grumbled. "It's freezing out here."

"He doesn't seem to mind." Henry nodded at the grizzled old fisherman standing in the front of the boat next to the controls. "He's not even wearing a coat."

"Alcohol dulls your senses," Janine said.

"Janine," Henry replied, a finger to his lips. "I can't believe you said that."

"*Please*, Henry. You can smell it on him."

Skye continued to stare out at the scenery until Janine and Henry dragged her down the short steps to the tiny interior section. It was filthy, and rubbish was scattered over the counter of the small kitchenette just opposite a single bed. Leven and Starion sat on a plaid blanket on the bed.

Janine picked up an empty beer bottle from the floor and set it in the basin on the counter. "This is disgusting."

"It's a short ride. It'll be fine," Leven replied.

Janine gave a snort of disgust.

Standing, Professor Leven handed Skye a package. Opening it, she lifted out a navy-blue corduroy front-pack baby carrier.

"Uh . . . thanks, professor. I'm not planning on having a baby anytime soon."

"It's for Starion. You'll have to carry him. In prairie dog form, he'll never make it down the trail."

Henry laughed and pointed.

"Put a lid on it, Valjean," Starion snapped.

"At least it isn't pink," said Janine, trying to keep a straight face and failing. "With ruffles and bows."

Starion shot her a nasty look as he took out a bagel with raspberry jam from the small lunch sack he'd brought along. "I'm not sharing." He paused and held it out to Skye. "Except with my princess."

"That princess thing is getting old," Janine said dryly.

Skye sat down on the bed next to Starion and took a bite of his bagel. At first, she'd hated the princess title, but now she rather liked it when Starion called her that.

"Your student Dylan is great," Skye remarked to Dr. Leven.

"Yes, he's a good kid now."

"What do you mean?" Henry asked.

Leven leaned against the wall of the vessel. "He's been in and out of juvenile homes. Dylan was one of those troubled souls that hurt animals. One of his community service projects was to help at a wildlife rehabilitation center when he was fifteen. That's where I met him. I recognized his potential and sponsored him to study at my university. He still says that helping injured wildlife changed his life."

Henry frowned. "Josh and his gang abuse animals."

"Who's that?" Leven asked.

"Some kid who kicked me when I was a prairie dog," said Starion.

Skye looked up from the brochure Dylan had given her about *The Lord of the Rings* sites. "Nothing can be done to help them. They're a waste of air, and that includes those jerks that shot the kangaroos."

Leven looked solemn. "Dylan is proof that people can change. I've seen success stories in my years working with troubled kids. Humane education works, Skye. Your mother published a couple articles about it."

Skye hadn't known that, but regardless, she didn't believe bad people could change. Dylan did seem likable though. His Aussie accent reminded her of Rob.

Slightly over an hour later, the boat docked at Glade Wharf. Embarking from the boat, Skye was so fascinated with the dense forest rising up in the distance she tripped. She would have face-planted if Starion hadn't caught her and then held her—just a little longer than necessary.

After everyone had assembled at the trailhead next to a large green wooden sign that read "Milford Track: Fiordland National Park," Starion exhaled loudly. "I have to change back. If any of the animals see me, it will be hard to explain my humanoid form. As I've told you, Janine and Henry, humans aren't allowed at the conference, but since you're with me, the animals will have to permit it. Most of them already know about Skye." He gave her an admiring look.

"Especially the animals from Australia." He motioned for all of them to come closer. "Form a tight circle around me so I'm hidden from view when I change."

One minute, Starion stood before them. The next, a prairie dog was at their feet.

"I'll walk with you until you meet up with the guide," Dr. Leven said. "Skye, please lead the group."

"Me? I don't know where we're going."

"Straight ahead. Stay on the trail."

Skye lifted Starion and placed him in the carrier. "Are you OK in there?"

"I'm perfect," replied Starion.

The group started down the trail. "Did you put the waist strap on this thing so I don't fall out?" Starion asked Skye.

"You can walk like the rest of us," Janine suggested.

"No, thank you," Starion replied sweetly. "Not big on hiking."

Dr. Leven explained that hikers from around the world considered the Milford Track to be one of the most beautiful walks in the world, and that to keep the environment safe, fewer than one hundred people each day were allowed to start the one-way walk to Milford Sound, a beautiful fiord. Glaciers had carved the fifty-four-kilometer-long Milford Track, forming U-shaped valleys full of beech trees — predominately silver, mountain, and red beeches, all with tiny leaves.

Skye stopped frequently to investigate this or that: huge bracket fungi growing out of the trunks of dead beech trees, giant crown ferns, a dome-shaped purple mushroom.

"Hurry up, Skye," Janine called out repeatedly.

Henry continued to complain about the cold, and Janine moaned about her new hiking boots. It didn't take them long — about twenty minutes — to reach Glade House, an overnight lodge closed for the season.

Janine peered in a window. "Nice. There's even a library."

Leven nodded. "This belongs to Ultimate Hikes. They're the only company licensed to escort hikers on the Milford Track. There are other facilities for independent trampers."

Past this, they crossed a suspension bridge over the Clinton River. The name was noted on a large green Department of Conservation sign. Henry ran back and crossed the suspension bridge a second time. He moved from side to side with exaggerated movements, causing the bridge to swing.

"Hurry up, Henry," Janine snapped. "I thought you were cold. What are you, five years old?"

"At least someone is having fun," Starion complained from the carrier. "Maybe we should have transported."

Skye shook her head fiercely. "No way. I wouldn't have missed this for anything."

Walking through a beech forest along the banks of the Clinton River, Skye thought she spotted a large bird, but then it was gone. "Starion," she said, "you promised I'd see kea."

"Don't worry. You'll see them."

Trailing the group, Leven called, "Skye, the elevation is too low here for kea. We have to be much higher. We're almost to the Clinton Hut; that's the lodge for independent travelers and our overnight stop. Our guide should be there, and I'll have just enough time to make it back to the boat launch before it gets dark. I'm leaving my pack with you; it has enough food for several days."

"Yippee," Janine moaned.

Starion peered out of the carrier. "Where's Valjean?"

"Henry?" Skye called.

Janine pointed behind them. "He's standing in the middle of the trail."

Skye walked back toward him and stopped. A bird — sooty-black with a white belly and undertail, a bit larger than a house sparrow but smaller than a starling — sat atop Henry's boot. The bird had strikingly long legs. Henry looked up at Skye with an expression of amazement.

"I'm not sure, but I think it's a South Island robin. I saw a picture in one of your books." He grinned. "He likes me."

Dr. Leven smiled. "Good onya, Henry. That's a spot-on ID. They're common on the Milford Track. They like to follow trampers and eat insects on the ground. They're naturally inquisitive."

"I admit it. It's cute," Janine said.

Skye smiled at the bird, who replied, "Hi hi hi hi."

"Hi to you too," Henry said.

"Hi hi hi hi." The robin flew off, saying, "Bye bye bye bye."

"Not the brightest bird in the forest, is it?" Janine said.

Henry frowned at her. "I like him."

"Me too," said Skye.

"I didn't say I didn't like it, only that it isn't . . . oh never mind." Janine started back down the trail with a huff.

Starion pointed to a patch of ground covered with short red flowers with pointed tips. "Those are sundews, a carnivorous plant that eats sandflies."

Skye bent down to investigate. "That's so cool. It's like a Venus flytrap but for mosquitoes." She noticed Starion's frequent smiles whenever she discovered a new treasure: an eel in the river, a fascinating rock, a bird called a fantail doing acrobatic dances. Starion seemed to be having fun watching her.

The temperature dropped slightly as the wind picked up. Skye was oblivious to the cold and wind as she stopped repeatedly, gazing down through perfectly clear water to investigate small fish near the banks of the Clinton River. She could see every rock on the riverbed. Leven pointed out a small picturesque waterfall, just off the trail.

"It's clean enough to drink," Leven said with a smile. "Fill up your water bottle."

"You don't need a filter or purification tablets?" Janine asked.

Leven shook his head. "Not at all. Perfectly safe to drink."

"Sweet," Henry said, filling his bottle and taking a drink. "Tastes amazing." He handed his bottle to Skye.

Taking a long drink, Skye said, "Wouldn't it be wonderful if we could drink water from lakes and rivers in our country?"

"Not happening," Janine said. "The fracking in northern Colorado is pumping all sorts of poisons into the ground."

Skye narrowed her eyes. "I know. And it wastes an incredible amount of water too."

An eerie sound rose above the trees.

"Stop," Starion ordered. "I hear our guide."

Keeeaah.

A raven-sized bird, mossy green in color, landed on a tree branch in front of Starion. It raised its wings, flashing bright-orange undersides, bowing low. The bird looked up with intelligent black eyes and a long hooked beak.

Skye gasped, euphoria cascading over her, and promptly fell backward into a bush. "It's a kea!" A huge smile spread across her face. "It's a kea!"

"Are you going to sit in this bush all day?" Starion asked from the carrier.

Skye clambered to her feet. "It's a kea!"

"Sorry to disappoint you," Starion said. "It's only Tane."

"*What*? I waited my whole life to see a wild kea and it isn't a real kea. I can't believe it. It's Tane." Her shoulders sagged.

"But they are real kea, Skye," replied Tane with a wave of his wing. A noisy group of four raucous birds descended to the branches below him.

The four kea began to swat at each other until the general silenced them with a look. "The hut is ahead. Star, may I have a word with you?"

"Princess, would you please unzip me from this thing?" Starion asked sweetly.

Skye lifted the prairie dog from the carrier and set him down on the ground.

"You sure you can walk by yourself?" Janine asked sarcastically.

Starion gave her an irritated glance as he ambled over toward Tane. Janine watched them, their heads close, their words quiet.

"What do you think they're talking about?" Henry asked.

"They better be talking about stopping this virus," Janine retorted. "There isn't much time."

"There's time — five days. We're almost there," Skye replied, still staring happily at the kea.

Professor Leven picked that moment to give her, Henry, and Janine last-minute instructions about safety and the weather, stressing the dangers of hypothermia.

"This is where I leave you," said Dr. Leven, when Tane and Starion returned. "Good to see you again, Tane. Everyone have a safe trip." Handing Henry the pack full of food, Leven started back, insisting he'd be fine alone. He had his cell phone and years of hiking experience.

Skye, still gazing at the kea, finally let out a squeal, "They're kea."

"Yes, they are," replied Tane.

"They're the smartest birds in the world."

"Wow," Janine said, shaking her head. "You're way too excited about a green bird."

Skye pretended to be horrified. "A green bird? I don't *think* so. Look at their feathers. They're absolutely beautiful."

The kea possessed feathers in varying understated shades of medium to dark green, many of the edges thinly outlined in dark green-brown. The primary flight feathers on the outside of the wings had an almost turquoise color on the top half, with the bottom half a dark brownish-black. When the kea was at rest, the bright-orange patch on the rump, above the tail feathers, was barely visible, the orange undersides of the wing hidden. The entire color scheme appeared, at first glance, to be quite plain, but like the kea mind, the feather colors were subtly complex and anything but ordinary.

The four kea laughed as they hopped to the forest floor, rushing over to investigate Skye's backpack, which she'd set on the ground. One pulled at the zipper with his deeply curved beak, while a second emptied the front pouch of its contents. A third grabbed a jar of lip gloss and rushed off to a nearby tree with it. The fourth got busy untying the laces on Skye's hiking boots.

"Cheeky birds," exclaimed Starion.

"Front and center, soldiers," barked General Tane.

Each of the four kea rushed to stand in a disorderly line in front of Skye. Still holding the lip gloss in his foot, one kea had succeeded in opening the jar and eating half of it.

"Do they have names?" Skye asked.

"Call them the four bads," muttered Starion.

"Really, what are their names?"

"You could not pronounce them," said Tane. "Refer to them as number one, two, three, and four."

"That doesn't sound right for such amazing parrots." Skye's words invoked more laughter from the four.

"You may name them," said Tane.

The first kea stepped forward, still laughing and awkwardly tripping.

"You can be Merry," said Skye.

The second kea snapped to attention in front of Skye. "Miss Skye, I will do whatever you need. No task is too difficult." He bowed low.

Skye smiled. "You're Frodo."

"I'm detecting a *Lord of the Rings* theme here," murmured Starion.

Skye pointed to the third kea, busily eating the remnants of the lip gloss pilfered from her backpack. "I think I'll call you Pippin." She pointed to the last kea. "That leaves you with the name Sam."

The fourth kea began to whine, "Why do I have to be Sam? That's such a—"

The sound of a gunshot cut off his words.

There was a sudden blur of feathers, shouts, humans diving to the ground. Another shot exploded into a tree, inches above Skye's head. She flattened herself to the ground, covering Starion.

"There he is," shouted Sam above the din, pointing a wing tip at a tree behind them.

Taking flight with the general, Sam headed for the tree, then swerved and crashed into the other bird. Skye could see the birds' confusion as both landed in a tumble. They wouldn't make it to the gunman in time.

Skye saw a rifle pointing directly at her through the trees. Covering her head with her arms, still shielding Starion, she shut her eyes in fear. A third shot rang out. Peering out, she saw —

Henry. Lying on the ground in front of her.

16

"Henry's been shot!"

Starion squirmed out from beneath Skye. Janine rushed over, kneeling next to them. "Henry, can you hear me? Henry?"

Skye reacted quickly, trying to cover her friends and the prairie dog. "Get down!"

"The kea got him," Starion said, motioning behind him. Blood decorated a tree where the gunman had been standing.

Soon Dr. Leven was shouting and racing back to the scene, bending over Henry, checking the injury.

"No . . . no . . .," Skye wailed.

Janine began to cry; it was the first time Skye had ever seen her do so.

Henry reached one hand up and tried to wipe the tears off Janine's face, but his hand fell limply down. Janine grabbed his hand tightly. She opened her mouth, but for once, it wasn't working.

Henry forced a brave smile. "Love you too."

Dr. Leven pulled a first-aid kit from the backpack at Henry's side. Placing Skye's hands on Henry's left shoulder, he said, "Press and hold." He turned to Tane and Starion. "We must transport him to your ship for medical care."

Tane shook his head, the feathers fluffed. "The doctor left after Starion recovered. None of my men would know how to treat him."

"Then transport Henry to the nearest hospital."

Starion and Tane gave each other a look before Starion spoke. "Have him magically appear in the middle of the hospital?"

"I see your point." Leven pulled out his cell phone, mumbling thanks that he still had reception. "Dylan, there's been an accident. Get a medical chopper to the clearing next to Glade House." He walked off to the side, speaking quietly.

"You'll be all right, Henry. You will, and you'll go to Broadway and be a big star like you said you would," Skye babbled on helplessly, blood drenching her hands, as Dr. Leven once again knelt down beside her.

"Skye, you've helped stop the bleeding. Good onya, you're doing great. Keep the pressure on. Henry, talk to me."

"Broadway," Henry mumbled.

Skye removed her shaking hands as Dr. Leven wrapped a pressure bandage around Henry's chest and shoulder, pinning his left arm and wrapping it, then looked over his shoulder toward Starion. "Tane must call the other birds and fly Henry to the trailhead. Dylan's calling for a chopper. Skye, grab that silver blanket out of the first-aid kit. We're going to put Henry on it."

"What can I do?" Janine wailed, still clutching Henry's hand.

"Help bring over some long pieces of wood. We're going to construct a stretcher. I put a whole bag of bungee cords and zip strips in the backpack I gave Henry."

Soon, a stretcher was ready. Skye continued to talk to Henry and watch for signs of shock. Though Henry was sweating profusely, he seemed to be breathing normally.

Starion leaned over Henry. "Why did you —"

Before he could finish, Janine pointed a shaking finger at the prairie dog. "I thought nobody was after us anymore. Tane said those Vangers were on his ship, under arrest." Janine's voice became an angry, hysterical shriek. "Sweet, gentle Henry. How could you put his life in danger?"

Leven put his arm around Janine's quaking shoulders. "He didn't know."

"He should have!"

Leven glanced at Starion, then down at the makeshift stretcher. "Henry, the kea will take it from here. Be still. Skye, I have every confidence in your ability to win over the delegates at the meeting." He attempted a smile. "She'll need your help, Janine."

"No." Skye gave Janine a tight hug. "Go with Henry. I've got this."

"But—"

"It's OK, Janine. You take good care of our Broadway star."

Pushing her cell phone into Skye's hand, Janine said, "Here. I know you lost yours. Dr. Leven's number is programmed."

"How fast can you run?" Leven asked Janine. The two took off.

A flock of over three dozen kea, assisted by Tane's soldiers, descended around Henry. Using their clawed toes, the birds lifted the stretcher. The air filled with the calls and wing beats of the birds led by Tane, who called down to Skye and Starion, "Go to the Clinton Hut. Turn left at the sign ahead."

The parrots were off, teetering in midair, then turning as one unit and flying slowly above the tree line. Skye watched until they disappeared.

"Starion?" Skye pointed to the still form sprawled under the trees behind them. "Is he . . ."

"Dead? Definitely."

Cautiously, Skye walked over to the figure. A bloody pit was all that remained of his left eye. His throat was a mangled piece of meat. Blood coated the ground and was splattered onto the trees next to the body. A rifle lay off to one side.

Skye felt dizzy and stumbled backward, sitting down abruptly. "I know he was trying to kill me. Why me?"

"I don't know why, but we will find out."

"Henry jumped in front to save me."

Starion nodded. "Valjean was quite brave."

"He's hurt because of me," Skye moaned.

"You're alive because of him."

Skye pointed at the dead body, her teeth chattering. "Is he a Vanger, like the others?"

"I don't know. He could be a Beholder. Tane will check when he returns."

"How can you tell, since he's dead?"

"There are certain minor anatomical differences."

Wrapping her shivering arms around herself, Skye mumbled, "I don't want details."

"You're cold," Starion said. "Let's go to the hut."

The Clinton Hut looked similar to camping lodges in Colorado. A bunkhouse on the left faced a kitchen building, with another bunkhouse perpendicular to the first forming the third side of a square. A wooden deck filled out the interior of the square. The bathroom structure was off to the right of the kitchen building. Entering the bunkhouse on the left, Skye set her backpack of supplies and Henry's pack full of food on the floor next to Starion.

Neither said anything for a long time.

"I'm going to put this in the kitchen," Skye said, picking up the pack of food, "and then go to the bathroom."

"I'll go with you. I need to make sure the gunman didn't have a friend with him."

The kitchen building was empty. No one was lurking outside. Skye dropped the pack of food on the kitchen counter. Starion sat on his back legs and looked around the perimeter, sniffing the air. "I think it's safe," he told Skye when she came out of the bathroom.

Skye sat at one of the dozen tables in the dining area, her head in her hands, and said nothing.

Tane and the four kea finally returned; Skye could hear their loud calls, and when she opened the door, the birds hopped inside. As the birds took turns telling Skye about the chopper and the transport of Henry, Tane and Starion excused themselves.

Skye tried to listen to the kea chatter, but her mind was too frantic over Henry and the gunman to pay attention. Who wasn't out to kill her? Animals, people from other planets, and now this unknown man. All because she was going to speak at the conference.

Skye broke out in a sudden sweat. Oma was a Beholder. Tane was a Beholder. Starion was a Beholder. Those men were Vangers. The dead gunman was probably a Vanger. What was going on between those two planets? A thought burrowed its way into her head.

No. Skye shook her head at the crazy thought that her father could possibly be a Beholder.

But.

If her father was a Beholder, then she was . . .

Starion and Tane looked grim when they returned. Before they could speak, Skye blurted out, "Was my father a Beholder?"

Tane and Starion looked at each other and shook their heads. "No," they insisted.

"Swear it," Skye insisted. "And if you lie, Starion, I will never forgive you."

"I swear on my life, Skye. Your father Pieter was most definitely, absolutely not a Beholder."

"That means I'm not half Beholder. Right?"

"Would that be so terrible, Skye?" Starion asked softly.

"I guess not. I mean, it would be cool to be able to turn into an animal."

"Can you?"

"No. Of course not," Skye replied.

"That's sort of proof, isn't it?"

"OK. I believe you," Skye said. "Now, who was that man who shot Henry?"

"An Earth human," replied Tane.

"What? I don't understand any of this," Skye exclaimed. "I'm trying to save humans. Why would another human want to kill me? Does he think maybe I can't do the job?" She put her hands on her forehead, her elbows on the table. "Why's everyone trying to kill me? Did he have identification in his pocket? Please. No more secrets."

"Very well," said Tane, receiving a nod of approval from Starion. "The man's wallet, which I retrieved from the body, contained only money—no identification or credit cards. However, there was a tribute, a promise of payment."

"Someone hired him then," Skye said. "Who was this payment promise from?"

Starion turned a small shiny paper, about the size of a business card, toward her. "The silver-and-purple serrated edges mark it as a promissory note." One side contained a black five-sided figure enclosing an embossed golden sun, the rays extending past the geometric outline. There was a four-digit number on the opposite side. "It could have been from my father's personal guard."

Tane sucked in his breath. "Or the Vijfhoek."

"If they exist," said Starion

"They exist." Tane looked grim. "And the number?"

Starion shrugged. "It could be anything: a combination, a post office box, an address."

"Wait," said Skye. "You're saying your father paid a human to kill me? Because I'm not supposed to be at the conference? Why does an important scientist like your father have a personal guard anyway? Is it a dangerous job?"

Tane cleared his throat.

Starion waved a dismissive paw. "Yes, it's a dangerous job. He's an important man on my planet." He paused. "I don't think my father knows about you, Skye. If he did, I'd be called home immediately."

"Definitely," Tane agreed.

"Then who's trying to kill me? Some of the animals are working for a Vanger. Or maybe, they want us all dead, and they aren't working for anyone. And now, greedy humans care more about money than the planet. They live here too. Is there anyone else who thinks this is insane?" She tossed a cup into the sink. "I have to give a speech to my animal friends, who probably hate me, and tell them that people are good and caring. How am I supposed to do that?"

Skye gazed out the kitchen window at the darkening sky. The wind howled as the first flakes of snow began to fall. She stirred a spoon absently in her third cup of now-cold cocoa. She felt numb all over. She was more worried about Henry than about her own safety — she believed Tane and Starion would protect her.

The kea repeated the medics' words that Henry's wound was not serious, but Skye was still afraid for her friend. Someone shot Henry because he was protecting *her*.

Not acceptable.

Skye was terrified about the conference tomorrow and worried she wouldn't say the right things. She wasn't afraid of public speaking; she just wasn't good at it, despite what had happened around the fire in the Outback. That was a fluke.

On top of everything else, she was so tired she could barely move. The stress, the hike, worries about her friends and the animals had all conspired to zap her remaining energy. She put her throbbing head down on the table.

"Skye," Starion said, "please let me walk you to the bunkhouse. You're exhausted."

Without a word, Skye put her coat on and stumbled after Starion to the building. A sleeping bag beckoned from one of the lower bunks. Closing the shutters on the window, she turned to the bed. Starion had transformed back into his human form.

"What if the animals see you?" Skye mumbled.

"They won't. You closed the shutters." He took Skye's coat and guided her to the sleeping bag. "Climb in, princess." He pulled the covering up and sat down next to her, his legs touching hers — only the sleeping bag separating them. "Try to get some sleep."

Skye stared up at him and felt . . . weirdly tingly. But she was too tired, too worried about Henry to think deeply about it. She shut her eyes.

Starion gently smoothed the hair back from her face. "Good night, Skye."

Skye woke early. She heard Tane and Starion talking outside the door. Rising, she peered out the window. New snow had fallen during the night, and it shimmered in the sunlight. The wind had calmed somewhat but was still making its presence known with a low whistling vibration across the glass windowpane.

Starion was talking about Oma, telling Tane that Katrina wanted him to stay away from Skye. He was complaining about the many rules she'd set.

The windowpane began to rattle, and Skye couldn't hear any more of what they were saying. When the noise finally stopped, she heard Starion's voice. "I know you have the virus on your ship. We have to find a way to stop it from being released."

"If the animals at the conference vote in favor of the humans then it will not be," Tane replied. "However, I heard a rumor that many of the delegates are believing lies about the humans. It then becomes an easy thing to pay them for a kill vote."

"I suspected it," came Starion's angry voice.

"Then there is nothing we can do," Tane stated flatly. "The vote determines the release of the virus. There is no way to open the console containing the virus canister. Any attempt to break in will jettison it. It is all on an automatic fail-safe system; the computer releases it thirty minutes after a negative vote comes in, just enough time to get all our people back up to the ship. Sorry, Star. There is no way to override it — unless we blow up the ship, and that I will not allow you to do."

"There's always something we can do, but I need your word that you'll help me. Maybe we can find another way to open the console. I may have an idea, but I need schematics."

"It is pointless," replied Tane. "The planet is probably lost. Go home, Star. Forget her. I am sorry, but the humans are as good as dead."

Skye stumbled back to the bunk before she heard Starion's reply. She didn't want to hear another word. She was getting out of here. *All I went through in Australia,* she thought, *believing I had to get back to New Zealand at all costs so I could speak at the conference. For what? So we could all die anyway? My speech isn't going to mean anything. They're voting against us no matter what I say.*

If they were all going to die, she wanted to spend her last hours with her best friends, not stuck in the mountains being lied to by aliens who were going to run off to their ship and leave them all to die.

She'd started to trust Starion. She'd even started to care about him. How could she have been so stupid? She angrily threw the remainder of her things in her backpack, placing Janine's cell phone in her pocket. She was tired of being a pawn. Was this all some elaborate game being played by two alien worlds?

Starion and Tane were so busy with their plotting they didn't hear her as she slipped through the trees back in the direction of the trailhead. She was sure the police would be coming. When someone was shot, didn't investigators come? There was probably a ride waiting, and she'd go back to Leven's apartment, take her friends, and go home. Starion didn't need her, and what was the point? A speech wasn't going to save them. Aliens were going to destroy everyone, and there was nothing she could do.

Pulling her scarf tightly around her neck, she plodded through the new snow. The trailhead wasn't far. She had an excellent sense of direction — not as good as Coorain's, but she'd navigated around the Rocky Mountains quite competently. That's why she didn't hesitate when she saw the path ahead and to the left. A shortcut. She'd be with Henry and Janine shortly.

Without thinking, she took the track and was soon crossing over the river and plodding up a steep slope, hoping to get a better view.

She should have known better.

Preoccupied and careless, she pulled out Janine's cell and looked at the time. "No bars," she murmured as she replaced the phone in her back pocket.

She didn't notice the ground beneath her start to shift. As the snow began to slide, Skye fought to stay on her feet. It felt as though she were glued to a magazine that was sliding across the floor. With a feeling of terror, Skye tried to jump to the side. All the signs she'd ignored fell into place: new snow, high winds, steep slope. She scrambled for a tree, attempting to grab it, knowing the slab of snow would shatter and slide off the mountainside, burying her under it. Her feet felt like sandbags were weighted to them as she tripped and fell headlong under a rocky outcrop, the tree just out of reach.

As the snow buried her and the world became a white blur, she thought she heard someone call her name.

17

At least Skye remembered to take a deep breath and hold it before the snow settled. Cupping both hands in front of her mouth, she created an air pocket, as she'd learned in a mountain-survival training course.

That was all she remembered.

Panic overtook her. She could feel her heart racing, her insides screaming. *I'm buried alive.*

How much time passed, Skye didn't know as she tried to gain control. *Don't panic. Think.*

With everything she had, Skye pushed the panic back a little. *Think. Think.*

More time passed.

She pushed the panic back a little more.

The terror gave way to anger, and she could think again.

Dying in an avalanche was such a pointless way to end a life. She knew she had about fifteen to thirty minutes to get out before she died of carbon dioxide poisoning. How much time had already passed?

Digging her way out was impossible. She wasn't sure how deeply she was buried, but the snow had already set like concrete. She couldn't move enough to reach the phone in her back pocket.

Starion and Tane hadn't seen her leave. They'd never find her in time. Hikers would probably come across her decomposed body in the spring — that is, if there were any humans left to hike by then. Maybe everyone on the planet would be dead. All her friends. *Everyone*.

Buried in the snow, about to die, Skye realized how selfish she'd been. Even if there was only a slight chance she could influence the vote, shouldn't she try? If it was true that she could save the world, then she had no right to be so wrapped up in her own problems that she gave up on humanity. There were good people: Janine and Henry, Coorain and Esh, Rob and Maka, Professor Leven, even Dylan.

Wait. There were more people than that.

Many more.

She'd let them all down because she'd been unable to accept that *she* was the only hope for humans, however slight. She'd wanted to believe she couldn't possibly be the one destined to save the world.

Maybe she was the one. Maybe Starion had picked the right girl. Maybe against all the odds she could prove Tane wrong and change the minds of her animal friends.

Her parents had always said she had a gift with animals. Janine and Henry told her she had a gift. Starion told her. Oma told her.

The animals in Australia had protected her. No one made them do it.

A few of the people on the bus had changed their thoughts because of her, because of her words. So what if the delegates were being bribed? Couldn't she appeal to their sense of fairness and justice? Couldn't she dispel false stories that had been spread about humans?

Maybe she was smart enough. Maybe she was brave enough. She thought about the runaway girl and her little dog. She didn't want the girl to die. Perhaps, she was the person to defend them and plead for a second chance.

She finally believed Starion. Oma trusted him, and the woman trusted no one when it came to her. Unfortunately, now that Skye was ready to trust Starion, she'd lost the chance.

She didn't want to die. Mostly, she didn't want to die alone.

She needed people, and maybe they needed her too.

Completely helpless and immobilized in the snow, Skye waited to die, full of regrets.

Was the snow shifting? Was that movement she felt? She heard scraping and the most wonderful call in the entire world. *Keeeaah.* Were those excited voices? The scraping turned into the sound of hammering—loud, insistent, frantic. Skye's chest threatened to explode, but not from lack of oxygen.

The kea—her friends—were digging her out.

She was going to get a second chance. And she was going to throw *everything* she had into a kick-ass speech.

"Miss Skye, Miss Skye," Merry called urgently as Skye pulled herself out of the snow, coughing and gasping. "Say you're all right."

Skye reached for the kea with shaking arms and cuddled him close. "Thank you," she whispered, gazing around at the group of about twenty birds that surrounded her. "Thank you, all of you, for saving my life." Their immense curved beaks were dotted with snow.

Her fingers stiff with cold, Skye pulled the cell out of her pocket and checked the time. She'd been buried twenty-eight minutes.

Slowly the kea took off, leaving only Merry, who perched on Skye's leg. Skye sat in the snow, relearning how to breathe.

"Don't tell Starion," she said to Merry in a shaking voice.

"Why?"

"Don't. OK?"

"I won't tell, Miss Skye." Merry pecked at Skye's cheek. "You're cold. Should we go back?"

"OK."

"Are you going to the conference?" Merry asked.

"How did you know I wasn't?"

"Because you ran away. I followed you. I called your name. Are you scared, Miss Skye?"

Skye rose to her feet and brushed off the snow. "Let's get Starion and Tane. I have to give my speech." Scared? She was *terrified.*

Skye, carrying Starion in the front-pack carrier, had been following General Tane for an hour. The bird flew from tree to tree, zigzagging across the snow-covered trail. Despite boots, coat, and gloves, Skye was becoming numb from the cold. Even the antics of the four kea, now referred to by Starion as the "Hobbits," couldn't make her laugh. On and on she stumbled.

She was going to do this. Failure? Not an option.

Under her parka, Skye was wearing the outfit she'd carefully picked out for the conference: her best gray pants, an ivory-collared shirt, and a black designer blazer — found by Henry at an after-Christmas sale. She'd added a teal and pink scarf, a present from Janine. And of course, she wore the delft locket.

Crossing over the Clinton River at the north branch, they plodded through the brush for what seemed like miles. After passing a lake and then a waterfall, Skye stared up at the spectacular peaks of Mackinnon Pass. The vegetation was changing to reflect the elevation — sparser shorter trees, rocky outcrops, soaring bare mountain crests.

Skye pointed to the mountain ahead. "Are we going up there?"

"No," Starion said from the carrier. "But that's where the kea hang out."

Walking was difficult. The snow had caused areas to become impassable, requiring the party to change direction and double back. Starion, with his short prairie dog legs, never would have made it without Skye. The high winds the evening before, combined with the new snow on top of older, weak snow, increased the danger of an avalanche. The snow became deeper as Skye trudged onward over rocky, uneven terrain.

Starion convinced her to drink water and eat a power bar. She was too tired to argue with him. Although Skye was in excellent physical shape, she began to slow considerably; she had never been on such a difficult hike. Finally, when she felt she couldn't go another yard, she heard Tane shout, "We are here."

She quickened her pace, following him toward . . . a huge wall of rock? Tane perched in a bush and nodded toward the side of the mountain. Skye dropped to the ground to take off her backpack as the Hobbits closed in around her. She removed Starion from the carrier and set him down in the snow.

"I don't see anything," Pippin complained.

"Me neither," said Merry.

Starion put a paw on Skye's arm. "You were great." Walking to the side of the mountain, he brushed the snow off a section of stone near the ground, revealing a small square metal box. On opening it, he entered a sequence of numbers on a keypad.

Two massive doors appeared in the side of the rock face. Starion turned back to Skye. "The meeting awaits."

Looking up, Skye saw a stone building jutting out the side of the mountain, blending in almost perfectly except for the round metal loops attached to the doors. She saw no knobs, no latches, only the round, hinged loops. She reached up on tiptoes and pulled frantically at them. The wide double doors, carved with symbols in the shapes of stylized animals, must have been thirty feet high, each door easily fifteen feet wide. Who could possibly need doors that big? It reminded her of the entrance to the Senate House in the Roman Forum where she'd gone on a family trip when she was a child. Her father had told her the Romans had built the entryway that tall so the Gods could fit through.

Skye shuddered. What was going to come through those doors after her? But she was too cold and too weary to think of anything but getting inside. She tried using the metal loops to pound at the door, but they didn't operate like door knockers, and did nothing to open the doors. The wind whipped her red hair about her as the temperature continued to drop. Snow swirled in huge eddies, obscuring the top of the stone building.

Skye was close to panic when Starion's furred body brushed her leg. He raised a clawed hand in the air, waved it three times, and made a series of guttural cries. The massive doors flung open.

"How did you do that?" Skye asked in awe.

"I'm just that awesome," Starion replied casually. "Impressed?"

Skye nodded enthusiastically.

Pointing a wing tip at the metal box Starion had opened before, Tane said, "It opens automatically, on a delay, after the correct sequence is entered."

"What's your problem, Tane?" Starion asked gruffly.

"Telling the truth."

Skye tried not to smile as Starion motioned for her to follow him and then tripped and fell headfirst into the snow.

"Need some help, Star?" Tane asked with a soft chuckle.

Starion brushed the snow off his fur, ignoring Tane. "After you, princess."

Skye gasped as she entered. The room seemed to go on and on; she couldn't see the surrounding walls. The teen and the prairie dog walked inside, accompanied by all five kea.

The doors shut behind them with a thud.

18
. . . .

"**B**ecause we tripped a sensor when we entered, the official count-down has started." Starion pointed up at a small glowing box. "It's counting down the time until the transport markers fixed to the delegates are activated."

Skye began to shake. The countdown. Her speech. Panic enveloped her.

"Don't look so scared, Skye," said Starion softly. "You're going to kill that speech."

Skye shut her eyes for a moment and thought of the snowcapped Rocky Mountains. *Her* mountains. Breathe . . . Breathe . . . Rocky Mountains . . .

She opened her eyes and looked around the dimly lit room. There were chairs and long tables arranged in a staggered seating pattern, like in pictures she'd seen of delegates at the United Nations. She wandered around the windowless room and thought to herself that it wasn't as much a room as a cavern. A huge sign hanging from the ceiling read "Terrestrial Ecosystems." There were arrows pointing to separate areas marked grassland, forest, tundra, and desert. In turn, these were divided into areas with names like tropical, rainforest, savanna, chaparral . . . A separate area sported a sign that declared "Island Ecosystems." The chairs and tables varied in size.

On the far side of the room, a similar sign hung from the ceiling that read "Aquatic Ecosystems." The chairs were glass aquariums of varying sizes, some small, some massive. Skye looked back at the aquatic-ecosystem sign and saw that it too had directions to separate areas: freshwater, estuarine, and marine.

At the front of the room stood a small wooden chair draped in purple with the words "President of the UEE." Two cloth banners pointed out from either side; one was a lapis-blue color with embroidered stars and tiny ships and some strange symbols, similar to the flight suit Tane had worn. The other banner was a seafoam-green color with more of the strange symbols and an image of a field full of crops that resembled an impressionist watercolor. A podium with a microphone stood in front; a small ladder led from the floor to a platform extending out from the back of the podium.

Wandering back toward Starion, Skye saw that he was now wearing a purple robe embroidered with the same odd symbols. In his clawed paws, he held a carved wooden staff topped with a gleaming black stone. The stone pulsed and glowed as Starion held it.

"Good afternoon, Mr. President," Skye said.

Starion bowed with a flourish. "We made it, with four days to spare. Go Team Skye." He glanced up at the glowing clock. "The representatives are arriving now."

Small bursts of light flashed from all around the cavern as the massive room went from semidarkness to stadium-bright. First, there were empty seats and tanks, and then animals occupied them. The quiet room erupted with noise. The pungent smell of thousands of creatures sailed through the air. Skye couldn't help but smile — she could understand their conversations, most of which centered on what type of food was being provided.

Starion leaned over and shouted, "Everyone can understand everyone else. There's a circle of protection around the entire building so that no animal may harm another." He waved the staff in the air, the black stone gleaming. "I've got some power in hand, in case it gets out of control."

"How does it work?"

"Think of it as a powerful type of magic." Starion grinned mysteriously.

From across the room came a thundering voice next to a sign that read "Arctic Tundra." "The pack ice is melting, or doesn't anyone care?" The voice paused and resumed in a whiny drawl. "Ahhhh . . . who ripped up my chair? That's rude. I'm endangered and the ice is melting."

There were peals of laughter from one of the tables in the front as General Tane bellowed, "Soldiers. Front and center. *Now*."

The four Hobbits hopped forward in a disorderly row. Merry was still laughing as he made a failed attempt to salute Tane with one wing. "Sir," they all cried in unison.

General Tane took a wooden baton in his beak and strode in front of each soldier. *Whack. Whack. Whack. Whack.* He popped each kea on the head and barked, "Apologize to the delegate from the arctic tundra."

The four kea recited in unison, "Sorry, Mr. Polar Bear Jackson."

"We were having a bit of fun with your chair stuffing," added Frodo.

Pippin called out, "Stupid whiner."

Tane whacked him again.

"Sorry," Pippin muttered.

Starion groaned. "This is not playtime for rascally kea." He sat down in his chair as more animals continued to appear around the room.

"Starion?" Skye asked. "Some of the animals have blue ribbons around their necks with a round silver disk that says 'DDU.' What does that mean?"

"Those are the delegates from Australia. The acronym means delegate from down under. There are various ecosystems on that continent so they don't all sit together, but they're a tight bunch and that's their way of showing solidarity. They've elected a leader to speak for their continent and the surrounding islands."

"Does that include New Zealand? General Tane and his soldiers aren't wearing the ribbons."

"Tane and the Hobbits aren't a part of the United Earth Ecosystems; they're here to help us. The fauna of New Zealand, which consists entirely of birds, two species of bats, and various marine mammals, doesn't like to be included with what they call the Australian riff-raff. That's why they aren't wearing ribbons. The Australian spokes —"

Before Starion could continue, every animal with a blue ribbon stood up; most were cheering and waving, and some ringing bells or pounding on drums. The ruckus seemed to come from all corners of the room as a five-foot-tall, 125-pound bird confidently strode in. Covered in black feathers with a bright-blue neck and long, fleshy red wattles, she looked mythical. A tall horn-like crest sat atop her head, and adorning it was a tiara covered in opals. She bowed slightly as a myriad of loud splashing noises came from the aquatic ecosystem area. Three reptiles the size of cocktail plates ran around on a table, their blue ribbons prominent as they shook diminutive feet in the air. The sandy-colored animals, small horns protruding from all over their flat bodies, darted madly around the table, flicking their long tongues rapidly.

"They're precious," Skye exclaimed. "What are they?"

"Don't let them hear you say that," Starion chuckled. "They think they're ferocious, but truthfully they're completely harmless except to about a dozen species of ants — their only food. They're called thorny devils and they're in the delegation from the Australian Outback. These three are from the town of Alice Springs. They're the animals I was supposed to have tagged when you came with me to Australia."

Gazing at the small animals, Skye said, "I never would have found them."

"Tane tagged them. Everything's fine."

Starion pointed at the giant bird. "That's the real powerhouse in Australia. Cassie is their leader. She's a southern cassowary from the oldest continuous wet tropical rainforest in the world — the Daintree Rainforest."

Merry flew over and perched on Skye's shoulder. "That cassowary isn't as smart as a kea," he said.

"Kea are the smartest birds in the world," Skye whispered to the parrot. Turning toward Starion, she asked, "Are there animals from the Great Barrier Reef?"

"A hawksbill sea turtle named Irwin is the spokes-animal for the Great Barrier Reef."

Skye heard a faint rumbling. It only registered in her brain because of the reaction of the other animals.

"Do you hear that noise?" she asked Starion.

"That's Cassie. She's trying to get the room's attention by booming. The cassowary has the lowest known birdcall, right on the edge of human hearing, so that's why you're having trouble."

The room was quiet when the cassowary spoke. "G'day mates. I see we've got a rodent in charge of these proceedings." She looked around the room. "What d'ya say to throwing a certain squirrel on the barbie?"

There were shouts of laughter as two of the thorny devils high-fived each other. Merry, still perched on Skye's shoulder, asked, "What squirrel?"

"She means Starion. Prairie dogs are ground squirrels," Skye replied.

"Oh." Merry hung his head. "Am I still the smartest bird in the world, Miss Skye?"

Kissing Merry on the top of his head, Skye said, "Of course you are."

Starion crossed his paws over his purple robe and stood to his full height of about a foot. He tapped his foot. "Right back at you, Cassie." Taking a gavel, he pounded it on the desk in front of him.

Skye looked up to see Starion's image staring down at her from giant screens. His voice echoed loudly around the cavernous hall. "Delegates, please go immediately to your appropriate ecosystem so we may begin."

19

....

Whining echoed through the conference hall. "What are we going to do about the melting ice?"

The four kea, perched together near the podium, all groaned in unison. "It's chair-ripping time again," Frodo said. Tane shot him a warning look.

"Everyone knows PBJ is a big baby," Pippin complained.

Skye leaned toward Tane. "PBJ?"

"The polar bear's name is Jackson so they came up with the nickname PBJ," Tane replied. "They think it is clever to name him after a sandwich. Extremely immature in my opinion."

The polar bear sat in an enormous chair, his legs flung out to the side, his gigantic paws draped over the chair back. Skye knew polar bears were ferocious and could kill in an instant, but there was something gentle, even amusing, about this huge carnivore. His nose twitched as he reached a paw up to scratch a small rounded ear.

Starion spoke into the microphone. "Mr. Polar Bear Jackson, we are all aware of the melting ice caps. Global warming is a threat not only to polar bears, but to animals everywhere. We know man is to blame. They drill and pollute and waste and hunt. They enslave and torture, not only animals but each other. On top of everything, they're too shortsighted to see that the increased emissions from fossil fuels are changing weather patterns drastically, causing flooding in inland places and droughts in others, allowing an increase in pests that decimate forests, creating more opportunity for wildfires.

"The question we are to decide is whether humans deserve to die. Can they change? I don't believe they deserve to die, but I am only the facilitator; I do not get a vote. You do. The fate of the humans will be decided by a majority vote, but not before we hear from our speakers, including a human."

The room detonated with shouts and boos amid roars of "kill the humans." There had been angry words about Skye's presence since the meeting started. She knew she wasn't supposed to be there, so she'd tried to ignore the grumbling and stay close to Starion. She felt herself slumping, trying to look more inconspicuous.

"No humans are allowed," came the rumble of a deep voice.

"Please step forward and introduce yourself," Starion replied.

A square-lipped, heavy slate-gray animal with a wide mouth and two horns stepped forward. "Name's Malanga. I'm a southern white rhino from Lake Nakuru National Park in Kenya."

"Thank you for coming, African delegate," Starion said. "I understand your concern, but the human poses no threat to you. What can it hurt to hear her words?"

Malanga pawed at the ground with one hoofed foot. "That's not allowed in the rules."

"I've changed the rules," answered Starion.

There was an outcry of rage from many of the delegates. Starion again held a paw up. "I see that you're not scheduled to talk, Malanga. Would it be acceptable for Skye to speak if I give you permission to also speak?"

After some hesitation, the rhino answered, "Yes."

Starion bowed slightly. "Thank you for compromising, Malanga. You may now address the assembly."

"My relatives — northern white rhinos — are gone. There are probably none left at all. What do those horrible humans call it? *Extinct*. And do you know why? Because of poachers. They killed them, and now they are after us southern whites. Those poachers cut our horns off to use in some crazy medicine that isn't medicine at all. Perhaps we should cut off their heads and make our own medicine."

There were more cheers.

"There's nowhere left for us to live," continued the rhino. "They've taken all the land away. I say kill all the humans. Especially the poachers."

Without thinking, Skye stood up. "Malanga, I am so sorry. You're right about the poachers, but there are good people trying to stop them. I'll bet you've seen uniformed officers with wildlife badges. There's even talk that drones could be used to catch poachers."

Malanga didn't answer.

"Have you seen the officers?" Starion asked kindly.

"I've seen people in uniforms but they're there to kill us. They're just waiting and watching. They make us think they're protecting us, but they're gonna sneak up on us when we're sleeping and kill us. I heard it. It must be true if I heard it."

A group of five corsac foxes, their gray-and-yellowish fur bristling, shouted, "It's true. They're going to kill all of you."

"That information is false," Starion said with disgust, pointing a claw at the leader of the foxes. "Dmitry, are you spreading conspiracy theories about wildlife officers? Please tell me you don't believe this nonsense."

"I believe it," snapped the rhino.

The foxes glanced at each other with smug looks.

"Dmitry," said Starion. "Knock it off or you'll be escorted home."

"The officers are there to watch for poachers, Malanga," Skye insisted. "They're trying to protect you. Please. I know you're hurting, but don't believe lies."

"It doesn't matter if it's a lie. People are bad. And I'm willing to bet you're bad too," Malanga replied, hatred seeping into her words.

Cassie's booming voice rang through the room. "You're bloody wrong. Perhaps other humans are bad, but not her." The giant bird paused and raised a three-toed foot, pointing one dangerous-looking claw toward Malanga. "Leave it off, or I'll kick your saggy bum."

The two animals began to advance toward each other. The foxes cheered, "Fight! Fight! Fight!"

Starion pounded his staff on the floor. "Stop. Now. That's quite enough."

Cassie dipped her head in respect and walked back toward the Australian delegates. Malanga lowered her head, snorting ferociously.

"Malanga?" Starion asked firmly. "Are you finished?"

Still snorting, Malanga moved back to her friends in the savanna ecosystem, giving Skye a hateful look as she went.

"That was your last warning, Dmitry," Starion snapped.

Tane hopped over to Skye and whispered, "Concentrate on Cassie's words."

While Skye felt elated about the cassowary's kind statement, she didn't blame Malanga for the anger. She hated poachers too, but she'd always believed the people who were to blame the most were the ones who bought the products made from rhino horns. If there were no market for illegal wildlife products, like ivory made from elephant tusks, there would be no money in it and hence no poachers.

"We must move on." Starion cleared his throat. "First, we will hear from our scheduled speakers concerning the threat that looms over them and the ecosystem they are representing. Our first speaker is a hawksbill sea turtle, a resident of Australia's Great Barrier Reef. He'll be speaking as a representative of coral reefs around the world. Please welcome Irwin."

There was a round of applause as a huge sea turtle pushed his way up out of an aquarium, leaned over the edge, and spoke into a microphone.

"It's a mess, that's what it is," the sea turtle huffed. "They killed the reef. The humans have killed the reef, and I'm not sure what we're going to do about it."

Using some colorful language, punctuated by a few four-letter words, Irwin described the oil spills, dredging, increased acidity of the oceans, warming temperatures, plastic pollutants, pesticides, and other chemicals spilled or dumped in the oceans. He described relatives burned alive at sea from fires set by oil companies trying to contain leaks, cousins washed up dead and covered in oil, a brother choked to death by a ring of plastic, his mother's sorrow at the babies lost forever — some eaten on shore by a pack of dogs, others collected by people and thrown into sacks.

The room was silent when Irwin finished.

Skye hung her head. Climate change was also to blame for the death of coral reefs around the world, but she doubted the animals understood just how serious it was.

Delegate after delegate gave speeches. Some were shaking with anger, while others seemed resigned to their fate. The stories were horrific: death, birth defects, suffering, habitat loss, and illness. All caused by humans.

"Where are we supposed to live?" trumpeted an Asian elephant.

"My home is gone," countered a red ruffed lemur from Madagascar.

"Mine too," squawked a scarlet macaw. "People came to my home in Brazil and cut down all the trees. They put my mate in a cage. I never saw her again."

"Save our rainforest," called a group of red-eyed tree frogs from Costa Rica.

Jackson, the polar bear, continued to interrupt, and Skye felt hopelessness crushing her.

One of the most poignant stories came from a little brown bat named Pim, shyly speaking in a slow Kentucky drawl, who told how exterminators had sprayed his entire family with chemicals. They'd been resting under the eaves of an abandoned, decrepit barn.

"We was sleeping," he squeaked softly. "Not bothering nobody. We was trying to be useful, eating all those 'squitoes that the people say carry that bad West Nile virus. Me and Fluff was having a contest to see who could eat the most. I gots six hundred in an hour, but Fluff, he gots a few more." A quaver in his voice, the bat continued, "But Fluff won't be gitting no more."

The room was quiet for several moments before he continued. "There was a lady with those exterminationers who said we was bad and ugly." Tears formed in the bat's eyes. "My momma used to say I was beautiful. My momma yelled for me to fly away before she fell down on the ground after they sprayed her. Then one of the men hit her with a shovel."

Skye began to shake with anger as the tiny bat continued.

"Then I went to the mine where my cousins live and my relatives was all dead except Aunt Mays. They all had a white yucky stuff over their noses and ears and on their wings. Aunt Mays says they came out of hibernation when it was still too cold and they starved cause there weren't no good bugs to eat. Aunt Mays yelled at me to leave and save myself and . . ."

Skye had heard about white-nose syndrome. A well-known bat conservation group was trying to find a cure for the deadly fungus that had already killed millions of bats. Skye whispered to Starion about the research.

"Pim," Starion said, "the people are trying to stop the illness, my small friend."

The bat's head drooped. "But they're too late. All my cousins are dead and I'm all alone." The bat began to cry in earnest before flying over to join some flying foxes that were easily a dozen times bigger.

Starion sighed sadly and motioned for Skye to come to the podium. "And now I think it's time to hear from Skye Van Bloem."

"Um . . . uh . . . hello," came a voice from the side of the room. "My name is Quyet and I want to speak."

The room exploded with heckles and calls to get on with it.

Starion pounded his staff once more. "Skye is scheduled to speak now. What is it you want to say, Quyet? Be fast."

"I . . . uh . . . I have something important to say."

"Then bloody well say it, you twit," yelled Cassie. "I thought monkeys were supposed to be smart." She ruffled her feathers in irritation.

Quyet reached for a bowl of leaves in front of him and stuffed several in his mouth, chewing slowly. "Uh . . . my name is Quyet."

Perched near the podium, Merry poked Pippin and Frodo, and together they burst into laughter.

"Merry, that's rude," Skye whispered.

"He's a weird animal with a weird name," Frodo replied. "Quit? What kind of name is that?"

"He needs to quit talking," Pippin added.

The three kea burst into laughter again. At least Sam was behaving himself.

"Quyet," Starion called out, "tell us where you're from and what you want to say."

There was a long pause.

"Look," shouted Pippin, "he fell asleep."

The monkey's eyes were shut, his long tail motionless. The crest of fur on the top of his head and the long cheek hairs obscuring his ears made him look like a stuffed toy. The black fur was gray-tipped, giving him a silvery appearance.

Cassie strode over to Quyet and pecked him with her beak. "Pay attention, monkey."

Eyes blinking slowly, Quyet reached again for the bowl of leaves. Cassie knocked the bowl to the floor with a resounding crash.

"This is ridiculous," muttered Starion. "Last chance, Quyet. Hurry. Up."

Scratching his furry underarm, Quyet said, "I'm a silvered leaf monkey from Vietnam. Sometimes I'm called a silvery lutung or a silvered langur." He held up his hands. "I have opposable thumbs." He pointed to his head. "I have a big brain."

"Bully for you," shouted Irwin.

"May I have some leaves?" Quyet asked in a sleepy voice.

"*No.*" The entire room shouted in unison.

Quyet frowned. "Did I say I'm from Vietnam?"

"*Yes.*"

"Oh . . . uh . . . I'm endangered."

"Most of us are," yelled Malanga.

"My family doesn't like people much, but there's a lot of people in Vietnam," Quyet continued. "We live on limestone hills cause there's not much forest left. It's steep, so the people can't live there, but you know what . . ." Quyet's voice trailed off as his eyes began to close.

Merry flew across the room and perched on Quyet's head. "Wake up. Miss Skye has to give her speech."

Quyet's eyes darted around the room. "There's a bird on my head."

"It's a bird that's going to bite you if you don't hurry up," said Merry. "*Quit* wasting time."

Up at the podium, Frodo and Pippin poked each other and laughed.

"People take limestone from the hills to make concrete," Quyet said. "When they're done, there's no hills left. It's all flat and then we have no home. The people call it mining." He paused. "Sometimes the people catch us and they eat us."

"They eat monkeys?" Merry asked, still perched on Quyet's head. "Yuck. Really yuck."

"There are poachers everywhere," shouted Malanga. "All the more reason to kill the humans."

Starion pounded his staff. "You spoke earlier, Malanga. You've had your chance. Quyet, that's a sad, sad story. Are you finished?"

"I vote to kill the humans." Quyet pointed a finger at Skye. "All of them."

The room was eerily silent as Merry flew back to a pale Skye. "He's really dumb, Miss Skye. Don't listen to him."

"What he said is true," Skye replied, her shoulders sagging. "But I wish he could meet Dr. O'Brien. He's spent years in the jungles of

Vietnam trying to save silvered leaf monkeys and Tonkin snub-nosed monkeys. They're super endangered."

"Am I endangered?"

"You're classified as nationally endangered, Merry. Kea numbers have been falling; there are less than five thousand of you. Some researchers think it's partly because you guys are always getting into things — like poisons from garbage and lead from roofing nails. But don't worry; the people of New Zealand take extraordinary measures to save their native birds and the Kea Conservation Trust is working on it."

Grumblings from the animals started anew and soon rose to an angry crescendo.

Starion pounded his gavel. "It's Skye's turn. Shut up and listen. I don't want to hear another word from anyone."

Please, Skye thought, *someone tell me the fate of the entire planet doesn't hinge on my words.*

She hoisted her backpack up onto the podium after Starion had climbed down, and she removed her speech notes. Taking out a small poster and unfolding it, she turned it toward the delegates. The huge screens flashed the poster's image around the room.

"This is a famous man who has tried to educate people about the problems facing our planet — especially climate change. He's made movies and written books about it. He wants to do something to help you."

The room was completely silent. A moment passed. Another. Then the room exploded in a mixture of jeers, heckles, and name-calling. A mango was lobbed at one of the screens displaying the poster.

Shaking, Skye stood at the podium, eyes shut tight, trying not to cry. She hadn't started and already she'd lost. Everyone knew the world was a mess. But what could she do? It wasn't fair. She didn't trash the planet. She did her best. Every. Single. Day.

Skye felt Starion take her hand. Opening her eyes, she stared down at him.

"I know you admire him," Starion said, indicating the poster with a flick of his head, "but don't use his words or his pictures. Use your own. I believe in you. Try again."

Starion held a furred paw up to the crowd. "Be seated everyone. It's Skye's turn to speak. Not another word from any of you."

As the room quieted down, Skye thought about all the people she loved. What was that NASA motto again? Oh yeah, failure is not an option. She adjusted her blazer and pulled her shoulders back. "I care deeply about this planet, and —"

"Why do you care? You're not human."

Everyone turned to the far-left corner. Out of the shadows, a shape emerged. As the cameras zoomed in, the overhead screens captured the image of a tall figure wearing a hooded black cloak.

"I say again," the figure continued, "you're not human. It's time to stop pretending."

Starion let out a low growl. "Oln."

Several things happened at once. Men in seafoam-green jumpsuits surrounded Starion and tightened a heavy tarnished-metal collar around his furry neck while two others moved toward Skye. Tane flew in front of Skye yelling for her to run. There was a loud pop followed by a thud, and Tane fell to the ground. Skye was vaguely aware of the noise in the room before a collar clamped around her neck and everything went numb. It was as though her entire body turned to jelly. She could see and hear, but she was powerless to move.

The black-robed figure loomed over Skye. Perched on his shoulder was . . . Sam? A kea, her favorite bird, had betrayed her? It made no sense. Sam was the one who'd attacked the gunman on the Milford Track.

The robed figure sneered down at Skye.

"Your Brilliance," said one of the uniformed men, "what shall we do with Starion?"

"Give him the serum."

Skye tried to protest but couldn't move any of her muscles — including the ones on her face. *Starion! What were they doing to him?*

A ringed thumb jabbed into Skye's gut. "I can see it in your eyes, your concern for that useless boy. Such a disappointment." Sam chuckled gleefully from his shoulder perch as the man barked, "Get her out of here."

Two men in green jumpsuits picked up Skye and threw a hood over her head. She felt herself being carried for what seemed like a long time. Finally, the hood was removed, and she was dumped unceremoniously onto a polished-metal platform — more a huge shiny box than a table. The men removed the collar and left. Her thoughts raced as she rubbed at her neck. The entire room, about twice the size of her living room back home, appeared to be made of rock — no windows, one solid metal door, and the silver-colored box.

It was only moments later when uniformed men dropped Starion on the hard-packed dirt floor, slamming the door behind them. Starion's collar was gone; he wasn't moving as Skye darted over to him, kneeling on the hard ground beside him. "Starion, wake up. Please wake up."

The prairie dog stirred, rolling over onto his chest. He slowly opened his eyes and, resting his chin on his paws, stared up at Skye.

"Are you —" Skye stopped midsentence as Starion's fur began to change shape in front of her. It was like a horrible sci-fi movie come to life as his body rolled and twisted, contorting, changing. It wasn't like before when, in a split second, he changed from one form to another. Groans of pain erupted from him, and then there was silence.

Starion, lying prone, with his chin propped on one hand, was completely naked. "Sorry about the presto-chango and for scaring you. Oln is evil for giving me that serum. It forces a rather ungraceful change and well . . ." He rolled over on his side, strategically hiding parts of his anatomy but indicating with one hand his nakedness, a grin firmly in place.

Trying to hide the blush spreading across her cheeks, Skye fought to come up with an appropriate comment. Nothing. She knew her face was probably the same color as her hair.

Before she could say anything, the door opened, and two guards dumped a man onto his knees, pulling the door closed behind them. Tane wore the same one-piece flight suit that he'd worn when Skye had first seen him in Australia. Standing, he reached out a hand. "Are you well, Skye?"

Ignoring his hand, Skye stood up. At six and a half feet, Tane was considerably taller than her. He turned to Starion, still sprawled on the floor. "Star, may I assist you?"

"It seems I have no clothes," Starion replied.

"Yes. Clearly he gave you the serum that returns us to our birth state."

Oh, Skye thought. *Guess Starion didn't do the naked thing on purpose.* Maybe that explained why he always went back to wearing the same clothes he'd had on before he turned into a prairie dog.

A chute opened above them, and a bundle of clothes dropped to the floor. Skye picked it up, throwing it at Starion before turning around. "Please get dressed so I can talk to you."

"Tane, mind telling me what happened?" Starion said.

"My forces were not aware that Oln was on the planet. Apparently, the kea Skye named Sam is not a kea after all. I take full responsibility."

Skye exhaled. Sam wasn't really a kea. It made her feel a little better.

"Skye, you can turn around now." Starion stood in front of her, barefoot, wearing black jeans, and holding a purple long-sleeved silk shirt, his chest pale and perfect. Dark ebony eyes peered out from behind strands of hair as he slowly put on his shirt, smiling seductively as he buttoned it.

Skye couldn't stop staring, but his little tricks were not going to work on her. Right now, she was more concerned with that man's statement that she wasn't human.

Before she could demand an explanation, the door opened, and in strode the man with the black robe, wearing dark glasses and with his hood partially hiding his face. Guards wearing seafoam-green jumpsuits flanked him. One tossed a pair of black boots at Starion.

Heated words in a language Skye didn't understand erupted from the man and were answered by Tane. Skye wasn't about to be left out of this. Holding up a hand, she said, "That's so rude. Speak English unless you want to teach me your language."

A bray of laughter escaped the man. "Very well, my dear."

"I'm not your dear anything." Skye stood in an aggressive stance—feet apart, arms loose but fingers clenched into fists, as she glared at the man.

"Well, well," Starion sneered as he turned to the hooded man. "If it isn't the great illustrious Prime Minister Oln." He waved his hand in the air mockingly. "Your Brilliance."

"Shut it now before I have my men put that collar back on you. I mean really, Starion. Is it such a chore to come home and do your royal duty? Your father agrees with me."

"Your English is quite good," Tane commented.

Starion raised an eyebrow. "Probably because he's been skulking around on this planet doing who knows what."

Skye nodded furiously.

"Perhaps I'm merely brilliant with languages," Oln answered smugly.

"Why are you here?" Starion demanded.

"I'm on a scientific mission aboard a Vanger agriculture ship. Imagine my surprise when I heard a rumor that you were not doing your duty. I felt it was my responsibility, as your father's faithful follower, to ensure his son was obeying orders. Naturally, when I contacted your father, he was grateful that I'm keeping a watchful eye on you. Let's have a chat, shall we?"

Oln motioned to his men to take Starion. As they dragged him from the room, Starion looked back over his shoulder at Skye. "I'll be right back."

"General Tane, you may leave for your ship. I would not want to keep a member of the Beholder military from performing his duty," purred Oln, a phony lilt to his voice.

"Is the female free to go?" Tane moved closer to Oln, and although Oln was tall, Tane still managed to look down at him.

"No."

Tane folded his burly arms over his chest. "I shall stay."

"Suit yourself. Enjoy the accommodations."

20
·······

"**W**here are we?" Skye asked, trying her best not to sound scared. Rob would have whipped out those knives of hers. Together they could have taken Oln down.

"We are still in the mountain, in the UEE complex," Tane answered. "There are dozens of rooms."

"Do you think the animals are OK?"

Tane gave Skye a pleased glance. "Yes, I am sure they are fine."

"Tell me everything," Skye demanded, the questions coming out in a heated rush. "First, why did that man say I wasn't human? You swore my father wasn't a Beholder. What is this royal duty? Who is that Oln person? Where did they take Starion? Why—"

Tane groaned. "Please, Skye. Starion will explain."

"Starion will not explain. You will. Please, Tane! Start at the beginning. I want it all, especially the part about whether you lied and my father really was a Beholder."

"I did not lie. Your father was not a Beholder."

Skye chewed at her bottom lip. Maybe that Oln guy was trying to insult her with that crack about not being human. "Let's have the rest of the story."

Exhaling with a long, weary breath, Tane began. "The two planets have a dependent relationship. My planet relies on Vanger for food-stuffs; they rely on us for other things, like ships to search for new agricultural samples. Therefore, we cannot simply ignore each other. King Magnus and Queen Opal, the rulers of Vanger, made a pact that the first-born child of their son Tarr would marry the first-born child of the Beholder rulers. Both sides hoped to end the constant bicker-ing through an arranged marriage. An edict was passed into law. It cannot be broken."

"An arranged marriage," exclaimed Skye. "That is so Middle Ages." She paused, looking thoughtful. "Wait. I'm confused. You mean the grandkid of the Vanger rulers is supposed to marry the kid of the Beholders? Doesn't the Vanger kid, what's his name . . . Tarr? Doesn't he get to rule?"

"No. Apparently, he did something that caused Magnus to refuse him the crown. It is widely known that Tarr is cruel and unpredictable. No one seems to know what he did, though it is likely that Oln does; he is the prime minister of Vanger. The crown passes through Tarr to his child."

"Who is?"

"Tempest, and she is quite spoiled. Her mother, Kemmie, is extremely beautiful, which is why Tarr married her, but I have heard rumors that Kemmie was, maybe still is, cheating on Tarr; half of Vanger gossips about it." He paused dramatically. "With Oln."

Skye gave Tane an exaggerated look of boredom. "Whatever. Half the politicians in my country are players."

"Who? They are what?"

"Never mind," Skye answered. "Who is Tempest supposed to marry?"

"The son of the Beholder rulers — King Pruet and Queen Anka."

Skye had a sickening feeling. She knew the answer before she asked it. "Who's the son?"

Tane looked toward the door and stiffened as he raked a hand through his close-cut black hair. "Prince Starion."

Skye sank to the floor, wrapping her arms around her legs. "His father is a scientist."

"Did he tell you that?"

"Not exactly, but he knew I thought so. He said his father was in charge of all this."

"He is," said Tane without any emotion. "Because he is the king."

"Starion's a prince," Skye mumbled to herself. Looking up at Tane, she repeated, "Starion's a prince."

"Yes. He is. He does not act like one, does he?"

Skye shook her head, not that she'd ever met an actual prince. What were they supposed to act like? Starion was a pompous, infuriating liar. Did he think she wouldn't find out he was a prince? That he was engaged? Did he think Skye would be his girlfriend on the side? The thought made her furious. He could just go back to his dumb planet and marry that dumb princess and have a dumb life with her.

Why did she feel terrible? Sure, he was gorgeous, but he was likely manufacturing that the same way he had the prairie dog façade. He was probably hideous, with a butt for a face and arms growing out of his back. You couldn't trust anything he said or did.

"Why doesn't Starion marry her?" Skye huffed.

Tane looked disgusted. "Starion dislikes the princess. He does not want to rule. On our planet, he is famous for his escapades. He has gotten into more trouble than any royal before him; nothing serious, mostly pranks. I think he just wanted his father to . . ."

Waving his hand rapidly as if to erase his last sentence, Tane continued. "When Starion was fourteen, his father sent him to Vanger for two years to study. Starion took to the planet and refused to come home. His father had to send someone to drag him back. Then Starion begged his father to send him on assignment to Earth. He was quite young, barely seventeen, when he arrived in New Zealand. He was supposed to be studying at the University of Otago, and helping with the UEE. He was in one of Professor Leven's classes. That is how they met, and it did not take Leven long to figure out what Starion was.

"Starion and the professor used to party nightly in a Dunedin pub called the Cloaked Sovereign. Their exploits became somewhat legendary. Starion's father heard about it and sent him to the United States because Americans are one of the top producers of the greenhouse gas emissions that are causing global warming and climate change. Starion was supposed to be studying the American humans as much as the animals while he organized the UEE."

"How long has he been in Colorado?"

"I believe a year or two."

"Can Starion assume any shape?"

"Yes and no. Technically it is possible, but he has to see the animal first and practice. Starion did just that while on Vanger. He is quite knowledgeable about behaviors of animals from several planets and has the somewhat rare ability to shift easily back and forth without a waiting period. For most of us, it takes several hours of resting before we can do it again. With some, it can take days. There is a serum, developed on Vanger, which prevents us from holding the shape of anything other than our actual true form. I am not sure how long the effects last."

"I heard Oln tell one of his men to give a serum to Starion."

"Yes, he was clearly given the serum since he reformed without clothes." Tane looked thoughtful. "This makes escape difficult, since the serum will prevent him from assuming any shape other than his real one."

Skye forgot how to breathe for a moment. "That's his real shape?" She'd meant it to sound casual, uncaring, but it didn't quite come out like that. She'd never believed that was his true form; it was just too perfect.

Tane smiled slightly before continuing. "Starion has a particular fondness for the fauna of your planet. His father wanted him to design Beholder cities, but though the prince is a gifted engineer, he was more interested in studying animal species." He shook his head. "And flying. Always the flight vehicles with him."

"Why has he been spying on me?" Her words did not come out as forcefully as she'd hoped.

Tane looked at the door then back at Skye, scratching his chin. "I believe he discovered you by accident. He is quite taken with you."

Skye waved her hand in a dismissive gesture. "I'm nothing compared to a princess—" She stopped abruptly. "Why does he call me princess?"

"I believe it is a term of affection. No doubt, he wishes it to be true. Tempest will be of age, eighteen, in a few months, and then Starion will be forced to marry her."

Skye felt like crying, or screaming, but she told herself she would not. Starion was a jerk who deserved to be married to a bratty princess.

Yep. A big jerk.

"I'm getting out of here," Skye stormed, walking around the room, inspecting the walls and the door, pushing on areas that looked different. She didn't want to think about Starion, so she'd concentrate on finding a way out.

Tane stood quietly watching her.

"Are you going to help me bust out of here?" she demanded. "Are you a general or not?"

A smile tugged at Tane's mouth. "I am beginning to understand what Starion sees in you."

"Are you making fun of me?"

"It is a compliment."

"Oh."

"There is no way out of here," Tane said.

"We're trapped?"

"Oln will not leave us in here."

The door opened, and in strode the man with the black hood again. "General Tane," Oln said smoothly, "I'm giving you another chance to leave for your ship." The man dropped the hood of his cloak and removed his glasses.

Skye gasped. He had thick, short hair, parted on the side, the color of a red poppy. The same color as her hair. His eyes were different colors — one a brilliant amethyst, the other black. Skye felt her knees grow weak.

No! Please! No!

"I'll stay," she heard Tane say. The red-haired man shrugged and left the room.

"His hair . . ." Skye could barely breathe.

Tane scrubbed at his chin. "Yes."

"But . . . but his eyes aren't the same color as mine." A strangled sound escaped Skye. "Are you implying that *he's* my father?"

"No. Of course not."

Skye broke out in a sudden sweat. She knew where this was going.

Tane exhaled loudly. "Most Vangers have red hair, though many choose to dye it — like one of the Vangers I put under arrest and most of Oln's men, it seems. Mismatched eyes are typical among Vangers. Your blue-green is a common color. You are obviously part Vanger. I say part because no Vanger ever had dark-green eyes."

"No." Skye shook her head vigorously. "No, no, *no*. My father was a Dutch botanist; my mother was an American animal behaviorist. They both had blond hair. I cannot be a Vanger."

"I believe your mother had forest-green eyes, did she not?"

Skye froze. That meant her father . . .

Tane shook his head. "It is best if I say no more. Starion should be the one to tell you."

Skye ranted at Tane until he told her the truth. "Your father was from Vanger. There are dyes which can color red hair."

"No, there aren't," Skye insisted. "Not my hair. I've tried. It doesn't work. If my father's hair was the same as mine, he wouldn't have been able to color it either. He was blond."

"Katrina showed me a picture of him, taken on Vanger, when he was young. He had the same hair color as yours. There is a botanical, not found on your planet, which can permanently color Vanger hair."

"But . . . why would he do that? He told me my hair was beautiful. He must have secretly hated it if he colored his own."

Tane frowned. "He was clearly in hiding and probably trying to pass for Dutch. Your hair color is widely recognized as being desirable. I am sure your father loved the very thing he could not have. You would have been safer had he colored it, but I suspect he could not bring himself to do it."

Skye grasped a strand of her hair and stared down at it. She set angry eyes on Tane. "I asked you, both of you, if he was a Beholder and you said no."

"He was not a Beholder."

"But that's a half-truth. You should have told me the real truth." Skye sank to the floor. "I'm an alien."

"Why should that make any difference?" Tane gave her a disapproving glance as he crossed his muscled arms over his chest. "I am one of those aliens, Skye. So is Starion. It does not mean I have horns growing out of my back."

"But you don't understand," wailed Skye. "Everything I thought I was is a lie. I'm not human. I don't know who I am." She put her head in her hands and tried not to burst into tears.

Tane sat on the floor beside her and put an arm across her shoulder. "Are there people on your planet who are adopted? When they find out who their real parents are does that instantly turn them into something else?"

"No. But . . . does Starion know I'm not human?"

"Of course. Anyone from our planet would only have to look at you to know you are part Vanger. It is not only the eyes and the hair. Your skin has a subtle glow peculiar to Vangers; it gives you away. And of course, there is your speed."

"Why didn't he tell me?"

"Because it does not make a difference, and I suspect Katrina forbid it. Clearly, she was a good friend to your father since he trusted you to her care. She is also quite brilliant — her botany texts are still used at several universities."

"My Oma?" Skye exclaimed. "But she talks to flowers and you're telling me she's brilliant?"

Tane quirked an eyebrow. "She is not just someone who washes your clothes and makes you dinner. As for talking to flowers, have you listened to what she is saying?"

"Uh . . . no."

"Maybe you should. Starion says she talks to your parents, not the flowers. Everyone grieves differently."

"You're right." Skye felt her cheeks flushing. All this time she'd been suffering through her parents' death and Oma had had no one. "She insists she's protecting me."

Tane ran a hand over his close-cropped hair. "Maybe she was trying to prevent Oln from killing you."

"What?"

"Calm down. I will protect you."

Skye jumped up and began to pace. "Super . . . just great . . ."

"Perhaps Oln was behind all these attempts on your life, though I have no idea why he would want to kill you. Perhaps his minions were so incompetent he had to take care of you himself. Perhaps he intends to use you to get something from Starion. Perhaps your father had a history with Oln and it is about payback."

"That's a lot of perhaps," Skye retorted.

"I admit to being confused. Katrina could answer some questions about you. Also, she would have known Sam was an imposter and not a kea."

"How?"

"Katrina has a rare ability among Beholders. She is a shapeseer. She can detect other Beholders in any animal form. Even Starion cannot do that."

"Oh . . . that's right. Starion told me."

Tane sat drumming his thumb on his leg. "Perhaps Starion can make sense of this."

Tane and Skye passed the time telling stories. Skye talked about her home and her friends Henry and Janine. She told Tane how the three of them had become best friends while on a field trip in the sixth grade. They had ditched the group and gotten lost in the Rocky Mountains for an entire night. As darkness fell and the temperature plummeted, the three became uneasy, then frightened. Janine tried to convince herself that search teams would see their tracks, find the scarf she'd accidentally dropped, and rescue them. Unafraid of the woods, Skye assured Janine and Henry that no wild animals would eat them, even telling her friends funny animal stories. Henry, steering them toward a sheltered group of pines, wrapped his skinny arms around both girls. When Janine began to shake, afraid that big spiders were going to climb on her, Henry sang for them, trying to distract Janine, who was several years younger than he and Skye.

The search team found them the next afternoon. The three were hungry and cold, but well. The incident was a bonding experience that convinced them they were a team. They'd been inseparable ever since.

Tane told Skye stories about Starion's antics as a child. Skye's favorite was the one about the baby jufons. Tane described the adults as frightening beasts, eight feet tall with massive wingspans, pointed horns with glowing yellow tips, and mouths full of razor-sharp teeth. Covered in long pale-yellow and orange-tan scales, jufons sported six-toed feet with ten-inch daggers for claws. They had short, stubby arms, long tails, and bright-orange eyes. Skye thought they sounded like an exaggerated version of a flying carnivorous dinosaur. Then there were the babies — tiny, defenseless creatures with stubs for wings and no teeth. They sounded . . . cute.

When Starion was eleven, he captured seven baby jufons, releasing them into the classrooms of his school late at night. The next morning, when the teachers arrived, they discovered havoc. The tiny beings were famous for their repulsive-smelling excrement that required clean-up crews to wear protective gear. The school closed for over a week. Starion became an instant hero to the students and a pariah to several of the teachers, including Skye's Oma. The school's president expelled Starion for the remainder of the term, embarrassing his father, King Pruet.

"What is Starion's mother like?" Skye asked.

"Queen Anka is famous for her parties and one in particular, which was held when Starion was about nine. He allowed a creature similar to your horse to run loose in the manor, breaking furniture, overturning food tables, and finally splashing punch all over the Queen's new gown."

Skye tried not to laugh. "What did his mom do?"

"She was furious of course, but if she spent even a fraction of the time on Starion as she did on her parties and clothes, he would have had a much better childhood. King Pruet beat Starion over that incident." Tane paused. "A doctor had to be called."

"That's child abuse." Skye was horrified.

"You cannot be punished if no one finds out. The King was careful to hide the abuse, and Starion told only me — and not until years later. He was a tough kid in many ways. When he was about thirteen, he started suffering from seizures. No one knew what caused them, but I do not think he has had any for several years now."

"Did King Pruet beat Starion when he let those jufons loose?"

Tane gave Skye a sad look.

Exhausted, Skye reasoned it must already be the next day. She finally dozed off, slumped on the hard ground. She woke, disoriented, when the door flew open and several uniformed men dumped a disheveled Starion on the floor. His silk shirt ripped, with a cut on his right cheek, Starion shook violently as he curled up in a fetal position, clutching his head between both hands.

21
·······

"**S**tarion!" Skye bent over Starion, whose body was quaking with spasms. All thoughts of the nasty words she'd planned to toss at him evaporated. "Tane, what's wrong with him?"

Tane lifted up one of Starion's eyelids; a dark eye rolled backward, unseeing. Sitting on the floor, Tane pulled Starion into his lap, gripping him tightly around the shoulders and waist. "Star, Star," he intoned in the kind of soft voice usually reserved for children. "I am here, my friend."

Skye stood by helplessly while Tane rocked a moaning Starion in his lap.

"They tortured him," Skye snarled.

Tane shook his head. "Except for the cut on his cheek, there are no marks."

"But look at him!"

Tane gently brushed matted hair from Starion's forehead. "I have seen these seizures before. It may be a while before he is able to communicate with us."

As Starion moaned in pain, Tane held his friend gently, reassuring him.

Eventually, Starion fell silent and dropped his hands to his sides. Hiding his face in Tane's shoulder, he peered out at Skye through a veil of tangled hair. When Skye smiled at him in relief, he quickly looked away.

"Starion, what's wrong? Aren't you better?"

When Starion didn't respond, Tane said, "He is embarrassed."

"That's ridiculous. He's been hurt. Why would he be embarrassed?"

Starion's muffled voice spoke into Tane's shoulder. "Because it's an embarrassing disease that only the weak get."

"Stop it, Star. That is your father talking," Tane scolded.

"Is it a disease like epilepsy?" Skye asked. "With seizures?"

"No, it is not like any of your Earth diseases," said Tane, lifting Starion's shoulders and resting his forehead against Starion's forehead.

"I thought the disease was gone," Starion sputtered.

"It is not a disease; I told you that years ago. You have not had a single attack since being on Earth. Think about it. And you never had any the entire time you were on Vanger."

"I can't think about it, Tane. That's the problem," Starion said, his voice barely a whisper. "When I try to think during an attack it gets worse. I've told you before; it's as though my skull is cracking in half and my insides are boiling. Whatever thoughts were there . . . they're gone. I've tried to get them back, but it can cause another attack, so I've learned to let it go."

The door opened and Oln walked in. "My dear Prince Starion, are you well?"

Starion rose unsteadily to his feet, assisted by Tane. "What do you want?"

"I came to make sure you were well. I didn't want the young lady to think I'd harmed you in any way." Oln's finely chiseled face held mock concern.

Skye glared at Oln and crossed her arms over her chest.

"I explained it to her," said Tane.

"Why thank you, General," said Oln, moving directly in front of Starion, taking his left hand out from under his cloak. A pulsing yellow light reflected from a ring as he reached up to casually scratch the side of his face.

Starion gasped and fell to the floor, convulsing, his arms and legs jerking wildly.

"Starion!" shouted Skye. "Tane, do something."

Tane quickly knelt down next to Starion and rolled him onto his side. "Stay back, Skye," Tane ordered.

Ten minutes later, Skye and Tane were still watching Starion to make sure he didn't hurt himself as the wild thrashing continued, his eyelids fluttering spasmodically. Skye was convinced it wasn't epilepsy. She'd never heard of such a violent attack that went on for so long. Oln had left, a smug look on his face as he gently rubbed his ring, which had a five-sided figure containing a glowing sun symbol on it and held a yellow gem.

Starion finally stopped convulsing. He resumed his earlier fetal position, head in his hands. Tane rocked him gently in his lap as before. Once again, Skye stood helplessly by.

There was a knock on the door, and a guard entered with a heavy tarp and a small clear tube that resembled a syringe. "Oln says this will help him sleep."

Tane took the items, and when Starion began to relax his body slightly, releasing the death grip on his head, Tane jabbed the tube into Starion's arm.

"I can't believe you did that," gasped an exhausted Skye. "There could be poison in that."

"I recognize the compound; it has a distinct color and luminescence. It is a common sleep aid used on our planet. The prince needs rest. Besides, if Oln wanted us dead, we would be dead, and although King Pruet does not particularly like Starion, he would execute Oln if he killed his only son. As much as Oln wants to believe it, he does not have the run of the planet."

Tane moved Starion, who was now quiet but still trembling, out of his lap and onto the floor. Skye took off her expensive blazer, wadded it up without a second thought, and placed it under Starion's head. She draped the heavy brown tarp over Starion, brushing the hair from his face. It was as soft as she'd imagined. "I think he's asleep, but he's really cold. And he's still shaking."

Tane nodded and leaned against the wall.

After a slight hesitation, Skye scooted under the tarp and wrapped her arms around Starion.

Skye had fallen asleep — for how long she didn't know. Waking on the hard ground, she rolled over and stared into deep-black eyes. "Are you OK, Starion?"

"Yes. I'm sorry that —"

Skye put a finger to his lips. "You shouldn't apologize for being sick. It's not your fault."

"I need to tell you something."

Before he could begin, Skye kissed him — quickly. Really quickly. With a closed mouth and open eyes. But it was a kiss nonetheless, Skye's first. So yeah, it was kind of a big deal.

A *really* big deal actually.

Skye was full of conflicting emotions. *He was dishonest and spied on me, but he protected me. He's supposed to marry a princess, but maybe he won't. He looks at me as if he cares for me. Should I trust him? Should I smack him? He's funny, clever, smart, sweet . . . He loves animals and is unbelievably gentle. He's even a vegetarian.*

Starion stared at her, wide eyed, before an enormous grin broke across his face. The man was unbelievably good looking, but with that smile, there was something else. Despite the pain he'd been through, happiness seemed to explode out of his dark eyes, filling them with light. He didn't try to kiss her back, as she'd expected, just gazed at her with those tender eyes, his smile increasing.

Skye giggled, and then covered her mouth in embarrassment.

"Skye." Starion tucked a strand of red hair behind her ear. "I need to tell you something and . . . uh . . . I hope you'll—"

The door flew open, and then Oln was staring down at Skye and Starion. An angry look crossed his face. "What's going on here?"

"Nothing now, thanks to your impeccable timing," groaned Starion.

"Get away from him," demanded Skye, sitting up, attempting to push Starion behind her. "He gets sick every time you're around him. Don't pretend you didn't do anything because we all know you did."

"Nonsense," Oln sneered, reaching down and grabbing Starion's head between his hands. "The boy is fine."

"Let. Me. Go."

"Or what?" Oln released his grip on Starion. "Your father has a message for you. Guards, bring him."

Skye flew to her feet and, without thinking, threw a fist at Oln. He caught her wrist and twisted it.

"Let me go!"

Oln released her with a laugh.

"Keep your hands off her, Oln," Starion shouted as two guards dragged him from the room.

"He better not come back convulsing," Tane threatened. "His father is going to be displeased when I report your actions."

"My dear general," Oln said, "King Pruet will be thankful for my watchful supervision, and I did nothing to harm the boy. It is not us you should blame for the prince's unfortunate condition."

"What does that mean?"

"What indeed?" Oln taunted. "It is not the Vangers who are the evil ones here, but the Beholders and their secret Vijfhoek group. Your own King Pruet is paying off delegates to vote against the humans, even spreading false information to influence the vote. To what end? We have always been able to take resources and move on; conquest implies ruling, and that has never been a goal. Vanger has never been interested in interfering in the affairs of other planets. I suggest, as a Beholder yourself, you find out why your planet is determined to pursue this course of action now."

Oln wheeled around to face Skye. "And you, the poor unfortunate half Vanger. Do you realize the prince is under orders from his father to bring back two humans? It is quite likely the Beholders will make science experiments out of the unfortunate pair. But wait, you know this. Why, you helped the prince by bringing your two friends."

"Starion wouldn't do that."

"Wouldn't he now? General Tane, what were the prince's orders in this?"

"Maybe those were the original orders, but he is not —"

"Are you implying that the prince was going to commit treason?"

"No, of course not, I merely . . . what I meant to say was . . ." Tane stammered.

Oln laughed loudly; the sound felt like a jolt through Skye. Still laughing, Oln shut the door.

"He's lying, right?" asked Skye, rubbing her wrist. "Please tell me Oln was lying about kidnapping my friends."

"Starion was going to tell you."

22

Only a few minutes passed before two Vanger guards tossed Starion back in the cell. He immediately fell to the ground, clutching his side.

"You've got fifteen minutes." Oln slammed the door behind him.

Skye's words were full of anger. "I want a yes or a no. No excuses. No explanations. Were you on assignment to take Henry and Janine, my best friends, back to your planet? Were they going to be science experiments?"

"Not exactly."

"Not exactly," Skye repeated, pointing an accusing finger at Starion. "That's all you have to say? I can't believe I felt sorry for you. And I take that kiss back." She glared at him and spit out the words. "Your Majesty."

Starion flinched. "I'm sorry I didn't tell you who I was."

"You're only sorry because I found out. And what is your excuse for not telling me my father was a Vanger?"

"Why does it matter?"

Skye furrowed her brow. "You don't think I'd want to know I was an alien?" She shook a wad of her hair at him. "That explains this awful color. I don't know who I am anymore."

"You're Skye Van Bloem—an amazing, compassionate woman whom I care for deeply. And your hair is the most gorgeous color in the universe."

"Shut up!"

Starion attempted to walk toward Skye, but it was more like crawling. Every movement caused his face to contort in pain. *How can I yell at him when he's been hurt?* With a groan of defeat, she said to Tane, "Tell him to hold still and I'll come see if he has any broken ribs. I can tell with animals, so maybe I can with people too."

Tane gave Starion a stern look as Skye approached.

"Hold still and don't even think about touching me." Skye found one rib she thought might be broken, maybe two. "How can Oln get away with this when Starion's father is the king?" She glanced from one man to the other. When neither one responded, she demanded, "What kind of father allows this? That is just sick."

"What should I say, Skye?" Tane said. "Short of permanent damage, the king appears to be remarkably unconcerned about his son. It could be that Oln was truthful when he said the king knew he was watching Starion."

"I don't know which is more sickening: that he allows it or that nobody speaks up about it." She shook her head in disgust.

"Help me sit up." Starion winced in pain. "I would never allow Janine and Henry to be hurt, Skye." He paused. "The vote is rigged—my father is paying off delegates and circulating false information about the humans. He intends to destroy the humans with the virus."

"We know; Oln already told us," Tane replied. "Now tell us what happened with Oln."

Before Starion could begin, Skye narrowed her gaze at him. "You're out of chances. I want the truth."

"Oln gave me a communicator pad with a message from my father. The note was short: Take vote immediately; wedding date is set for next festival."

Looking away, Skye felt her face redden.

"Skye, I —"

"I don't care," Skye sputtered, facing Starion, but not looking at him directly. "You can marry whoever you want."

"He does not want to marry her," Tane said. "However —"

"But does she want to marry him?" There was a long uncomfortable pause. Skye glanced from one to the other. "Does she love you, Starion?"

Starion shrugged.

"I see."

"I don't love her, Skye, and I'm not marrying her," Starion said. "I've been in tight spots before. Like when Father refused to send me to Earth. But yet, here I am."

Tane coughed.

"With help from Tane," Starion added. "Father isn't going to get his way this time. I'm not marrying Tempest and I won't let him destroy Earth. I care about you, Skye. I care about your friends."

"The edict is law, Star," Tane said.

"Laws were made to be broken," Starion retorted.

Tane frowned. "Not this one."

"There it is," Skye said, throwing her hands up. "That's why he's trying to kill me. He thinks you won't marry that princess because of me."

Starion turned to Tane. "I've never discussed Skye with anyone, except you, Katrina, and Richard. How could Oln know I care about her?"

"You say you care about me," Skye said, "But yet you didn't tell me I'm part Vanger. You must know about my father." She crossed her arms over her chest. "Well? Did you?"

Starion gave Tane a cautious look. "Your father, Pieter, was the younger son of Queen Opal and King Magnus, the rulers of Vanger."

Skye's mouth dropped. "Am I a princess?"

"No," Tane and Starion replied in unison.

"It does not work that way on Vanger," Tane added. "Vangers have only one child; it is not the law exactly, but people follow it. A second child is automatically cut from any claims to property or titles as a way of discouraging more children. Though he was probably loved, I am afraid your father was simply a playmate to Prince Tarr and nothing more."

"Obviously, since my real grandparents never cared about me either," Skye replied bitterly.

"I do not think they know about you," Tane suggested.

"I never heard them mention you while I was on Vanger," Starion replied.

"You know them?"

Starion nodded. "They aren't bad people."

"Whatever," Skye said. "But Tarr isn't going to rule, right?"

"And we're all thankful for that," answered Starion. "Tarr's seriously disturbed."

"Get to what Oln said," Tane replied impatiently.

"He told me to go home and marry Tempest. He said in exchange, he'd let Skye live as long as Kemmie thinks she's dead."

"See," Skye retorted, "I'm right."

"Why did Oln break your ribs?" Tane asked.

"I may have called him the evil villain of Vanger and accused him of wanting me to marry Tempest so he and his mistress, the vain Princess Kemmie, could control her and, through us, rule both planets."

Tane groaned.

Skye stared at Starion. "Why would you say that? You must have known he'd hurt you. Cause apparently evil dad doesn't care."

Tane shook his head in resignation. "He does not think before he speaks."

"Oln says he's the only one who can negotiate with Father to abandon this planet." Starion smiled weakly at Skye. "He gave me fifteen minutes to say good-bye to you."

"But," Skye stammered, "does he think—"

Terrified shouts resonated from the hallway, interrupting Skye. Screams preceded shrieks of pain. It sounded as though a war were going on outside their door as shots were fired and soon were followed by several crashes. Cries and the pounding of running feet split the air. An odd growling noise rose above the chaos. Finally, everything was quiet.

Wild pounding vibrated the door.

"What is going on out there?" Tane demanded.

"Stand away from the door," came a familiar voice.

Tane pushed Skye toward the far wall, dragging Starion with him and wrapping his body over both. A boom reverberated through the room as the door exploded inward, blowing pieces across the room.

"Are you all right?" Tane asked.

Skye and Starion nodded as they rose unsteadily to their feet, Starion leaning on Tane. In the door stood Jackson the polar bear, and on his shoulders perched three kea. Two capuchin monkeys held weapons that looked like grenade launchers; dropping them, they ran off down the hallway.

"Where's the president?" asked the polar bear.

Skye pointed at Starion. "Don't tell the others. OK?"

Jackson scratched one ear in confusion, staring at Starion.

"Please, Jackson," Skye implored. "Don't tell them he's not really a prairie dog."

The polar bear nodded reluctantly.

"Miss Skye," called Merry, holding a small oval container in one foot. "Frodo, Pippin, and I are here to save you."

"I'm here too. Don't forget me," whined the polar bear.

"And PBJ too," the kea shouted in unison.

Each kea held an aqua-colored oval disc, about the size of a quarter, in their claws. Jackson's white fur was dotted with red. A putrid smell of excrement and electricity permeated the hall, flowing into the room.

"Where did you get those transport modules?" Tane barked at the kea, motioning at the three discs.

"Where is the general?" asked Frodo.

"I am the general, you insufferable birds. Answer the question."

"I took it out of the guard," said Pippin proudly.

Skye swallowed loudly. "Is that blood on your feathers?"

Frodo strutted along the polar bear's wide shoulders. "I got mine out of the guard after PBJ ripped his arms off."

"Me too," chimed in Merry.

Skye sat down abruptly, her face pale.

Attempting to squat down next to Skye, Starion instead fell to the floor with a groan of pain. "Skye, the guards were going to kill you."

"I . . . I thought no animal could harm another because of some weird force-field thing."

Starion put his arm around Skye. "It doesn't include humans, Vangers, or Beholders."

"Come," urged Tane. "We must leave before Oln returns." He turned to the three kea. "We already have transport modules, you dense birds."

Pippin made a rude gesture at Tane after the man had turned his back. Merry and Frodo thumped wings and laughed quietly.

The entire group moved out of the room and down the hall, with Starion directing the way while leaning heavily on Tane. Skye covered her nose and mouth with one hand as she stumbled forward. Jackson brought up the rear as the kea flew about looking for more guards. The halls were empty except for the signs of the fight; blood and other bodily fluids decorated the floors and walls. Bodies lay in heaps. Two mangled arms rested against a wall.

"Look," Pippin said, pointing with one foot to a side room.

Sprawled in a pool of blood, lying face up, was a chubby, balding man with small black eyes. His asymmetrical face showed surprise. One hand was thrown out to the side. His ring finger was a bloody stump.

"You didn't kill him, did you?" Skye asked.

"No," all three kea answered in unison.

Tane looked into the room and frowned. "He is a Beholder Council member named Chee. I believe he is under investigation for misdirection of funds from Vanger food shipments. He was, I believe, the one pretending to be the kea named Sam."

"I'm sure he was working with Oln," said Starion. "I always knew Oln was a thief. He probably sent Chee after Skye."

"And then killed him," Tane said. "Maybe this is a Vijfhoek plot. I have heard Chee was a member."

"Who's the Vijfhoek?" Skye asked. "Oln used that word."

"I only know it is a secret organization run by Starion's father, King Pruet."

Skye turned to Starion.

"Don't look at me," Starion said. "I don't know anything about them. Let's go. We've got to get back to Leven's and then up to the ship to disable that virus."

"Why Leven's?" Skye asked.

"I need to get my secret weapon for disabling the virus." He scratched his forehead. "I *hope* it's my secret weapon. I have to check some drawings first."

"What's —"

"Later," Tane commanded. Assuming point position, he motioned for the polar bear to be his rear guard while the three kea surrounded Skye, who was supporting Starion. Holding a sleek gun he'd taken from a dead guard, Tane burst through a door at the end of the hall. A half dozen of Oln's guards immediately began firing weapons. Tane rolled to the ground, twisting, and took out three guards in rapid succession.

Starion clutched Skye tightly with his free arm, his face contorted in pain, as he attempted to turn her away from the fight.

Gunfire echoed around the room as the polar bear began dismembering a fourth guard, who shrieked in pain. The three kea descended on the fifth as Tane downed the last.

Attempting to remove transport modules, the kea ripped at dead guards. The polar bear wiped blood off his muzzle, licking his enormous paws delicately.

"Let me go," Skye mumbled to Starion, who released his grip on her. He hobbled over to the computer consoles lining the walls. Three-dimensional maps of places around the globe lit up several screens. Smoke curled out of sections of a paneled grid.

"Get over here, Tane." Starion pointed to a blackened section of the grid that had been hit by gunfire.

Tane groaned. "With that panel knocked out, we cannot do position-to-position transport on the surface. Our modules will only get us to my ship or the transport control ship, and there will be a record of everything, including our destination. Fortunately, I was able to delete the previous logs. It is likely Oln has his men on the TCS, in which case your father must be giving him permission to do so. Oln could be monitoring transport to my ship as well. I do not know what is going on, but we cannot let Oln get the coordinates of Leven's apartment." Tane began typing rapidly on a console on the far wall. "I am sending a message to Leven to send a chopper to meet us at the trailhead of the Milford Track. I am also getting a message to a couple of my men to go to the TCS. Everyone is supposed to have authorization to transport, but I suspect Oln is somehow bypassing that. He needs to be stopped immediately."

"Fine. Let's get going," Starion said, falling to the floor with a moan.

Skye rushed over to help him up, saying angrily to Tane, "There's no way he can walk back to the start of the trail."

"He can if the serum has worn off. Unlike most of us, Starion can change form even when he is hurt, and when he changes back to human form that usually heals most injuries. Has the serum worn off, Star?" Tane asked.

Starion shut his eyes and took a deep breath. Opening them, he nodded, then gritted out, "Let's destroy that virus."

23
....

The polar bear, like the other animal delegates, was not able to leave the building because of the transport tags. The devices acted as containment units, and they couldn't be removed by the animals themselves.

Skye was hesitant about leaving Jackson, but Starion insisted the animals would be safe. Tane assured Skye, once again, that King Pruet would never allow the virus to kill his only son. Therefore, the humans were also safe.

For now.

"But the animals —"

"Skye, they will be fine. Beholders and Vangers are vegetarians and value animal life," replied Tane.

"Yeah, right, and I'm a math genius," she snapped.

Since the kea were untagged and not a part of the UEE, they would be able to go with them. Pippin brought Skye's backpack to her, which he had retrieved from under Starion's podium.

"But, I have to give my speech," Skye insisted. "Don't I?" She removed her speech papers from her backpack and stared at them. One torn corner had clearly fallen victim to a kea beak.

Tane and Starion gave each other a look before Tane said, "Perhaps, but the mission has now changed."

Skye hugged Jackson and wondered if she would see him again.

"Be safe, little girl," Jackson said to her. "I'll miss you."

Skye waved good-bye and blew Jackson a kiss. He pretended to catch it, and then put it in his mouth, chewing with exaggerated motions, his lips raising up, showing his big teeth.

"Bye, PBJ," the kea shouted in unison.

"You're scary," yelled Pippin.

As soon as the group cleared the building, Tane said to Starion, "Change, my friend."

"Skye, would you like to go for a ride?" Starion asked, grinning despite the pain.

"Just so you know: I'm still mad at you."

Starion exhaled loudly. "I swear I would never hurt your friends, and I'm going to do everything I can to save your planet. Give me another chance. Please?"

"Maybe."

"I have a plan to save Earth, but I'm going to need some schematics of the ship and some technical advice to double-check my figures."

Tane nodded. "I have people working on it now."

Starion began to change. When he did, what stood before Skye was not a prairie dog but a huge midnight-black horse with a silky flowing mane. In the center of the animal's forehead was a single white star-shaped patch. The animal had immense black eyes — Starion's eyes.

Skye gasped as years of confusion evaporated. She finally understood. No wonder she'd felt a connection to all those animals over the years. Though each animal had been different, the eyes were always the same. They had always been Starion's eyes. The rabbit on her sixteenth birthday, the mouse that lived in a shoe box in her living room, finally a prairie dog . . . always the same eyes.

Starion's eyes.

"You were the rabbit. And the mouse. And . . . the things I told you . . ." *Her deepest fears. Her secrets.*

The horse whinnied and pawed the ground.

"I am not getting in the middle of this. I will meet you at the trailhead." Tane was a kea again and rose into the sky with the other three birds.

"Climb on, Skye." Starion's voice seemed odd coming from the body of the stallion. He knelt down on one front leg.

Skye backed up slightly, her arms tightly folded across her chest, and shook her head.

"You were so sad," Starion said quietly. "Katrina said I could stay and be a friend, but only if I remained an animal and helped protect you." He paused. "I'm sorry I didn't tell you who I was."

Skye remained silent. She was too emotionally exhausted to argue right now. And embarrassed. Her mind raced. The things she'd said . . .

"Skye, please," Starion begged. "I know what you're thinking. You never said anything that I didn't experience myself. You must know by now how I feel about you."

Skye continued to stare at the ground, arms folded tightly across her chest.

"Skye, we need to go."

After some hesitation, she climbed on.

"Don't let go," Starion said.

"I've been riding since I was seven," she mumbled.

"I'm not a horse. I copied this from another planet I visited." He spread enormous wings out from the undersides of his body, fanning them rapidly as he climbed into the sky.

Looking at the ground pass below her, Skye forgot her embarrassment for a moment. She was riding a flying horse. Like in a Disney movie. With a prince. And talking animals.

This was utterly impossible. But wait. Hadn't everything been since she met Starion? She was sure he was being truthful about Oma making him stay an animal; she wasn't sure if she was mad about that anyway, though she was distressed, thinking of things she'd said. In a way, she was glad to know — at last — what had happened to the little mouse. If only he hadn't lied about Janine and Henry. How could she forgive that? She was exhausted, shaken by all she'd seen. She wanted to go home to Colorado.

Attend the university. Have a life. Be normal. Forget about all this. She'd never see Starion again.

The thought tied up her insides, made her nauseous. She didn't want to feel like that. She wanted to hate him. But . . .

Skye clutched Starion tightly as he rose higher and higher. In the distance, she could see the rugged grandeur of the fiord with its deep blue water surrounded by mountains. It was the most spectacular scenery she'd ever seen, perfect and untouched in its palpable beauty.

The sun was descending, and fingers of pink and orange paraded across the western sky. The air was bitterly cold. Starion had wrapped Skye in a thick parka as they'd left the UEE structure, but she didn't want to think about where the coat had come from. Maybe a dead guard? Her cheeks were stinging from the wind and cold, her fingers becoming stiff despite the gloves, but she didn't want the ride to stop. She continued wrestling with her feelings for Starion even as she clutched him tightly.

Soon they overtook Merry, who flapped along beside them for a minute and finally perched gracefully on Starion's back. "Isn't this fun, Miss Skye?"

"It is, Merry." Gripping Starion's neck tightly, Skye rested the side of her head on his soft mane. Was that the sound of the wind or a chuckle?

When they descended, a short distance from the head of the track, Tane was waiting in his human form. "That is it for me. I will not be able to change form until tomorrow."

Sliding down Starion's back, Skye couldn't resist the urge to pet him, forgetting — in her exhaustion, for a brief second — that he was Starion and not a magnificent flying horse. "Absolutely gorgeous," she murmured.

Before she realized it, she was stroking Starion's hair. Starion was back in human form.

"I'm gorgeous, huh?"

Skye tried to cover her embarrassment with a frown.

"I hear the chopper," Tane said. "Ribs OK, Star?"

"They're fine."

Skye turned to the three kea resting in a tree above her.

"I'm going to miss you," she said to the birds as they flew down to perch on her shoulders.

Merry leaned over and gave Skye a peck on the cheek. "I would vote not to kill the humans, Miss Skye."

"Me too," chimed in Frodo.

Pippin spread his wings around Skye's neck. "Me three."

Skye tried to speak, but no words came out. She gave each bird a kiss on the top of the head. Merry was last, and Skye whispered to him, "You saved my life, Merry. You're the smartest bird in the *whole* world."

Merry beamed.

Starion bowed low before the three birds. "We owe you our lives. Your help will not be forgotten."

All three birds rose gracefully into the air, the undersides of their wings flashing a brilliant orange in the darkening sky. Their cries could be heard even when they flew out of sight.

Keeeaah.

Skye ran to Dylan, who was standing next to the chopper—its bright lights illuminating the area. "How's Henry? Is he OK?"

"Yes," Dylan replied. "Recovering well; minor injury according to the doc. Henry's a good mate. Your other friend was hovering, stuffing food down him, ordering him about. She's a bossy one for such a pretty lady."

Skye smiled. "She is. Pretty, I mean. Bossy too, I guess, but it's because she cares about Henry."

"We're meeting everyone back where I picked you up in Queenstown," Dylan continued. "There's a landing pad on the roof. The professor says Starion will give the pilot directions." He motioned at the pilot. "This is Tim."

Tane, Dylan, and Skye climbed into the rear of the chopper. Starion motioned for the pilot to move to the left seat.

"Starion," warned Tane.

"Excuse me," said Tim, removing his headset with a quick yank. "This is my bird and there's no way in hell I'm letting you fly it."

"I'm not going to hurt your precious MD 500E. One hundred fifty-two knots max speed isn't that impressive. I can handle it, trust me."

Tane groaned from the back seat.

Starion flashed a smile at Skye. "I've never flown one of these before."

"That's it," snarled Tim. "Get your ass in the left seat."

Starion turned to Tane. "Take care of this so I can fly."

"No."

Skye looked from Starion to Tane. Clearly, Starion was used to getting his way. *What a brat.*

Starion looked confused for a moment. "But—"

"If you don't get in the left seat," Tim interrupted. "We're not going anywhere."

Starion slowly moved to the left seat and folded his arms over his chest. Turning to look over his shoulder at Skye, he said, "I'm a better pilot."

"Someone's full of himself," Skye muttered as the chopper rose into the air.

Leaning toward her, Tane said, "There is not a flying machine made that Starion cannot fly. He was the youngest person to ever graduate from flying school on our planet. The instructors at the flight academy all kept it a secret. King Pruet was furious when he found out."

"How old was he?"

"Twelve."

24

It was completely dark when the chopper landed on the rooftop of a nondescript gray building on the outskirts of Queenstown and everyone piled out. Starion continued his commentary on the pilot's flying skill — or rather, lack of skill, as he put it.

"Shut the hell up," Tim said to Starion as he thrust a piece of paper at Dylan. "I'm charging extra for the pain-in-the-ass pretty boy."

Dylan handed the paper to Skye before getting back in the chopper with Tim. "Give this to the professor. He pays the bills."

Starion motioned for Skye and Tane to follow him as he disappeared down a flight of stairs. Pressing a code into a box near a closed door, Starion pushed inward on a metal door, which opened into a short hallway. Skye and Tane trailed after him until he reached the end of the hall, entered another code, and passed into a spacious room decorated with modern paintings and containing several plush black couches. The view of the Remarkables was still as incredible as it had been the last time Skye was here. But now the apartment was even better because of who was sitting on one of the couches.

Skye tossed the bill at Leven. "Henry!"

Henry winced as Skye squeezed him. "Ouch, watch the shoulder. I'm glad to see you too."

"You OK? You've been gone for days," Janine asked.

"Starion's a prince. His father is the Beholder king."

Janine gave Skye an incredulous stare. "I didn't see that one coming."

"And there's something else." Skye ran a hand over her hair. "My father was a Vanger."

Henry and Janine stared wide eyed at Skye. "You mean . . ."

Skye nodded. "I'm part alien. At least now I know why I look like a freak."

Henry shook his head and groaned. "You're smarter than that, Skye. People look at you and are blown away."

"Sure they are."

"Oh please, Skye. Henry's right. Everyone's noticed how Starion looks at you," Janine insisted. "Prince Hottie could have anyone."

"Richard, I've changed my mind about choppers," Starion said loudly. "Of course, that pilot was an idiot."

Tane looked at Leven and shrugged before the professor could answer. "You know he cannot help it."

"Poor Tim." Leven looked down at the bill. "What is this extra charge?"

"Because someone was being a brat," Skye answered.

Janine regarded Starion with a frown. "What's happened now, Your Royalness?"

Starion ignored her as he clapped Henry on the back. "Glad to see you're well, Valjean. How's the injury?"

"It's OK. I'm on antibiotics and got a couple stitches. The doctor said the bullet didn't hit anything important."

"I owe you lunch, my brave friend. Just the two of us."

Henry gazed at Starion with awe. "But aren't you a prince? Why would you want to hang out with me?"

Starion gave Henry a pointed look. "Because I like you. I didn't ask to be a prince, and I never want to be the king. Uneasy lies the head that wears a crown."

"You read Shakespeare?"

Janine groaned. "No quoting Shakespeare. It's so dull."

Henry shook his head sadly. "For someone so smart, that makes you sound dumb, Janine."

She shrugged.

Henry turned to Starion. "Does that mean I shouldn't bow?"

"You'd better not."

"Do you have to bow to your father?" Henry asked.

Tane made a choking sound before feigning a cough.

Starion ran a hand down the side of his face. "Henry, treat me like plain old Starion. Can you do that?"

"I can," Janine replied.

Oma appeared in the doorway. Skye hugged her, telling her about *Prince* Starion and his frightening seizures, Oln's attempt to kill her, and the rigged vote. She demanded an explanation of why she was the last to know about being an alien. The whole story erupted out of her in an incoherent mess. She decided to let the years of Starion's animal spying slide for now; she knew what Oma would say.

Skye's grandmother motioned for everyone to sit down. She explained patiently why she hadn't told Skye about her Vanger heritage: Pieter wanted Skye to be normal, like other Earth kids, and he'd made her promise not to tell.

"Now," Oma said, "one at a time. I want the general's report first."

"Well then," Janine snapped at Starion, after she'd heard the entire story, "why don't you go back to your planet and marry that princess? Then the prime minister will go away and leave Skye alone and talk your power-hungry, abusive father into leaving Earth."

There was a long uncomfortable pause as Starion looked off to the side of the room. Tane coughed. Leven wandered off into the kitchen. Oma sat completely still.

Henry finally spoke. "Please, Janine. You're supposed to be smart."

Skye rose from the couch in a storm of anger. "The princess can have him. I don't date guys who stalk me, lie to me, and put my friends in danger. Oh yeah, and act like an entitled jerk." She glared at Starion. "Guess you thought because you wanted that helicopter, you could take it."

At least he had the sense to look embarrassed.

"That is something his father would do," Oma said.

Tane stiffened. "That was inappropriate, Katrina."

She shrugged. "Calling it like I see it." She looked around the room. "Is there any hope for an honest vote?"

Starion repeated Oln's words about the rigged vote and his promise to save the planet if Starion married Tempest. "It's true I dislike Tempest, but Oln doesn't know that. He made some bizarre statement about letting Skye live as long as Kemmie thought she was dead."

Oma paled noticeably. Starion stared at her for a long moment and then said in a warning voice, "You know something. What is it?"

She made excuses, pretending not to know, and finally retreated to the kitchen. Skye heard Oma's angry words in that same foreign language as Starion followed her, finally guiding her into a back room and shutting the door loudly. Leven scurried back into the living room and sat next to Tane.

Skye drummed her foot nervously on the floor as she looked at Tane and Leven. "I want to know why Starion is, was, whatever — why he thinks he can take my friends."

"What?" Henry asked. "Are we going to their planet?"

"Cool," added Janine.

Skye turned to them. "Not cool. You're going to be science experiments."

Henry and Janine stared at each other, then back at Skye.

"Skye," Tane said. "Starion does not intend to surrender Janine and Henry. King Pruet ordered him to work on the UEE, already in progress, take the vote, and bring back two earthlings — all when Starion was seventeen years old. That was long before he knew any Earth people."

"I trust Starion," said Henry. "I don't believe he was going to turn us over to be science experiments. He has a Mephistophelian father, so he had to pretend he was going to do it."

"What? A Mephi-what?" asked Skye.

Henry dropped his gaze. "I'm trying to expand my vocabulary. I've been reading Marlowe's *Dr. Faustus*. The word is a reference to the devil Mephistopheles to whom Faust sells his soul."

"Oh please, Henry," scoffed Janine. "You got that word from one of the characters in the musical *Cats*. I know you've watched it a zillion times. Anyway, Mephistopheles was a bit of a tragic figure. I don't think Starion's father has even the tiniest particle of goodness in him so I would use a different adjective to —"

"Stop," shouted Skye. "What are you talking about?"

"Who put drying agent in your extraction?" Janine groused.

"Skye," pleaded Henry. "Sit down. You're making us nervous with your pacing."

She plopped down on a chair and turned to Dr. Leven. "What do you think, professor?"

"Starion would never hurt you," Leven answered without hesitation.

Skye was reluctantly starting to believe it; she longed for it to be true, but she was afraid she'd never truly understand the real Starion.

"Do you think he's a good person?" Skye asked.

"Yes," Tane replied. "He is my prince."

"He's my prince," Janine corrected. "Using contractions isn't like synthesizing some unknown compound."

Tane said in a flat voice, "He *is* my prince."

"Whatever," Janine muttered. "Just trying to help."

Skye turned to Tane. "He's your friend. I've seen you with him, the way you protect him. That's not just duty."

"How did you meet?" Henry asked.

"I saved Starion's life when he was ten."

Skye moved closer to Tane. "What happened?"

"Starion was on a class field trip to a construction site. I was in my third year at university and I was studying at the site. Starion apparently got bored and started climbing on a couple of the towers. Even as a boy, he liked heights. He climbed up to the top. The building had a serious design flaw and Starion's weight was enough to collapse an entire section. He fell almost thirty stories."

Skye gasped. "But how could someone fall from that height and still live? Did he change into a flying animal?"

"No. I did."

"What did you turn into?" Skye asked.

"A jufon. They are swift fliers. I reached Starion right before he hit the ground. After I saved his son, King Pruet promised me a monthly salary if I would spend time with Starion. At first it was a chore; something I did to get money, but we quickly became friends. We used to have our own code when we were young, special phrases to get us out of jams, things that sounded innocent to anyone else but were codes for something entirely different."

Tane chuckled, but his face quickly took on a solemn cast. "King Pruet was always good to me, but sadly, he treated me better than his own son. He is determined to make Starion into the man he wants and will stop at nothing to break him. Knowing Starion, you know that he cannot be broken. The situation is a bad one, and it has been escalating in recent years. I have grown afraid for Starion."

"But yet he implanted that device that transports Starion to your ship if he gets hurt," said Skye.

"King Pruet makes a public show of caring for Starion, but the truth is something quite different," said Tane. "He has not yet learned the device has been removed. When he does, Starion will be punished. You asked if you can trust Starion. The answer is yes."

"Are you going to be able to stop the virus?" Henry asked.

"I do not know. I have a couple excellent engineers analyzing some drawings. Starion thinks you, Henry, can stop it."

Henry squeaked, "Me?"

Tane nodded. "Starion will—"

The sound of a slamming door startled everyone. Starion stomped back into the living room and flung himself onto a sofa at the opposite side of the room. Looking at him, Skye could tell something profound had happened. He looked different — his eyes held a fierce joy, but his mouth drooped. Skye heard her grandmother puttering in the kitchen. It sounded as though the woman was crying. She quickly rose to her feet, pointing a finger at Starion. "Did you make my Oma cry?"

Starion crossed his arms over his chest. "She's keeping secrets."

"Yeah, like you don't," Janine retorted.

Skye turned abruptly and walked into the kitchen. "Oma," she said. "What happened?"

Katrina wiped her tears with the back of her hand. "He's the prince."

"I don't care if he's the king of the universe. He has no right to treat people like that." Skye took Oma by the hand and guided her into a chair. "Thank you for taking care of me. I know you loved my parents. I miss them too."

Oma nodded as the tears fell.

"What's this secret you've hidden from Starion?"

Oma looked down at her hands. "Nothing you need to worry about."

Skye hesitated. She knew she could badger the truth out of her grandmother, but somehow, in the woman's state, it seemed wrong. Later, she'd press her for the truth.

Right now, she had a spoiled brat of a prince to deal with.

After Oma left for the bathroom, Skye stomped out to the living room and stood in front of Starion, hands on her hips. "Stop making my grandmother cry and I want to know what this secret is."

Starion shook his head. "You'll have to ask her. It's her secret. I'm sorry." He took Skye's hands in his. "Please excuse me. I need to speak with Tane."

Tane followed Starion into the kitchen, leaving Skye standing in the living room.

"That's not awkward," Janine mumbled.

Professor Leven cleared his throat. "The phone is on the stand by the front door, Henry and Janine, if you need to call your parents. Then I think we should all get some rest. We cannot help Tane and Starion analyze engineering drawings. It's extremely late and it's been a long day for everyone." He looked at his watch. "It is the next day."

Skye wandered down the hall toward the bedroom with the incredible view. Passing the kitchen, she heard Starion say, "Katrina's right. She said if I loved Skye, I would do what is best for her, and I will. Because I do love her."

Skye inhaled sharply. *He loves me*. The words bounced around in her head, searching for a place to rest. *He loves me*. Skye's stomach tumbled, in free fall.

She shut the door to the bedroom and sat on the floor, her head in her hands.

He loves me.

25

∎∎∎∎∎∎∎

Skye hadn't slept well, and she was still exhausted when she staggered out to the living room.

"He's got a plan," Janine said gravely, handing Skye a glass of orange
juice. "Henry is some sort of secret weapon to disable the virus. They
worked all night on it, but we can't implement it until tomorrow.
They're checking out some data and waiting for more information.
Oh, and looking for that Oln guy." She motioned with her head toward
Tane and Starion, talking quietly on the far side of the room, their
heads bent over a tablet-sized screen.

"What is it?" Skye asked loudly. "What's this plan?"

Starion explained his plan, keeping the details to a minimum.

Skye, Henry, and Janine sat staring at each other as he left the
room with Tane. Picking up empty glasses, Oma and Leven went into
the kitchen.

"I hate Starion's plan," wailed Henry.

"Let's be glad he discovered a design flaw, though it's the weirdest
thing I've ever heard. Anyway, I can do my part," said Janine calmly.
"It doesn't seem all that difficult."

"You have to think," Henry pointed out. "I have to *perform*. There's
a big difference. I don't want to be his secret weapon. What Starion is

asking me to do is . . . there's too much pressure." His face was ashen, his lips trembling.

Janine and Skye wrapped their arms around Henry.

"Yes. It's a lot of pressure," Janine whispered. "But we believe in you."

"You can do it, Henry." Skye added, "We can't let everyone die." Her mouth was dry as she said, "Tomorrow I give my speech. I will try as hard as I can to make it the best speech of my life so you don't have to be the secret weapon."

"If the vote is rigged, it doesn't matter if you give your speech," Janine said.

"She's got to try," Henry insisted. "Please, Skye. Starion says he's going to confront all the animals. He thinks he can get them to vote honestly."

Skye squeezed Henry's hand. "Of course I'm going to give my speech."

"Didn't Tane say that Oln guy might have lied about the vote being rigged?" Henry asked, desperation bleeding into his words.

"What if they honestly vote to kill us?" Janine asked.

"Not after Skye's speech." Henry twisted his hands together. "Right, Skye?"

Skye gave Henry a thumbs-up and tried to smile in spite of her hammering pulse. Grabbing both her friends by the hand, she dragged them into the kitchen. "Let's make breakfast."

Starion was staring into the refrigerator; Tane and Oma were leaning against a counter.

"Let's talk about those seizures, Star," said Tane.

"Why aren't you looking for Oln so we can return to the conference? And double-checking that design flaw? Why are we wasting time on this?"

"Experts are working on it, Star," said Tane. "I have my sister's friends verifying our calculations. My men are searching for Oln. Now, about those seizures."

Starion twirled an earring but remained silent.

"Did you know your father's chief medical advisor was doing controversial research that attempted to induce memory loss after a traumatic event?" Katrina asked. "And then died a few years ago under odd circumstances?"

"What if he is responsible for covering up some event that happened to you?" Tane gave Katrina a glance before continuing. "Perhaps it is not a disease at all but a type of conditioning. What if something went wrong during the conditioning, perhaps embedding a trigger in your brain that causes seizures? What we need to do is figure out what the trigger is and what event happened to you."

"I'm not doing this right now," Starion said and walked out of the kitchen.

Janine whispered in Skye's ear. "I have a theory. And it's a really good one."

It was late in the evening when Starion asked, "Where's Tane?"

Oma handed him a note.

Starion glared down at the note, then angrily crumpled it into a ball. "We don't have time for this. What could have come up that's more important than finding Oln so we can return to the conference? Time is running out. Skye has to give that speech tomorrow. It's our only chance." He looked around the room. "Are there any questions about the plan?"

Henry was still whining; Janine felt confident in her role; Oma answered affirmatively; Leven nodded.

"If my speech doesn't work, and you take my friends up to the ship, then . . ." Skye paused. "Am I supposed to just sit here, with no way to know what has happened? I should go up to the ship too. To help." She stared down at her hands nervously. "If my speech doesn't work."

"Skye. Please," Oma said quietly. "You need to stay here with me. Let them disable the virus. Your job is to give the speech."

Opening her mouth to speak, Skye stopped when she saw Oma's expression of panic. Skye was fairly certain Starion and Tane wouldn't let anything happen to her friends, and even though she felt she could take care of herself, Oma was worried, maybe terrified. She poured all the love and gratitude she felt for her grandmother into her smile. "OK, Oma."

With a flourish, Starion produced a small silver bag. "You will be able to see everything."

"Where did you get an S-Eye?" Oma asked.

"Being the prince has its rewards."

Janine made a sound of disgust.

Starion squatted down next to Skye. "You said you'd give me another chance." He placed the silver bag in her lap.

Skye looked down, then back up at him, her face softening. "What does it do?"

Starion removed a small black case from the bag and opened it.

"Are those contact lenses?" Skye asked.

"Not exactly." Starion placed one clear round device over the pupil of his eye, then did the same with the other. "S-Eye is short for Spy Eye. They're highly regulated on my planet, for obvious reasons." He took a palm-sized screen from the silver bag and handed it to Skye. "Touch the screen."

When she did, she saw herself. Then she saw Henry and next Janine.

"What's it doing?" she asked.

"Look where my eyes are moving," said Starion.

"You're looking at me." Skye looked down at the screen. "Wait, I can hear myself."

"A microphone is embedded in the lenses," explained Starion. "You are more than my eyes. You're my ears too."

"Thank you, Starion."

He squeezed Skye's hand gently, then he took the lenses out of his eyes and put them back in the bag along with the screen. He set it all on the console next to the television. "No one move these and I'll put them in my eyes before we go up to the ship."

"Why don't you leave them in so Henry and I can see what you're doing at the conference?" Janine asked.

"I can't wear them as a prairie dog. Sorry."

"I still want to see the ship," Skye said.

Starion knelt down in front of her. "If all goes well, I will take you to see it someday. Maybe I'll take you in a plane I built myself and we'll go on a picnic."

"Did I miss anything?" asked Tane, appearing in the room.

Starion rose to his feet, wisps of dark hair framing his face, his short ponytail lying across one shoulder. "Glad you saw fit to join us," he replied sarcastically. "We'll go first thing in the morning. Everyone try to get a good night's rest."

"Is everyone ready?" Starion gazed around the room.

"Those are cool guns you and the general have," said Henry, leaning forward in his chair. "Can I see yours?"

"No," said Tane in an irritated voice. "Guns are not for children."

"I'm almost eighteen," Henry protested. He pointed at Starion. "He's only two years older."

"The prince has had years of training with weapons," Tane replied gruffly.

Henry whispered to Skye, "I checked it out when they weren't looking. I'll bet I could fire it."

Janine, sitting on the other side of Henry, gave him a stern look. "Guns are bad, Henry."

Without a word, Tane slapped Richard on the back and gave him a stiff hug.

Starion held his hand out to Leven, palm up. "Hand it over."

"Kids, would you like anything to drink?" Leven asked, ignoring Starion as he started into the kitchen.

Starion grabbed his arm. "What's in your pocket, Richard?"

Oma looked at the three and frowned.

"We must be leaving," Tane said. "Now."

"I don't think so," Starion replied. "Hand it over." Leven reluctantly handed Starion a small black device the size and shape of a cell phone.

Looking over Starion's shoulder, Oma said, "It's some type of signaling device."

Starion waved it in Tane's face. "What's this?"

"Time is running out."

"We're not going anywhere," Starion warned, "until you tell me why you gave Richard a . . ." His face paled as he turned the device over in his hand. "How could you sacrifice our friend?"

Crossing his arms over his chest, Tane replied, "He volunteered. You wanted a backup plan in case we fail to open the console. This is it."

"But—"

"If the virus enters the Earth's atmosphere, we're all dead anyway," Richard interrupted.

"I'll find a way to transport you to the ship, Richard," Starion said.

Shaking his head, Leven said, "I'm not leaving my son to die. Or Dylan, or my other students."

"You're going to die with them?" Starion exclaimed.

"No. I'm going to save them. Someone has to do it." He looked over at Oma. "Katrina, don't even consider it. I believe you made a promise to Skye's father."

"What's going on?" Skye asked.

"Let me guess," Janine said. "Professor Leven is going to sacrifice himself by attracting the virus canister with a signaling device." She pushed her glasses up on her nose. "Doesn't the canister open when it hits the Earth's atmosphere?"

"Not if it detects a signal from this device. It opens when it makes contact with the signaling device," Tane said.

"How big is the canister?" Henry asked.

"Length 22.63 centimeters and circumference 21.17 centimeters. It is 167 times as dense as osmium," answered Tane.

"Huh?" Henry glanced at Skye, who shrugged.

Janine put her arm around Henry. "It's about twice the width of a big tube of toothpaste, and a bit longer. Osmium is the densest naturally occurring element on Earth, though under certain conditions iridium wins." She paused. "The virus itself weighs nothing, so this canister must be super heavy and composed of an element we don't have on Earth."

Tane nodded.

Janine's eyes blazed as she grabbed the sides of her face. "That is so awesome."

Skye could tell Janine had completely forgotten the plan. She was now in chemistry-is-so-cool mode as she spoke in a breathless voice. "What is it called? Where does it fit on the periodic table, and—"

Starion interrupted her. "I promise to tell you about it. Later. We have a planet to save right now."

Janine's shoulders sagged. "Fine. Put the signaling device in space."

Tane shook his head. "It is complicated, but the signaling device does not work in space."

"But we'll still die," Janine exclaimed. "It still gets released."

Tane shook his head. "When the signaling device is activated the canister will embed like a high-speed bullet in the body of the person holding it. The virus will probably be contained within the body."

"Probably? What do you mean *probably*? Has it been tested?" Janine demanded.

Tane maintained a blank face. "It is extremely new technology, somewhat experimental. There was no time for tests. The virus could still spread."

Janine threw her hands up in the air.

When Skye began to protest, Dr. Leven held up a hand. "I'm the only one. I'll stand on the helicopter pad, away from everyone. No one else will be hurt. Katrina, you'll need to call this number." He handed her a slip of paper. "Tell them I've been exposed to a virulent contagious disease. They'll come with the proper containment equipment."

"Containment equipment?" Janine scoffed. "For an alien virus? Think that'll work?"

"Starion, how can you let him do this?" Skye demanded.

Tane and Starion exchanged looks. Oma finally spoke. "You're quite brave, Richard."

Skye brought a shaky hand to her forehead. "But shouldn't it be—"

"Don't make this harder," Oma said. "I don't think there's another option." She looked at Tane. "Where did you get the device?"

"That is classified information."

"Your sister?" Starion asked.

"My sister is dead."

Henry raised his hand. "The plan is going to work. We won't need the professor to do this. Right?"

All eyes focused on Henry.

"That's up to you," Starion said.

Henry paled.

"And me," Skye said. "The animals are going to vote in our favor after I give my kick-ass speech. Right, Henry?" She forced a confident smile she didn't feel as she clutched at the speech notes in her pocket.

"Yes, of course they are, honey," Oma said with a smile. But Skye knew her grandmother well enough to know the smile was forced.

"Your speech will be excellent," Starion added. But Skye knew Starion too. His body language screamed defeat.

Skye looked around the room at the grim faces. Her animal friends wouldn't vote to kill them, would they? She had to give a perfect speech. Even if it didn't go well, even if the animals did vote to kill them, there was Henry.

An idea began to form. She knew the location of the fire escape and the empty building across the street. Five floors down, a run across the street, another six flights up. She'd have to be fast. And covert.

Phase one of Starion's plan commenced. After some awkward good-byes, Tane and Starion activated their transport modules and disappeared.

26

One minute, Skye was looking at Henry, and the next, Starion was holding her. "What happened?"

"You fell," Starion said with a mischievous grin. "Sometimes transporting is disorienting. We're back in the conference hall for phase two of my plan. Don't stray away from Katrina or me. OK?"

Skye nodded, her arms around Starion's neck.

"What took so long?" Oma asked.

"Apparently a Vanger agriculture ship is, or was, in orbit. We can't find Oln. We were further delayed because Tane cannot locate a couple of missing guards; one was a friend, the only Vanger in his crew, and he's concerned about him. Tane is on his ship monitoring the vote, and then depending on the result, we'll be on to phase three."

Skye gazed at Starion. "You can put me down now."

"Do I have to?"

"Starion," scolded Oma. "Turn back into a prairie dog before any of the animals see you."

"We're in a closet. They can't see."

"*Starion.*"

"The professor orders and I obey," said Starion, releasing Skye and turning to bow at Oma, who simply snorted in disgust.

"Oma, do you have to turn into an animal too?" Skye asked.

When she nodded, Skye said, "Make it a native Colorado animal."

Oma turned to Starion and gave him a sharp glare. "Behave yourself, little prairie dog." In an instant, she transformed into a black-footed ferret.

Popping his jaw in irritation, Starion muttered something under his breath before reassuming prairie dog form.

Skye tried not to laugh as she opened the door. Black-footed ferrets ate prairie dogs.

The main assembly room was a mess, food was running out, and animals were beginning to pick fights. The smell was dreadful, and there was trash everywhere. The greenish water in several tanks smelled like urine. About twenty assorted species of ducks were hiding near Starion's podium, and a tiny marmoset clung precariously to a chair, crying for its mother.

Skye pried the miniature primate from the chair. It wrapped its diminutive claws around Skye's finger in a death grip, staring at her with wide black eyes, curling its striped tail around another finger. The marmoset's small mouth opened, and a birdlike chirp fell from it. It increased its hold on Skye's finger, pressing its miniature face, covered in soft gray fur, to her finger. Spotting its mother, Skye reluctantly handed the baby back.

A giant panda from China, complaining about the lack of tasty bamboo, sputtered, "I want to go home."

"It's total pandemonium in here," Skye quipped.

Starion chuckled. "Pandemonium . . . good one, Skye."

The panda stared at them, made a distasteful sound, and returned to his ecosystem.

With a flurry, the three kea flew over to Skye and perched on her shoulders. "We missed you, Miss Skye," exclaimed Merry.

"We came back to see what happened," added Frodo.

"Are you going to give your speech?" asked Pippin.

Skye nodded. "I'm so happy to see all of you again."

Word soon spread that Starion was back. Animals scurried to their voting places, chattering and shouting.

"QUIET!"

Starion pounded his wooden staff loudly on the floor. "It has come to my attention that certain members of the UEE have been offered bribes to vote against the humans. There will be *severe* repercussions if I discover that anyone had a part in this. The vote must be honest and fair. To do otherwise is an affront to everything the UEE stands for. Are we clear on this?"

Murmurs of assent echoed around the room.

"ARE WE CLEAR?"

Shouts of yes resonated.

"All right then," continued Starion. "Please give Skye Van Bloem your full attention."

Slowly, Skye walked to the microphone. She knew what she had to do. She ripped her speech into bits, scattering the paper onto the floor.

The only way she was going to win over the animals was by speaking from the deepest part of her being. She wanted to live in a world full of wonder and diversity, and she appreciated all animals for the unique roles they played.

Skye took a deep breath. "I watched three boys kill a Great Plains toad and did nothing. Because I was afraid."

There were gasps as all eyes focused on Skye.

"Those days are over. I will *not* stand by quietly while an animal is tortured. I will *not* accept the loss of another species. I will *not* believe there's nothing I can do to help this planet." Skye leaned over the podium and looked out at the animals she loved. "I'm eighteen now, and, for the first time, I can vote. That is a powerful thing. I will check the records of every single person who runs for office. If they don't vote *for* the environment — if they vote *against* it — they will find themselves without a job."

The three kea cheered and high-fived each other while the rest of the room remained silent.

"I've been told that if people don't change and stop destroying the planet, a horrible virus is going to be let loose. It won't kill any of you, just humans. The virus is going to enter through the atmosphere, the thing we're destroying. There are gases with names like carbon dioxide, and methane, and nitrous oxide, that are creating a sort of big heavy blanket over the planet. The heat gets trapped and can't escape into space. That raises the temperature on the planet, and that's a bad thing. Not only does it get hotter, but ice melts and goes into the oceans and then coastal places get flooded. Warm ocean water kills coral reefs and makes storms stronger. Some animals can't live with the hotter temperatures and some pests, like mosquitoes, like it better. It upsets the whole ecosystem puzzle.

"These greenhouse gases come from things like gas-powered cars and factories and burning coal. We need to stop doing those things—especially burning coal. I know you don't want me to talk about the man in the poster I showed you before, so instead, I'm going to tell you about my two best friends.

"Janine Franklin and Henry Wilkinson are good, kind people. Janine went snorkeling on the Great Barrier Reef with her family a couple summers ago. She was careful not to touch any coral, not to leave any trash, and not to disturb any nesting birds on the island they visited. She even got in a fight with some guy because he threw a cigarette overboard.

"I've known Janine since I was in sixth grade, and she has always stood by me. She's honest and ethical and the world is a better place because of her. She recycles everything and always carries her green bag. She doesn't use plastic water bottles and plastic straws. Last year she talked her parents into putting solar panels on their house. She loves chemistry and genetics, and I know she will make an important scientific discovery that could help the entire planet, because she's that smart. But if the Beholders release the virus, she'll die. Henry is my other friend." Skye's voice began to crack. "He was just released from the hospital because he protected me from a bullet."

The room became noisy, and Skye was forced to stop. Starion held up a paw to quiet the animals. "We're looking into it, but we cannot question the gunman. The general and his soldiers have put a quick end to him."

The three kea strutted and took bows.

"Henry is a hero, and he's a good person. He loves to sing, and he has this amazing voice. He volunteers to pick up trash for the parks department." Skye held up her wrist. Around it was a simple bracelet containing clear beads strung on a blue cord. "Henry bought this for my birthday last month. It's made from recycled plastic water bottles and recycled glass bottles. It pays for one pound of trash to be removed from the oceans." She sought out Irwin with her eyes and said, "It reminds me not to use plastic, and I tell other people that plastic kills animals who live in the oceans." She glimpsed the sea turtle nodding. "Henry rides his bike instead of driving because he knows about global warming and wants to put less pollution in the air. He likes polar bears and worries about them drowning if the pack ice melts."

"Finally," Jackson called out. "Someone is concerned about us."

Skye gazed sadly at the polar bear. "I'm sorry about the melting ice, Jackson. People love polar bears, they really do." She didn't want to tell Jackson there were environmental groups that predicted polar bears would be extinct in the wild in her lifetime. In a way, they were the poster children for global warming. She felt an acute heaviness in her chest for the creature. He was so majestic, so fiercely beautiful. To think there would be a world without them in the wild was beyond tragic.

"I know other people like Janine and Henry. My parents were good people who cared about the planet. There are hundreds of environmental groups working every day to fix these problems. Many of them are unpaid and those that are paid make little money. Political activists march and protest and keep an eye on our elected officials. There isn't an easy solution, but more and more people are taking responsibility for climate change, habitat destruction, and scores of other issues. My parents always thought education was the key, and one of my ideas is to get an environmental educator in every classroom teaching kids how they can help the planet. They can tell their parents not to ruin their world, but if you vote to kill us, they'll never have a chance. I have some other ideas too, which I'd like to tell you about."

Skye felt her whole being explode with passion as she began to outline her proposals. In an instant, the helplessness she'd felt about fixing the planet faded. She could do this. She *would* make a difference, because the alternative — giving up — was not acceptable. Skye had never quit trying to conquer obstacles in her life, not even that confusing math class. She'd always wanted to help animals, but in that moment, she realized she couldn't live in a world without polar bears, sea turtles, prairie dogs, elephants, kangaroos, and all the other animals she'd added to her list of friends. They mattered because the wonderful diversity of the planet was what made life rich and whole and worth living.

"We have to stop using fossil fuels and switch to green energy, like solar and wind. We need to stop building pipelines that carry dirty oil. These pipelines break and spew oil into precious water supplies. The native people in my country know this. They protest and have always tried to protect the land — their land, which was stolen from them. We must all support them and stand behind them. We will not let corrupt politicians and big business destroy our planet for money. We are all responsible and doing nothing is not OK."

She paused, squaring her shoulders. She spoke slowly, loudly, each word said forcefully. "Every single person can and *must* help."

Several of the Australian delegates cheered.

"Some people don't know how to help the planet, but they can be taught. Even little things like not using plastic and walking instead of driving will help. Stop spraying toxic chemicals that hurt bees." She glanced over at Pim. "And bats too."

"I eat 'squitoes," called Pim.

"We help pollinate," shouted a group of leaf-nosed bats.

Skye gave the bats a thumbs-up. "Everyone must be taught kindness — toward animals and people. Humans are not all bad. We have gone to the moon, made great discoveries, produced beautiful art and literature. There is music. And science. And philosophy. All this will be lost if the virus is released."

Malanga the rhino gave a disgusted snort and muttered something to the group near her, but still, Skye pressed on.

"In conclusion, I'd like to say that if you give us a chance, I think people will do the right thing. Social change sometimes takes time. A young girl named Anne Frank kept a diary during one of the most horrible wars on our planet. She was hiding in a warehouse with her family so the Nazis wouldn't take them to a concentration camp. In the middle of all this, she wrote, 'Despite everything . . . I still believe in the inner goodness of man.' Sometimes I forget her words, so I need to remind myself of them. They make me want to be more courageous and to believe in the goodness of people, even though it's hard. I get angry with people too and wish they would take better care of the planet and make better choices. Sometimes I even hate them, like those men in Australia who murdered the kangaroos. *For fun.*"

Everyone had heard about the kangaroo slaughter and Skye's rescue of the joey. There were shouts from around the room. Most of the delegates seemed to like Skye, but they clamored that she was only one good person out of billions of evil humans.

"What about Coorain?" Skye called to the Australian delegates.

The Australian members looked at each other knowingly. "He's a good bloke," Cassie admitted.

"Yes, he is," Skye insisted. "He'll die if you condemn us. I believe in Coorain, and I believe in Janine and Henry, and others like them. I believe that Starion has a plan to help. Please vote to give us a chance. Please don't condemn all humans to death." She spread her arms wide as tears began to fall. "I care about you. All of you. I never intended to spend my life defending humans, but in defending you, in learning about and protecting the animals of Earth. I don't know where my life will take me: maybe doing field research, or working as a wildlife rehabilitator, or becoming a humane educator. If I get good enough at chemistry, I'd like to work as a climate scientist. Maybe I'll run for public office and make sure laws are passed that protect all of you. Whatever I end up doing, I know that I will not sit quietly by while another species goes extinct. I will fight for you — all of you. Please give me a chance to do that."

The room was silent as Skye sat down. "That was incredible," Starion whispered to her. "No one on this entire planet could have done better."

Moving back to the podium, Starion announced, "Please enter your vote via the screens in your ecosystem. Touch the green circle to give the humans a chance. The square red box indicates you think they should all die. Please consider your vote carefully. You have thirty minutes to make your selection. If you need assistance, please call one of the capuchin monkeys over to help. After the final result is posted, we'll begin transporting everyone home. Once you're home, the tags will be removed."

"How will we know if the vote is fair?" Skye whispered.

"We may never know."

Skye began nervously drumming her fingers on the back of Starion's chair. "What if the vote is fair, but they decide we should all die? Even if you destroy the virus, won't the Beholders come back later with more of it and kill us anyway?"

"Maybe."

"That's not fair. Is your planet so breathtakingly wonderful that you can condemn others? What makes the Beholders so perfect that they can wipe out entire races? Instead of killing us, why can't they send people to help us? I think they have some other reason for wanting us dead. If I ever meet that father of yours, I'll tell him so."

Starion scratched at his fur. "I think you would. You're brave enough to do it." He looked over at Oma. "Did you hear that, professor? Our Skye would be one amazing ruler, ramming through some long over-due reforms."

Oma glared at Starion through masked eyes, twitched her long whiskers, and opened her mouth to show sharp teeth.

Starion returned a bored expression. "Whatever."

Skye continued to fidget, looking around the room at the chattering delegates. *What were they saying? How would they vote? Had her speech been good enough?*

The overhead monitors flashed in unison: "Vote closing in ten minutes."

"OK," Starion whispered to Oma and Skye. "If the vote is against the humans, Tane is going to immediately transport us to Leven's. Katrina, take Skye down that empty hallway. No one will see you. I may be a few minutes behind you."

"Why?" Skye asked.

Oma replied, "Remember, I told you we can't transport in animal form. Starion will need a minute or two to hide somewhere and change back. Don't worry. He'll be right behind us. Of course, if the vote is in favor of the humans, then we have more time."

"But we won't have to destroy the virus if that's the case. Right?" asked Skye, pulling nervously at a strand of red hair.

Starion looked slightly stricken. "No, we still have to destroy it."

The monitors flashed that the results were in. The entire room went eerily quiet. Now Starion was fidgeting as Katrina motioned for Skye to follow her into the deserted hallway. "You'll still be able to see the monitor." She changed back into her human form.

Skye clutched the chain holding her locket. A thousand images flew through her head as she reflected on the people who would die if the animals voted against them. Coorain, Rob, Maka, Esh. Starion would save her, Janine, and Henry, but they'd be all that was left. She thought not only of famous artists and performers, but also of regular folks — people working every day to help the environment, zoo keepers and wildlife rehabilitators toiling long hours to care for animals. She thought of the young waitress at the Asian Café down the street from her home who was saving for college. There was Henry's mom, working exhausting hours as a hospital aide, doing her best to support Henry, and Janine's parents and little sister.

All doing their best.

They'd all die.

Her entire life Skye had wanted to save animals, and yet here she was trying to save people. Once, she'd thought it would be a good thing if some disease wiped out humans because other species would then have a chance. The planet would be better off without destructive people. Maybe at the beginning she'd secretly agreed with the animals at the conference — people deserved to die.

Now, she was trying to save people. Could anything be more ironic?

It was wrong what humans had done to the planet, to animals and their habitats. It was terrible what those hunters had done to the kangaroos, what Josh and his gang might have done, but . . . Maybe no one had ever treated them kindly, so they were taking it out on others. Skye hated it that she was thinking about them, instead of the wildlife heroes she had always admired.

She thought of Dylan, what he'd been, what he could have been if Dr. Leven hadn't helped him.

Did people deserve another chance?

Maybe the exterminators didn't understand how important prairie dogs were to the ecosystem. Maybe those hunters in Australia didn't appreciate how amazing kangaroos were. Maybe they needed to spend time learning about them. Maybe if they'd had humane education when they were children, they wouldn't think it was OK to poison intelligent animals or shoot a national symbol. Maybe they needed a mentor like Dr. Leven. Maybe, like Oma had said, the system itself was broken.

Could people like Josh be taught to treat the planet with respect, animals with compassion, and other people with empathy? Dylan had learned. Maybe education was the key. Her parents had believed that.

There were good people on the planet besides Janine and Henry. The past several weeks had taught her that. Once, she'd believed paradise would be living without people. She took a long, weary breath. Did she still believe that?

The screen began to count down the vote. 5 . . . 4 . . . 3 . . . 2—

```
Every ecosystem has voted to destroy
the humans
with the exception of the ecosystems in
New Zealand.
The Australian vote was tied.

The virus will be released in thirty
Earth minutes.
```

Skye barely had time to read the screen before she was standing in the living room of Leven's apartment, Oma next to her. They looked at each other. Oma's face was pale, and Skye, horror struck, began to shake.

All those people, thought Skye. *They'll all die if we aren't successful.* She took a shuffling step backward, her heartbeat racing, fingers touching her parted lips.

She couldn't let everyone die.

Henry jumped up from the couch. "Janine. Professor Leven. Come quick."

Leven came running, followed by Janine, zipping her jeans. "Henry, this time I really was on the . . ." She stopped midsentence when she saw Skye. "They're going to kill us all, aren't they?"

Henry sank to the floor.

"Now, son, don't go to pieces on us," said Leven, lifting Henry to his feet, careful of his injured shoulder. "You know you can do it. Do you and Janine have those transport modules securely on you?" Henry and Janine nodded. "Then stand here together and wait for Starion. He should be —"

Starion appeared in front of them. Putting his hands on Henry's shoulders, he stared into his eyes. "You can do it."

Skye, still unable to speak, her mouth like the dry dirt of the destroyed prairie dog colony, walked over to Henry and Starion on weak legs. She fell against them, gripping the two as though they were all that kept her from plunging down a deep chasm. Janine, Leven, and Katrina soon joined them in a desperate hug.

"Are you ready?" Starion asked Janine and Henry. They nodded. "As soon as I activate my module, Tane will see the signal, activate your modules, and fold space around the two of you. We now have twenty-six minutes until the virus is released." He looked over at Skye and reached for her hand. Taking it in his, he said, "I'll see you soon."

"Please, can I come?" Skye said in a strangled voice. "I have to do something."

Starion shook his head. "You promised Katrina. And you'll have the S-Eye." Taking the small silver bag from the spot where he'd left it, he removed the case with the lenses and inserted them in his eyes. He handed Skye the small flat screen, activating it with a touch. "It will be as though you're sitting on my shoulder watching and hearing everything through me."

Skye took the device. Her pale face stared out from the screen.

Starion kissed her on the forehead, and then they were gone. Phase three had started.

■ ■ ■

"Do you remember Starion's instructions for —"

"Leave the girl alone." Katrina gave Leven a wilting stare as she glanced over at Skye, curled up on one end of the sofa, clutching the screen. "She knows what to do." She paused. "Skye, honey. Can I get you something?"

"Do you have some iced green tea?"

"Let me get it," Leven said, heading for the kitchen.

Skye stared down at the screen in her hand and looked through Starion's eyes.

"Oma," Skye asked, "are there any crackers left?"

Skye threw her plan into action. There was no time for panic. Leven had a son who needed him. And students, like Dylan. She knew exactly what to do, and she wasn't going to think too deeply about it. *Get it done.*

At the same time Oma disappeared into the kitchen, Leven handed Skye the tea. Setting the screen to the side, Skye pretended to reach for the tea, but instead jumped off the couch, bumping into Leven, spilling the tea, and knocking him off balance. She grabbed at him as he stumbled.

"I'm so sorry," she exclaimed.

"No worries," replied Leven, wiping at his shirt. "I'll get a cloth."

After he left the room, Skye tucked the signaling device into the waist of her pants and pulled her shirt down over it. She'd slipped the transport module and her cell phone — which she'd finally found under the dresser in the guest room — into Leven's back pocket when he'd stumbled. With luck, he wouldn't notice until it was too late.

When Katrina and Leven returned, Skye was curled on the end of the sofa holding the S-Eye screen.

"Interesting," came Janine's voice.

As Skye watched the screen, she saw Janine, then General Tane, who was standing against a far wall, working on a computer.

Janine's voice again. "I know I'm on a spaceship, but where's the bridge? The viewscreen?"

Skye heard Starion's voice. "What did you expect, Miss Genetics Whiz?"

"Not a room that looks like a computer lab at school, minus the windows," came Janine's response.

The tables and chairs appeared to be made of a bronze-colored metal. Three huge screens hung from the ceiling: one showed a live picture from the assembly hall at the UEE, one had a map of the world with colored blinking dots in random places, and the other was blank. The sound for all the screens seemed to be off. Computers lined the walls. A see-through enclosed booth about the size of a small walk-in closet, containing a table with a panel of lights across it, stood against a corner. That must be where the virus was kept; Starion had described it accurately. Janine, with Henry following, moved toward it. Two men in uniforms similar to Tane's stood on each side of the booth.

Tane spoke to the two uniformed men who nodded and left the room.

Skye saw hands — Starion's hands — open the booth door and point to a canister embedded in the center of a floating solid table without legs that was covered by a see-through panel. *The virus.*

The whole assembly looked complicated — a chute extended from the side of the table. Starion had explained that in 0.01 seconds the capsule was automatically loaded onto a blindingly fast delivery mechanism and then fired from the ship.

"Are you ready, Valjean?" Starion's voice.

Henry nodded nervously, staring down at the table.

Starion pushed buttons on an overhead screen above the table and a holographic image composed of colored dots of varying shapes appeared. Pushing and spinning the images with his hands, Starion formed an odd matrix of arrows and small colored circles, all contained in various geometric shapes. Looking satisfied, he turned to Henry. "OK, Henry. Doesn't look too difficult to sing. Any questions?"

"What is that?" gasped Henry. "Some weird alien musical notation? I don't know what that means. How am I supposed to read that?"

Starion glanced at his work and grimaced. "Sorry. The computer will translate from my system to yours." He pressed several buttons and spun the images. Soon, five horizontal lines appeared, followed by a treble clef on the left side. The colored shapes turned into musical notes and moved onto the lines. More lines of musical notation appeared. With a quick movement of his hands, Starion twisted the entire image to face Henry.

"Here we go, Valjean. Take a deep breath. You're going to do great. To review what we said, you have two tries, just two, before the computer locks you out for a period of two hours. We don't have two hours to sit and wait. We're down to nineteen minutes before the automatic control fires the virus canister into the atmosphere. It's loaded onto a mounting device that is unbelievably fast; nothing, and I mean *nothing*, will catch it before it reaches the Earth's atmosphere. There's no way to stop it once it goes.

"Henry, make it count the first time; every note has to be dead on or the lock mechanism on the panel won't open. Janine needs time to figure out how we're going to destroy that virus. Be thinking, Janine, while Henry dazzles us with his voice. Remember; sing each note as a one-syllable word like la or fa."

Any tampering with the panel above the canister would automatically fire it, so they couldn't simply pry it open. When Starion had explained the design flaw to Skye, she couldn't believe that a series of highly accurate sounds could cause it to open. The question was whether Henry could replicate them — exactly.

Janine kissed Henry on the cheek. "Pretend you're on Broadway. It's a packed house and you're a star."

Henry smiled weakly as Starion and Janine walked out of the booth. Before Starion closed the door, he said, "Cough, sneeze, do it now before I activate the sound. Once I shut the door, nod at me when you want me to turn it on. You'll see me do it and then you can start singing."

It took fewer than thirty seconds before Henry nodded at Starion, who reached up, pushed the button, and gave Henry a thumbs-up.

Though no sound could penetrate the booth, Starion and Janine could hear every note through the computer speakers. By the sixth note, the computer screeched a lockout warning. Starion quickly opened the door as Henry fell to the floor. "I can't do it," he wailed.

Starion put his arm around the other man's waist and lifted him up. "Take deep breaths. Relax."

"We believe in you, Henry," Janine said, "but man up. I can't believe I'm saying this, but don't let Skye down." She twisted her hands together as she mumbled, "Or my little sister."

Skye watched Leven go to the front door of the apartment, toward the elevator. Katrina said something to him, and then he was gone. He would discover Skye's switch when he got on the roof, so she had to be fast. She'd climb down the fire escape and then activate the device when she reached the roof of the abandoned building across the street. She glanced down the hallway toward the door that led to the fire escape and mentally prepared for the last race of her life.

She'd failed to win the animals over with her speech. She was the one responsible. Was there something else she should have said? Maybe she shouldn't have ripped up her speech notes. Her miserable failure rocketed around in her head. All this was her fault.

She didn't want to die, but what was her life compared to millions? And she wasn't about to let Professor Leven sacrifice himself because she'd screwed up. She had to be the one to do it.

Looking back down at the screen, Skye inhaled sharply and waited to see what Henry would do.

Henry took a tissue from his back pocket and blew his nose. Shifting from foot to foot, he ran shaking fingers through his blond curls. "You're right. You're absolutely right. I can do this."

Starion turned to Tane. "If we fail, immediately transport Katrina and Skye to the ship."

■ ■ ■

Skye walked toward the door that led to the fire escape, still looking down at the S-Eye screen. *Please, Henry*, Skye thought in desperation. *I know you can do it.*

"There's one thing I didn't tell you," Starion said quietly. "When I reboot the computer, the lights will rearrange themselves on the staff. The notes will not be the same this time. We don't have time for practice. The computer will fade the notes in less than two minutes, which is about how long you're going to need to sing them. It's a security thing since the first attempt failed."

Henry took a deep breath. "You love Skye, don't you?"

Watching the small screen in her hand, Skye couldn't see Starion's face, only Henry's reaction, and she knew Starion must have nodded yes.

Skye felt her chest tighten. Then she heard Henry say, "Activate it."

The notes did as Starion predicted and reassembled in a pattern that required a singer with an incredible range. Henry gasped.

"Come on, Henry. When you sang 'Bring Him Home' for *Les Mis*, the range was way bigger than this." Janine huffed and turned her back to the musical staff. "I'll be outside with Starion when you've rocked this music."

Skye was betting Janine had turned her back so Henry wouldn't see her terrified expression. Everyone on the planet depended on Henry.

The door closed.

Henry pulled his shirttail down and stood tall and straight. He nodded once at Starion to push the button. Henry sang, using the word "Skye" to represent each note. The sound poured from him in a symphony of perfection, each note clear, flawless, powerful.

It was *glorious*.

One hand on the door leading to the fire escape, the other clutching the screen, Skye paused in awe of Henry's mastery of the music, and when the locking mechanism on the panel slid open, she wasn't surprised. She could hear Starion's sharp intake of breath, see Janine's expression of amazement. Even Tane was transfixed. It seemed in one blazing moment that Henry could have sung anything into opening. Skye clutched the screen to her chest in thanks before shutting the door and moving back to the living room.

Henry had saved them all.

She looked down at the screen.

"Incredible. He is as good as you claimed." Tane frowned at a computer screen. "Starion, there is a problem at the TCS and—"

"Not now, Tane," Starion shouted, yanking the booth door open. "Janine, how are we going to destroy the virus?"

Ignoring Starion, Janine gave Henry a huge kiss on the cheek. "Perfection, maestro. Absolute perfection. Look out, Broadway."

Henry could only stare, a big grin plastered to his face.

"Janine," Skye heard Starion bark.

"Yeah, yeah. You didn't need me for this. It's simple. Throw the canister out into space and fire something at it to open it. As long as it doesn't get near the atmosphere, it'll be fine. No virus can withstand the cold of space. The canister isn't loaded onto that super-fast-thingy, so it will float around out there. Do you have a garbage chute to throw stuff off the ship?"

"Yes."

"And then can you aim one of your death ray guns at it and explode it?"

"Yes."

"Then do it." She smiled at Henry. "I did have the easy job. I admit it."

"Tane," Starion shouted. "I can't lift this thing. Put it in the receptacle."

Skye watched Tane deposit the canister in a chute, his muscles bulging. It was incredible that something so small could be so heavy. A screen lowered from the ceiling near the booth. Skye saw stars and the black of space, then the canister ejecting from the ship. When it was a safe distance away, a missile fired. The detonation was small, but the monitor captured it, zoomed in, and showed the container exploding into bits.

Cheers and shrieks exploded loudly, bouncing around the room. Starion spun Janine in a circle as Henry sang an encore.

Skye noticed that Tane seemed nervous as he motioned for Starion to look at something. But Starion was distracted by the victory and continued to ignore him. Two Beholder guards entered the room.

Was it over? Skye wondered. Somehow, it seemed too easy.

"You know what I thought before I started singing?" revealed Henry. "I thought that as mean as Josh and his gang have been to me all through high school, they didn't deserve to die. I know that's messed up, but that's what I was thinking."

Janine hugged Henry. "That's why you are such an unbelievably good person and one of my best friends."

Starion clapped Henry on the back. "I don't call you Valjean simply because of your voice. Skye is lucky to have you, both of you, as friends."

"You weren't really going to turn us over to be science experiments, were you?" asked Janine, once again.

"Starion," Tane implored. "Come and—"

"In a minute," Starion snapped at Tane, then turned back toward Janine. "I was not." He clutched at his chest dramatically. "You wound me. You wouldn't like my planet anyway. I'm not going back. You might say that you've captured me. A reversal of fates, so to speak. That's phase four: I'm staying. I can't wait to take Skye on a real date. You're invited if you don't mind flying with me. A few loops, a few spins; it'll be fun."

Janine and Henry laughed and said in unison, "No thanks."

"Tane," Starion commanded, a happy lilt in his voice, "Transport us back to Leven's apart—"

The front door of the apartment flew open and Leven shouted, "Skye, give it to me *now*."

Skye handed the signaling device to Leven without a word.

Katrina gasped. "What were you thinking, Skye?"

"It doesn't matter now, does it? My best friend saved us all." She grinned. "With his amazing, incredible, perfect voice."

Katrina was shaking as she held Skye in a tight grip. Noticing tears in Oma's eyes, Skye whispered, "I had to do it, Oma. Please don't be angry."

"She's an exceptional young lady, Katrina," said Leven. He handed Skye her transport module and her cell phone.

Turning, Skye attached the module to her bra.

As the two headed for the kitchen, Skye called after them, "I'm ordering takeout. What do you—" Skye gasped and dropped the S-Eye screen.

He was here, in Leven's apartment. He pointed a gun at her.

Everything happened quickly. Leven rushed toward her. Skye didn't hear a shot, but Leven fell to the floor, blood gushing from his leg. The signaling device flew out of his hand, and Oln fired at it. Crashing to the floor, the device imploded, forming a black smoking lump on the ground. Oma tried to wrestle Oln, and he jabbed a silver cylinder into her side. She gasped and fell too.

Skye screamed and lashed out with fists, but Oln, much larger, seized her in a headlock, lifting her feet off the floor. "Hire incompetents, you get an incompetent job," he muttered.

As the room spun, she heard Oma frantically wail her name.

The scream faded into nothing, and Skye was no longer in the apartment.

28
·······

"I believe there's been a change of plans, Prince Starion."
Starion wheeled around at the sound. Oln, one arm wrapped tightly around Skye's neck, held a gun to her head.

Starion advanced toward Skye, snarling at Oln. "Let. Her. Go."

"I don't think so, my dear prince. Take another step forward and the girl dies."

Skye felt tears streaming down her face.

"Skye, has he hurt you?"

She could barely breathe. "I think he killed Oma and the professor."

The color faded from Starion's face as he stumbled, clutching onto a chair. "Richard? Katrina?"

Skye stifled a sob.

Starion spun around to face Tane. "There's only one way Oln could get the coordinates to Leven's place. One of your men is a traitor."

Skye thought she saw Tane flinch.

"Richard . . ." Starion mumbled, looking back at Skye. "Your Oma." His posture stiff, he advanced toward Oln, hatred flaring in his eyes. He raised his fist.

"Do it and she dies," Oln hissed.

Starion stopped.

"He killed Skye's Oma," squeaked Henry.

Janine's lips were trembling as she stared at Skye. "And Professor Leven."

"General Tane," Oln said, "perhaps our prince would like to speak with his father. He's expecting to hear from us. Would you activate the communications screen?"

Walking over to a console, Tane entered some information and then announced, "Sire, everyone is here." Turning to Starion he added, "I have activated the translator."

An image of an older version of Starion filled the previously blank overhead screen. The man's hair was considerably shorter, and he had a short pointy beard and mustache, but the features were so alike, there could be no doubt as to the man's identity.

"Father," said Starion, "when we were on the Milford Track there was a gunman with a tribute to kill. He came after . . . well . . . he was trying to kill someone and the promissory note looked like it came from you, but—"

"What are you babbling on about? If I were going to kill someone, you'd know it. I don't sneak around passing out tributes for death."

Recognition bloomed in Starion's eyes as he glared at Oln. "You've been trying to kill her for years. You wanted me to think it was my father's guard." His eyes widened. "Did you kill her parents?"

Oln clutched Skye tighter and smiled. "Why, my dear prince. I have witnesses who will verify my location during every one of these attempted assassinations."

"You won't get away with it," Starion shouted.

"*Enough*," commanded King Pruet. "I received the transmission concerning the vote. Have you released the virus, Tane?"

Tane stepped forward and bowed. "Sire, the virus was destroyed before it could be fired."

A snarl echoed from the screen as King Pruet's nostrils flared. He pointed at Oln. "Explain. *Now*."

"King Pruet, how good to see you," said Oln, bowing slightly from the waist while still keeping a hold on Skye.

"Enough with the pleasantries, Oln," snapped Pruet. "Who are you threatening today? Why are you on my ship? You told me you were going to collect your plants and go home."

"Yes, your Majesty, I did come as a diplomat on a Vanger agriculture ship, and it has returned home. However, I felt it was my duty to stay and inform you of the traitorous activities occurring here."

"Oln," Pruet said, a warning edge in his voice. "I will feed you to the jufons if you don't tell me what I want to hear."

"Your Majesty, I am only doing as you requested — keeping a watchful, yet respectful eye on your dear son." Oln bowed again. "Your son has compromised his mission for this girl. The vote went against the humans and he destroyed the virus — for her. He thinks royalty has no part in the governing of our planets and intends to defy the edict." He paused dramatically. "Such a shame. Princess Tempest will be extremely disappointed. I believe the marriage date has already been set."

"She's obviously a Vanger," said Pruet, motioning at Skye.

"Indeed. She's the daughter of Magnus's late son Pieter and a human."

"Does Magnus know?"

"It is of no concern to him."

Pruet leaned forward and glared at Oln. "If you are deceiving me, Oln, I will have you strung up from the highest building in Rotsblok."

"Your Majesty, would I deceive you?"

Pruet gave a derisive snort. "Just a moment."

The monitor immediately went blank, and as Starion inched closer to Skye, Oln said in a warning tone, "A compromise then, Prince Starion, quickly, before your father returns."

"I won't compromise with a murderous coward. You'll pay for the deaths of Katrina and Richard. You know who Skye is, and when my father returns I intend to tell him."

Oln pushed the gun harder to Skye's temple. "Do you think your father will care? There is only one compromise possible. You forget what you know, and I will convince your father to abandon his plans for Earth. Without me, he will release a new virus. The girl can return to her home unharmed, though we will all maintain that she's dead. It will be our secret."

Skye let out a slight sob.

"Don't make me say it again," Starion demanded. "Let her go."

Pruet was back on the screen when Oln released Skye, who immediately fell into Starion's arms.

A loud, braying spurt of laughter sounded out from the screen. "It's the girl, is it, my son?" Pruet leaned forward and leered at Skye. "Yes, she is quite the beauty, but then, so is the princess."

Despite everything, Skye couldn't help the shock she felt. *A beauty? Her?*

"Father, if you would allow me to introduce Skye."

"My dear son, I will allow you nothing. You are to come home immediately. You have undermined this entire mission. What am I to tell the Council? Now you shirk your responsibilities to our planets by refusing to marry the princess. There will be dire consequences for your actions. I fear for you, truly I do." Shaking his head in mock sadness, he looked over at Oln. "Prime Minister, what is this nonsense with the girl?"

"Your Majesty," Oln said. "I am merely here to ensure the prince returns and marries Princess Tempest, as the edict demands." He sneered at Skye. "She is preventing that."

Pruet sat drumming his fingers on his chair. "Tane."

"Yes, Sire." Tane snapped to attention.

"Complete your mission and bring my son home. Arrest him if he won't come willingly."

Tane put his right hand on his chest then dropped it quickly to his side. "Yes, Sire."

"And Tane. Get me that report." Pruet paused. "You know the one."

"What's Tane up to?" Janine said a little too loudly.

"Sire, what should I do with the girl and her friends?" Tane asked.

Pruet directed his attention at Janine, then gave Henry an appraising look. "Ah, so these are the sample humans . . . lovely coloring on the female. Tane, bring them. Oln, get rid of that girl; your Vanger dramas do not interest me. Her death may be a just punishment for my son. I want that ship home now so we can manufacture and send back a second virus."

Janine gasped. Henry fell to the floor.

"No, Father. *Please.*" His face drained of color, Starion crumpled to his knees. "Please, Father. May I have a moment to offer a compromise?"

"Why, Starion. I don't believe you have ever begged me for anything. And on your knees. How refreshing." Motioning to one of his assistants, Pruet took a large glass of purple liquid and settled himself into the chair. "I'm absolutely dying to hear your proposal and an explanation for your behavior. Destroying that virus is going to cost you dearly." He leaned forward. "You have two minutes."

Starion gazed up at Skye, and she saw a myriad of emotions in his eyes. He stayed on his knees as he looked back at his father. "I'll come home and marry Tempest."

Skye sank to her knees beside Starion and whispered, "Starion, no."

Starion continued to look straight ahead at the computer screen. "I'll go back to school, finish my engineering studies, and design your cities. I'll take political strategy lessons and attend Council meetings." He took Skye's hand in his and squeezed it gently. "And I'll stop flying."

Tane gasped.

Janine, having helped Henry back to his feet, shouted at the screen. "How can you be so cruel? Can't you see they care about each other?"

Pruet snorted. "Touching. My heart is breaking. I'll bet the prime minister's is as well, eh, Oln?"

Oln coughed. "Indeed, Your Majesty. Indeed."

"Let me guess," Pruet continued. "There are conditions for your oh-so-wonderful new promises. Aren't there?"

"Yes, Father."

"Out with them. Stop wasting my time. I need that ship back here."

Starion, though not looking directly at Skye, wrapped his arm tightly around her and said in a voice threatening to crack, "Skye, Henry, and Janine are to be returned to Earth unharmed. You will not release the virus. I need parts to fix the transport control in the conference arena so I can return the animals to their ecosystems. Oln must be punished for the deaths of my Earth friend and a Beholder professor."

"I care not for the life of some Earth friend, but this matter of killing a Beholder, well, that is serious. Oln? What do you have to say?"

Oln bowed and said, "Sire, the Beholder is Katrina, formerly of the University of Rotsblok. I have proof she was in contact with the resistance. One insurrectionist was right here hiding on General Tane's ship — a fellow Vanger, sadly. There was also a member of the resistance manning the TCS. I'm afraid we had a little difference of opinion."

Pruet spoke to someone standing beside him and then waved a dismissive hand. "I have given orders for a clean-up vessel to fix the transport control and return the animals. Those three children will be unharmed, and you, my son, are finished with this business and will return immediately. The Council will rule on the death." He paused, a murderous look in his eyes. "And there will be another purge. Anyone suspected of assisting the resistance will be executed."

"How do we ensure the prince will keep his word?" asked Oln, smoothing back a thick wave of red hair.

"If my son does not keep his word, if he fails to be the absolute model of princely behavior, I will send another virus and that, as they say, will be that."

"That's not fair," shouted Janine shrilly. Henry quickly covered her mouth with his hand.

Pruet pointed a finger in Janine's direction. "You realize I can kill you all where you stand."

Janine was shaking as she batted away Henry's hand, but she looked up at Pruet and said, "Do we have to live in fear for the rest of our lives that if Starion has one moment of happiness you'll kill us all? Are you going to torture him with more seizures?"

Pruet flew up out of his chair, smashing the glass of liquid on the floor, and roared, "Who told you this?" His pointed beard quivered with anger, his nostrils flared.

"No one told me," Janine stammered. "I . . . I . . . figured it out. How could you do that to your own —"

"*Enough.*" Pruet sat down roughly in his chair and pointed at Tane. "One more word from her and I want her terminated."

"Yes, Sire."

Henry clamped his hand over Janine's mouth and kept it there.

Skye's eyes narrowed as she stared at Tane. It was all becoming clear now. He was a traitor.

She looked into Starion's eyes. The mischievous sparkle she had grown to love was gone — replaced by despair. There was one thing she could do for Starion. She was willing to beg. If she were successful, his life would be bearable, at least. She had to be cautious. One wrong word and she'd get them all killed.

Still on her knees next to Starion, Skye looked up at the screen and said, "Your Majesty, may I have permission to speak?"

Pruet made an exaggerated yawn. "Out with it."

"Please don't punish Starion because of me. I'm sure he'll do everything you ask, but please let him have his flying. Please." She stood up and made the most gracious bow she could, then went back down to her knees. "Please."

Pruet stroked his beard and leaned forward. "I think not. No flying. My son has offered his compromise and I'm willing to accept it. Starion, are you willing to honor your promises if I return your Earth friends and put the planet's destruction on hold?"

"Yes, Sir." He squeezed Skye's hand.

"I do like you on your knees in front of me with the 'Yes, Sir.'" A wicked smile curled Pruet's lips. "Tane, return those three to Earth and make sure their transport modules self-destruct when they get there. The clean-up crew will mop up the mess my son has made."

"Father," Starion said, "may I have a few minutes alone?"

Pruet waved his hand again. "Make it fast. I find this whole business nauseating."

The viewscreen went blank. Starion rose shakily to his feet, lifting Skye with him. Releasing her, he walked over to Tane, a fist raised as he snarled, "You lying murderous traitor. After all we've been through together, how could—"

"Maybe the sunrise will be purple on the Festival of Five."

Starion immediately froze, his fist still in the air. Tane reached up to take Starion's hand, lowered it, and pressed something firmly into his palm, closing his fingers around it. "Say good-bye to your princess."

"Oln. Guards," Tane barked. "Let us go into the other room for a few minutes."

"So they can escape again?" Oln scoffed.

"Prime Minister, I do not believe there is any way for them to escape King Pruet." Tane pointed to the door, then followed Oln and the guards out.

Starion returned to Skye and wrapped his arms around her in a tight embrace. "I'm so sorry about Katrina. She was a wonderful woman, and I know she loved you very much."

"I know," Skye said in a strangled voice. "And I'm sorry about the professor. Starion . . . your flying. Maybe if I'd said—"

"There's nothing you could have done, but I will never forget what you tried to do for me. It took great courage to stand up to him."

Skye swallowed loudly and, with everything she had, tried to fight the tears.

"Have a happy life, my princess," Starion murmured. "I wish you tailwinds, always."

"You're sacrificing your entire life for me."

"You make me want to be a better person. For once I'm going to do the right thing." He winced. "I guess I've never done that before."

"Come back, Starion. I . . . I think . . . I forgive you."

Releasing her, Starion kissed her forehead and stepped away. "I won't be able to come back. I have to do what my father wants now." He made a slight motion with his head at a computer on the far wall; a light near the bottom was steadily blinking.

Panic flowed through Skye. She couldn't lose Starion. Not now. Not after all they'd been through. He was going to give up everything for her, her friends, her planet.

She threw herself at Starion, wrapping her arms around him tightly. She kissed him, and this time it wasn't a chaste kiss. She tried to pour herself into him as he kissed her back with desperation. The kiss became frantic, and Skye felt a deep grief bubbling up inside her. She clutched at him as he gripped her, anguish rolling over him and onto her.

When they finally broke the kiss, Skye saw tears in Starion's eyes. She kissed them away and whispered fiercely over the tightness in her throat, "I will *never* stop trying to find you."

With one arm wrapped around Skye's waist, Starion turned to Janine and Henry. "Take care of her for me."

Janine nodded and stifled a sob. Henry, tears streaming down his cheeks, saluted Starion as the door whirred open. Oln and Tane reentered, without the guards.

"Send those children back, Tane," snapped Oln.

"Take out your transport modules and hold them," Tane ordered the three. "I am sending you back to Leven's. Drop the modules as soon as you arrive. They are going to destruct and you do not want to be holding them when that happens."

Skye clutched Starion with one hand, the transport module in the other. Lifting her chin, Starion kissed her gently on the lips. "Think of me when you see a prairie dog." He moved her hand off his waist and kissed it, then, with his back to Oln and Tane, slipped something into her hand and closed her fingers around it. A large ring with a black stone flashed on Starion's finger; Skye had never seen him wear a ring before.

So softly that Skye could barely hear him, Starion whispered, "On the Festival of Five, my *only* princess." He furtively showed Skye a gold-colored square of plastic the size of a credit card, and then he slipped it into the back pocket of her pants.

Starion turned to Henry and Janine and bowed.

As Skye was about to ask Starion what he meant, she was back at Leven's, Janine and Henry beside her. "Drop the modules," Janine shouted as they began to burn and smoke. In a matter of seconds, the modules were ashes.

Skye looked down at her hand and opened her fingers. In it was a bronze-colored ring with a square black stone, like the one on Starion's staff at the UEE and the one on the ring Starion was wearing. In the center of the stone sat a tiny silver star.

"Oma!" she shrieked, dropping the ring into her pocket and racing to her grandmother.

Janine gasped at the two bodies. The floor was slick with blood.

"Are they dead?" Henry choked out the words.

"Call for an ambulance, Henry," said Janine, trying to sound calm. "Skye, help me move your Oma off the professor."

As Skye and Janine moved Katrina, they could hear her labored breathing. Janine motioned at Leven. "I think your Oma made a tourniquet. It looks like a laser sliced through half his leg." She put her ear to Leven's chest as Skye cradled Oma's head in her lap. "He's alive. Henry? The ambulance?"

"On its way. What can I do?"

"I think he's in shock or passed out. Get blankets off the beds."

"Oma, can you hear me?" Skye sputtered, her lips trembling. "The ambulance is coming."

Skye felt her limbs going weak, her mouth dry. She'd lost her parents. She couldn't lose Oma. They had so much to talk about, so much Skye wanted to learn. So many questions.

I didn't tell her enough that I love her, Skye thought desperately.

"I love you, Oma," Skye cried out between shallow breaths. "I love you!"

The woman opened her eyes, her face contorted in agony. "My beautiful Skye. Forgive me."

"Don't talk, Oma. Lie quiet until the ambulance comes." Skye gently trailed a shaking hand down Oma's cheek.

"Transport module. Take out. Put in." Katrina tapped lightly at her right upper chest, just below her shoulder, then at the same spot on Skye.

Janine bent over Katrina while Henry arranged blankets on Leven. "Why do you want your transport module in Skye?"

"Prince . . ."

Janine looked at Skye in confusion, and then said to Oma, "Starion went back to his planet to save us. His father came for him."

Katrina continued to tap at her upper chest, gasping for breath, her eyes wild as she began to thrash around.

"Oma, what is it you want us to do?"

"Cut out . . . must have . . . princess . . ."

Katrina let out a horrifying shriek as the thrashing became worse and blood began to seep from her eyes and nose.

"She wants you to cut it out of her?" Janine's voice was a breathless whisper.

"But why?" Skye asked in panic, wiping frantically at the blood.

"Never see prince again." Katrina's eyes closed, her hand falling back to the floor. "Princess."

"You have to cut it out," came Leven's faint voice.

Janine gave a hard shake of her head, waving her hands in front of her chest. "I'm not cutting anything out of anybody. Look at her; I could hit an artery and kill her. Do I look like a doctor?"

"It will deactivate when her heart stops," Leven said.

"No it won't. We used one to transport," Janine insisted.

"The Vangers have different transport modules," Leven said in a pain-filled voice. "All Beholders implant modules at birth, and they deactivate when they die. Right, Starion?"

There was no response.

"Where's Starion?" Leven asked.

Skye, her voice quivering in panic, gave an amazingly coherent Leven a short version of the story.

"Katrina knows she doesn't have long to —" Leven began.

"*No!* She'll be fine. You're not a doctor." She gripped her grandmother's hand tighter. "You'll be fine, Oma, you will. The ambulance is coming and you'll be fine, and we'll have movie nights at the hospital while you're getting better and . . . and . . ."

Leven's voice rose weakly. "Katrina saved me, tied a tourniquet around my leg to stop the blood. Oln hit her with the silver cylinder. Starion explained it to me once." He inhaled painfully before continuing. "Nothing we can do. No cure. Katrina knows. I'm sorry. You've only minutes to get that module out; do it before the ambulance arrives." Leven nodded toward a khaki cloth bag on the corner of the couch. "There's a knife and duct tape in my field bag. Get them, Henry."

Rummaging through the survival bag, tossing out notes, field guides, water, medical equipment, pens, and power bars, Henry finally found the items and dropped them next to Janine. It was obvious Henry was too frightened to think, appearing to be on automatic control.

Leven forced himself to speak between clenched teeth. "Cut the module out, Janine. Skye, immediately hold it in the same spot that Katrina has it. Henry, duct tape it until we can get it embedded in Skye."

"Embedded," cried Henry. "This is crazy."

"I am *not* cutting it out," insisted Janine.

Leven glanced at Skye, then back at Janine. "You're the only one who can do it. If you don't, there will never be another chance. *Ever.* Starion is as good as dead."

Katrina's eyes began to flutter as she mouthed, "Love you, Skye."

"Oma." Skye put her ear near the woman's mouth. "She's not breathing!"

Janine grabbed the knife and plunged it into Katrina's shoulder. As blood poured from the cut, Janine dug fingers into the incision she'd made, lifting the quarter-sized oval disc, frantically wiping the blood off the device with her other hand. Unlike the Vangers' aqua-colored modules, this one was a deep-purple color. Roughly pulling the sleeve of Skye's shirt down, Janine slapped the bloody module onto Skye's skin. "Henry, *tape*."

Skye, her eyes frantic, was oblivious to the taping as Katrina gave a lurch and then went still. "Oma, don't leave me. Please don't leave me. *Don't leave me all alone!*"

The door flew open, and several paramedics rushed into the room.

29
∎ ∎ ∎ ∎ ∎ ∎ ∎

Four weeks later

Skye sat at a desk in her bedroom at the Queenstown boarding house and tried to read. She twirled the ring Starion had given her. She'd thought the black stone had some sort of power, but it simply sat on her finger. It didn't pulse or glow or anything.

She finally threw the book against the wall. She couldn't concentrate; she had no appetite; she had trouble sleeping. She'd cried. A lot.

Oma was gone.

Starion was gone.

She was alone.

Her insides ached and burned.

She placed her hand over the spot under her right shoulder where Dr. Leven's doctor friend had implanted Oma's transport device — no questions asked. The small scar had already faded to a thin white line. It was all pointless though. The stupid thing didn't work. She pressed it repeatedly and said the words she thought Starion had said. *Those were the words he'd said, weren't they?* Janine thought the TCS had left anyway.

A knock sounded on the door. The owner of the boarding house pointed to the phone on the desk. "You have a call."

Who would be calling her? Perhaps it was Dr. Leven; the hospital was releasing him today. Dylan was driving them all to Dunedin. She, Janine, and Henry were supposed to board a flight to Los Angeles, via Auckland, and then back to Denver. She had orientation at Colorado State University in a couple days. If she missed it, she would lose her scholarship — no exceptions. She wouldn't be able to attend her parents' alma mater this year.

She picked up the phone. "Hello?"

"Do I have to fly over there or are you going to bloody well let those friends of yours help you find Starion?"

"Rob, how did you find me?" Skye exclaimed.

"Henry called my parents' hotel. He told me the whole story."

"He did?"

"Too right. I knew that big guy was bad news. Janine says he kidnapped your bloke." Rob paused. "She says the police haven't found him yet."

They'd all agreed to tell the police the same story: One intruder — matching Oln's description — had killed Oma and injured the professor. A second man — matching Tane's description — had kidnapped Starion.

"Starion left me a card that Professor Leven thinks is a key to Starion's place in Dunedin. I'm going to try to find it. Maybe there'll be a clue about where he went."

"I can be there to help," Rob said enthusiastically. "We'll have another bloody good adventure, Skye. We'll find him."

"I don't want you to get in trouble with your parents."

"Friends come first," Rob said.

"It means a lot that you called to help." *Please don't get dragged into this*, Skye thought. *Not you too.*

Rob sighed dramatically. "OK, but let Henry and Janine help."

"Janine has a scholarship and Henry has auditions."

"Friends. Are. More. Important."

Skye smiled, though she knew Rob couldn't see her. "They told me the same thing."

"Henry's a doll. Really. He's bloody ace."

"He's not available, Rob."

"I got that. Too bad."

"What happened with Maka?" Skye asked.

"We gave it a burl. Didn't work out."

"I'm sorry."

"No worries. I've got a new bloke. He's one of the Maori on the team." Rob's voice was upbeat, carefree.

Skye tried not to let the sadness bleed into her words. "I love that about you, Rob. You don't let anything get you down and then you're off on a new adventure."

"I'm shallow with blokes. I get that."

"No, I didn't mean that. I meant you're a survivor. Does that make sense?"

"We both are, Skye."

There was a long pause, but it wasn't an awkward one.

"Difference is," Rob said, "you found the one. He'll always be it for you. That's why you need to find him."

Skye knew what she had to do. She loved her parents and wanted to make them proud, but sometimes the right decisions were not the easy ones.

"Go after him, Skye, and stop mucking about or I'm flying over there."

Skye finally laughed and Rob joined her.

"Thanks for making me laugh," Skye said.

"It isn't right," Rob said, "about your grandma. I've never lost anyone, but I know it's got to be . . ." Her voice trailed off.

"I miss her."

"Bloody right, you miss her. That's how you know she was really, really, *really* ace." Rob paused. "Do you need me?"

A knock sounded at the door. "Come in," Skye called.

Janine and Henry walked into the room carrying their suitcases and backpacks. "Dylan's here," Janine said.

"Who's that?" Rob asked.

"Janine and Henry. We're going to get Dr. Leven. He's being brave about losing his leg. The hospital's releasing him today and we're driving to Dunedin. Hang on and I'll get you the number."

"Got it. Janine gave it to me. She's pushy, but I'd let her at my back anytime. Hold the phone so I can shout out at them."

Skye held the phone toward Janine and Henry. Rob yelled so loudly she could probably be heard in the hallway. "DON'T MUCK ABOUT FINDING STARION OR I'M COMING."

"That's Rob for you. Loud," said Janine.

"YOU KNOW YOU LIKE ME, JANINE."

"Bye, Rob," Skye said, putting the phone back to her ear. "You're the best."

"Too bloody right."

Skye put the phone down and turned to Janine and Henry. "I have to find him."

Janine crossed her arms over her chest. "You know you're going to lose your scholarship if you're not on that plane."

"We knew you wouldn't leave," Henry said, looking at Janine. "But we can't let you stay here alone."

"You have to go back," Skye insisted.

Janine smiled. "Our parents gave us permission to stay, the Fioretta people are more accommodating than CSU and they're holding my scholarship for a semester, and Henry says there'll be other auditions." She paused. "If you argue we'll call Rob and tell her to come." She glanced at Henry. "Apparently she carries knives."

"We're agreed then," said Henry. "We're the three musketeers. All for one, and one for all." He extended his hand. "I'll be Porthos."

"I'm in," said Janine, placing her hand over Henry's. "You can call me Aramis."

Skye placed her hand on top, gently wrapping her fingers around the stack of hands. If she could have lifted her heart out and placed it there, she would have. She knew with every part of herself that her friends didn't just have her back; they had her heart too. She was getting Starion back, and truthfully, she did need their help.

"That leaves you the name Athos," Henry said. "Do you have a plan?"

Skye's eyes narrowed. "We get Starion away from Father Evil and then Oln *dies*. After that, I keep my promises—to Jackson, to Pim, to everyone."

It looked like college would have to wait.

Skye had a prince to save.

Dear Friends,

Just because you're too young to vote, that doesn't mean you can't make a difference. You can write letters to your local newspaper and your school paper. You can read about climate change and talk about it on social media. You can start petitions and protest in a peaceful way. You can talk to adults about environmental issues and tell them this is your planet too. Janine would tell you to take science classes.

You can tell your friends to read this book because a bunch of the money from its sale is donated to environmental organizations. Write to the author for more information. She loves hearing from readers.

If you want a bracelet like the one I wore at the conference, then check out www.4Ocean.com. You will sponsor the removal of one pound of trash from the ocean. Irwin is excited about that.

We can all do a better job of helping the planet. I'll see you in the next book, "Holding."

With much love,

Skye

About the Author

Carol Fiore is the author of *Flight through Fire*. She holds three degrees and is a licensed pilot. Carol donates most of the proceeds from the sale of this book to environmental charities. Visit her website at www.carolfiore.com.

CPSIA information can be obtained
at www.ICGtesting.com
Printed in the USA
FSHW011948270619
59516FS